BEAST

BEAST

By Lulu Allison

Bluemoose

Copyright © Lulu Allison 2025

First published in 2025 by
Bluemoose Books Ltd
25 Sackville Street
Hebden Bridge
West Yorkshire
HX7 7DJ

www.bluemoosebooks.com

All rights reserved
Unauthorised duplication contravenes existing laws

British Library Cataloguing-in-Publication data
A catalogue record for this book is available from the British Library

ISBN 978-1-915693-32-7

Printed and bound in the UK by Short Run Press

1

A
fall.
A summons.
These cursed revolutions

Demon strokes my back, hooks a finger into the crevice of my neck, scratching gently. It is lovely. I close my eyes and allow myself to enjoy these last moments.

Soon he will stop.
Soon it will be over.
He will be gone and I will be nothing.

All this I know.

I enjoy the attention but know well he pets me for his own comfort, not mine. I am, I always was, his consolation; I provide a service. He wants me as a child wants a teddy bear: for a sense of security, something to know, something to own. I do not hold it against him.

All these years, some three times my allotted span, I have been charged with such power, such knowledge. I have seen the mind of a divine creature, dabbled in human dreams, skipped the realms of earth; marble palace, puddle-grimed shack, endless tundra and silent forest. I could go on. So much I have seen on earth. And I have been allowed to witness a little of the might and majesty of the cosmos.

All I have seen.

My ordinary state had not prepared me. No woodland creature, nor human, no beast of any kind, is prepared for the mighty charge of the divine. But there are those who call it down, and we must deal with the consequences as best we can.

Soon this deal will be done. A wager that both may feel they won – though it concludes with bliss on one side and oblivion on the other.

This oblivion is as to become a pelt, the cast-off of a once living thing, worn for another's comfort. But this oblivion is for the fate to be known. To remain eternally knowing, inert and powerless.

This is the meaning of losing your soul.

My own imminent end is not oblivion. Death is a comfort. A return to the quiet side of existence. Simply and unknowingly to be; elemental, diffuse, part of all.

To be wordless and in ignorant bliss.

Death is a kindness.

Eternity is for the damned.

All this I know.

Demon settles on the grass. I hop from his arms, nibble at the softly bitter herbs scattered near the cliff edge, growing lushly where no feet tread. My divine body requires no sustenance, but with divinity's unsought imposition came much pleasure and I eat for enjoyment.

Demon lies on his back, looks past the curtain of sky, seeking the blackness beyond. He longs for this final act to be complete. To be free to once more part the curtain and head into darkness. At journey's end a centuries-long night of sleeping, softly cocooned in brotherhood.

He comes from a brood, settled nightlong like our rabbit kittens, tucked so softly together as to almost become one. Though no little rabbit is pulled from blissful shared sleep and hurtled across the universe to a distant planet in fulfilment of an ancient bond. I am glad for them that they are not.

But I too have been transported into another realm. Or I would not have the capacity to tell this tale. Luckily for me, the transformation came softly, as a gentle settling, a spell of awakening. Demon and his kind experience their call to work as a dreadful wrench. He waits now only to return home, with a new soul to speed his journey, to line and warm his den. I feel the impatience of his longing almost as though it is my own. For a moment, I am sad that I will not be going with him.

I do not think they ever really know each other, as we rabbits do, in our burrow communities. This strange spawn, held afloat in the dark of space like the glass creatures of earth's deepest seas. Though they are unknown one to the other, they long to be together. I have learned ways to console Demon, but nothing can fully assuage the discomfort of being torn from his brothers.

I believe I have enjoyed myself more than he, during our time in each other's company. For all his divine provenance, for all his ancient might, he is an anxious, unsettled creature.

All this I know.

All this I know and yet so much is hidden. How it all came to be. Why this slow and sorry story, so tuned to the calibrations of a mortal mind, must keep revolving. It is as though, in order to be told at all, the tale must be repeated, endlessly.

Told once, who knows when? That first time is lost. Told again, told again and again. Told in slips and slides, slanting over centuries, with new players, new stages changing this detail or that outcome. A fireside tale reformed and retold forever, with parings and embellishments, new-shaped in every revolution of its repeating. A clock of human life.

And demons must, like the hands of the clock, be there to make the telling.

I have become attuned to the value of stories in my time with Demon. I have learned their worth. Stories make sense of the things that do not hold still before our eyes. Stories have the power to shape events. They are a kind of spell.

We rabbits have no stories for our minds exist behind a veil and are not condemned to grapple with what we cannot see.

Again and again life sets out to prove that life has no reason. Or if there is reason it is hidden deep within the darkness we cannot see. But for humans it seems, absence of meaning is intolerable. Life swells and drags past, as wantonly as a flooded river, changing the landscape, bringing debris, taking treasure. Bringing the new, changing the order of the old. Life, so often in full flood, can rarely be dammed, but stories tame the waters of understanding, allowing a little navigation.

This much I know.

I have become a teller of tales. To mollify, cajole and flatter. To gather meaning from the shadows, the echoes, flits and glimmers, the wraiths and wrecks and wilderness. To make the first pressing, the second veil, the third layer, the fourth shadow knowable. And yet so much remains hidden; even wrapped in the most elaborate and delicious of tales, there is so much we cannot know.

Why, for example, demons came to be sleeping, then to be woken, as though even in their divinity, their great might, they must come as servants to the feeble, greedy, needy humans.

For that they are. This much I know.

All that I know, until the depthless, lightless fathoms are reached.

The explanation ends with a rip across the page. The lees, dark in the bottom of the glass. It is one of Demon's torments, that he must do this work, it has always been so, yet he does not know why. None do, I think.

He is compelled. It is his fate. And that is all there is to it.

When I was a natural rabbit, I could do no more than obey the need to seek out the sweet herbs and tender grasses of the hedgerows, dig an earthen home, jump to tension at any sound that may signal predator. This was survival. And though I know of course that Demon has more than the frail protections of an earth rabbit, he feels the peril of survival the same way; the desire to return home is to him as urgent as life. It is true, the consequences of failure are great. But failure is so unlikely.

I have known fears of course. Foxes, cars, the stupid, lascivious interest of dogs. But each day gave its own measure of bliss. The evening sun on a grassy bank, the earthy smell of home, tucked in warmly with sisters and brothers, our pelts banked against the chill of night. The wild and wondrous call of another's scent. A new grown patch of tender leaves under a hedgerow jewelled in dew. Our lives are, were, so simple. Just being, in a world that allows us to be.

A small but mighty joy.

All I have learned and the great wealth of all I have seen and still I find reason to set my ordinary lost blessings high amongst the treasures. To need little and to find it. To wordlessly, thoughtlessly enjoy existence. This is the true bounty of animal life. Perhaps our easy way to contentment is the reason Demon does not come to harvest rabbit souls. The more needy the soul, the easier it is, and perhaps the more valuable too. But who am I, with my divinity a loan soon to be rescinded, presuming to guess at the value of a soul?

Such calculations are long lost; secrets darkly fermenting in the lees.

All that no one knows.

2

**I
have
no choice.
I am bound, forever,
in service to this sacred cycle**

It was a sunny day, more than twenty years ago. Demon pulled me from the grass and held me. I slid from dandelion hunter to divine creature at his touch. My natural self shrank, though it is still shadowed inside. Outside I darkened, like Demon, to an inky, marbled, shifting shade; the night sky, the depths of a well, old meat. I shimmered with the petrol lustre of the cosmos. Marks like dip-pen spells scratched in a child's hand or tattoos grown into ancient skin flickered over me. My old dappled markings were for woodland camouflage. These sighing patterns have a different utility – revelations, runes of belonging to an ancient and mighty order; thus I show myself as divine. Like Demon, though few may catch sight of me, I am terrible and wondrous to behold. I wish sometimes there were more to observe my magnificence.

Not long before we came by accident together, Demon had been woken from his sleep and dragged at hurtling speed through the cosmos by the dreams of a human girl. Such a slender, half-formed creature, yet she had the power to call the divine. It hardly seems credible.

As he neared his destination, he became once more a creature with a body, with a kind of skin, with something like weight (enough at least to make a temporary compact with gravity) and his hurtle became a fall. He arrived on the banked edge of a field still spinning, anxious and groggy, a creature pure of the cosmos becoming one at home on earth. He arrived without my notice, had pulled me to him before I knew he was there. But perhaps I only knew it at all because he made me his. He pulled me to him and held me close, buried his blunt face in my fur. I fizzed and dazed and sat, frozen, in his arms.

The first thing I knew was that this creature is confused and a little afraid. I was puzzled, not understanding that I had changed; I was no more used to wondering at the state of fellow creatures than I was to climbing the tarry telegraph poles that edged the field.

As he endeavoured to gather himself in, against the sickening rush of his arrival, I began to push myself out into the full capacity of my new being.

We became companions.

We lay in the grass all afternoon. His travel sickness subsided, his shock receded and I was able to comfort and help him with that.

I learned with wonder (I learned to feel wonder at all) of what he told. Such sparks flew into me, formed thinking where there had been no thought. We lounged in the grass and I listened, heard the story of my new companion; in truth, my master.

Demon has told me since that he had other companions on previous visits. A snake, a mouse, a puppy that a score of years stayed puppy. He misses Puppy still, I think. The sweet trust, and love. The playful silliness. Even now, though I need fear nothing, it is hard to let go of a prejudice against dogs.

But the vacuum of space is an airlock and demons must return alone, cloaked in a newly acquired soul. Earth's creatures, even when invested with the divine, cannot bridge the two realms. I do not know that he would invite me. And though I face the end, I would not go with him if he did. It has been tiring, living in a body that carries so much. I have longed, now and then, to slide back into those short and dappled years, sitting on a grassy verge, low sun warming my back. And for that to be all and enough.

As I will, Puppy died when Demon left. It is better that way. All this I know.

'It will be done soon,' Demon says, and we feel the nearing. We wait.

3

I
wish
it were not so

Yes, my rabbit mind, in seeing only what survival demanded, was in many ways, blessed. When Demon pulled aside the veil, I was beset both by knowledge and by curiosity. Curiosity, infuriating and demanding, never settled. I hope still, before we go, if allowed by Demon, I will have some final answers. Curiosity and knowledge – a tale cannot exist complete without a measure of both.

So many questions jostle, dammed behind my desire not to pester and provoke Demon. But how they torment me. There is still so much I do not know.

How did Demon finally unlock her? How did the years-long story reach the ending for which we now are waiting?

Back then, I wanted to know about the beginning.

He told me of the gentle brush of fingers that on reaching for the divine had woken him and bid him attend.

A call is made, it strikes a certain note, is born through the cosmic hum. If the caller is one who possesses the spark of divine creation, if their call flies on wings of yearning, sometimes it hits a frequency that carries it all the way. And this is what brings a demon. A bold dreamer, a soul in need, a heart filled with longing, an imagination daring to aspire to the divine. A voice crying love me, hear me, heed me. A little moment of meeting the right conditions in the mighty cosmos.

And a key made this way may turn subtle pins, unlocking the divine sleep of a demon and bidding them obey. The demons must, like common traders, like costermongers, come to make a deal.

Oh how Demon resents his bondage. He told me so in those first hours together. For the barest moment, I sensed his fearsome might. I cannot in words do justice to the dread that overwhelmed me, held in hands hot and twisted by a fury that raged outward from his core. I was afraid that his control would snap, and those hands become the expressive tools of a destructive urge. Every part of my being, rabbit and divine, trembled with fear. I felt as though I were coming apart.

I knew then, how powerful he was. I knew that if his contained anger were so dreadful, unleashed it would be unendurable. Though I only once encountered it to the same degree again, it was a caution, a stark reminder that behind his more familiar disappointed and tetchy demeanour, there was ancient and overwhelming might.

I felt it rage, for the briefest moment, and then it was gone. He held me on his lap once more in peace, and I listened to him bitterly tell the nature of his looped and endless chore. How a human dream or desire catches him, how he like a leashed dog must come to heel, through all the wild inclines of the cosmos, in the service of that dream.

No other animal but the human can call down the divine. They have a special talent for it. Other creatures are, I can say having been one, too settled. They have not the skill because they have not the need.

All this I know.

Suddenly he was tired of talking.

'Enough. You must learn the rest yourself. Come,' he said, as though I had a choice. To my astonishment, we two were airborne. As he lifted me I slid into a different consciousness. I heard the stories Demon had to tell not by listening to his words but as though they floated from his mind into my own. Our two centres, linked by the twisting threads of memories and stories.

My curiosity grew as Demon shared his memories. The old marks, spooling backwards in time, the complex knots of the many deals undoing as I watched, as I absorbed them in the place where my own memories lived. A wild variety of tales unwound. I saw places I could not have imagined – villages that had grown to cover acres, until they also pushed up into the sky, all the land cemented, no plants but those placed by human hands for their own pleasure. Fields of grit that I learned to call sand, desert. Trees that dripped in wet and punishing heat cast by the overhead sun. My sun had always risen at a sloping angle. I saw all this before I had the naming of it. Now of course I must know more words, more names than any rabbit who ever lived. A part of me would love the chance to go back to my former fellows and preen before them. But I think they would run away.

I explored all that he knew and it became my own. His words and his thoughts enlightened me. Layers of wonder unfolding within as I learned the shape of this strange, magnificent being. And all the while thinking why me? Why this? So many thoughts that I had not the time to resolve, for it was clear to me even in this strangely uncertain state, my role was to serve. I found that I could also share, with this new way of hearing and seeing, this new way of knowing, the way he felt. As his memories unfolded into me, I felt with him what they meant.

Through the dim approach of night we drifted. I saw it all in pictures, slipping into my memories like dreams. It was not quite like sleeping, more a tuning out, sliding between layers of being. Something like familiarity, seen in a broken lens, recalled imperfectly.

The next time I was fully within myself, I recognised from the high vantage point the fields and copses of my home lands below us. The hill slopes and woodlands I had thought covered all of the world. That world, my world, had ended in vague mystery and with that I had been content. I knew the village, knew it was where people and their animals lived. But I had never been there, and never thought there was anything beyond.

Demon carried us over fences, gardens, rooftops, into the village. We came to rest on the tower of the church. I blinked away my foolish astonishment, looked across the houses on one side, and the familiar slopes of distant hills on the other.

It was the first of many surprising journeys. Those wanderings have been a highlight of my time with Demon. Over our long years together we have found ourselves in secret parts of the world. The many wondrous places without humans, so Demon could rest, far away from their terrible demands. In realms of ice, in forests and grasses. Island, desert, mountain, tundra. A city park at night. A haunted garden. A summer camp in winter.

Places where other creatures thrived; we waited for time to pass in the company of giraffes (ridiculous), migrating butterflies (pretty, annoying) and kangaroos (I did not trust them).

We went, once, against my wishes, into the dank and musk of a badger sett, and Demon laughed at my disdain. Stupid, shuffling things. We explored the abandoned warren of other rabbits, amongst heather and the roots of pines. We were not too big after all, for our form is a shifting thing. No burrows were plugged by my magnificence. I slept truly, for a while, in the comfort of just enough space between snug earthen walls.

Sometimes we travelled far beyond the mantle of the earth. Oh I longed to enter what lay beyond the darkness, the realm from whence my new and only companion came. I could see the shimmer, the shift of meaning, far still on a new horizon. I could not speak but still I begged Demon to take me. Somehow in that distant light, I saw in him a beauty that did not shine under the sky's mantle. A beauty of such strange order. It pulled at me and wordlessly I begged. Each time I pleaded, he would turn his calm and newly noble face to me, I caught unexpected shards, shimmers of longing, and wordlessly he told me I could not go there. Nor could he return, until a soul had been secured.

And as morning came it was as though I had dreamed it all. So many nights spent in that wondrous passing.

Yes, over the years I have seen something of the cosmos. To let go of the rules we live by here. To be free of the order, the soft hold of earth. To miss it, and recognise the gentle embrace upon return. It is a thrill, a strange wonder that sits close to fear; everything is rewritten.

But this became true the moment Demon made me his.

The darkness of evening slid in around us. Demon was quiet for a while, then his mind quickened to a sacred labour. He listened to a far away silver thread of sound. A distant horn calling. Not now, not this minute, but soon; the call to hunt.

Demon was no longer interested in talking to me. It was up to me to fill the gaps, to understand what I could. All his thoughts were turning to the mark, the one who had called him; the being at the end of the reaching hand. As his strength returned, the old habits emerged; he began to feel relish for the game of it.

'The quicker we tie this knot, the longer we have, without fear of failure, for the diversions of earth' he told me. I felt a surge of excitement, and again a curious rising desire for experience, for knowledge – brashly surprising tastes, previously hidden sights, unexpected learning. No such need had existed before. Surprise, after all, in the life of a wild rabbit, is not joy but peril.

Demon picked me up in his arms once again. Feeling more accustomed to our movement, I had the time to notice the new qualities of my weight, or mass, or heft. I had some, but was still somehow airborne and careless, as weightless as sunlight in my new form. Light enough to travel the air as though a petal borne on friendly breezes. An ancient compact with gravity, reworking her pull as a courtesy, one sacred power to another, allowed us this magical freedom. Another of those ancient lores, the reasoning no longer knowable.

We slid over the low parapet of the roof, across the village green and landed weightless on the grass.

4

Girl,
are you
brave enough?
And strong enough?
I hope, for both of us, you are

And there she was, the one who had pulled down the ancient wreathings of the divine. The trader, the dreamer, the mark. Eve.

We found her in the dark of approaching night, a few hours after Demon's dizzying arrival and my own equally dizzying transformation.

Yes, we were three transformed creatures: Demon from blissful sleeper into unwilling practitioner of ancient lore, me from drab rabbit into divine companion, Eve from an angular, awkward child into a musical explorer who had summoned the divine.

I could not tell it on that first sighting but I came to like her very much. I care for her still. I like too who she became, which is not always a given for those who cross paths with Demon or his brothers. All this I know.

She was sitting on a bench on the village green, overlooking a model village. We could tell from her settled comfort that she liked this spot, enjoyed the absurdity of the little houses with their blind windows and painted roses, felt soothed by a corner of the world set at a manageable scale. She still loves it. And the secret hidden at the heart of it, near the crossroads. Not many knew it back then but this girl, Eve, was soon to become one of them. Now it is common knowledge. She has done well from the keeping and the telling of that secret.

The model village was built on what had been a tennis court in the grounds of the dilapidated house behind. The boundary had shifted so that this patch, once private garden, was unofficially conceded to the common land of the village. The house was hidden behind a swathe of dark rhododendrons.

It is not a copy of the village that surrounds it. It is an invented place, and thus for Eve, free of the expectations of others. It demanded no accounting for her belief that she did not fit in, that she was too awkward to belong.

The real village had evolved into a satellite of a larger town seven miles away; it was pretty, quiet, ruled by cars. There was a pub where friendship grew, joy was created, disapproval gloomily aired. There was a shop that sold biscuits, tinned soup, j-cloths, vegetables in polystyrene trays. There was a church that barely scraped a reason for its existence from Sunday to Sunday, but still offered a community for the older residents, with its fete, the harvest festival, Christmas carols. There were ordinary families; some rich and some too poor. Most doing fair to well. There was a rowdy family with a history of enmity with the dour local landlord. Normal families with normal values. So they like to think.

Demon's mark sat lazily angled on a bench. Smoke and breath clouded the winter evening above her pale face and dark hair. She was deliberately unkempt, or carelessly kept. She marked herself either way, I was to learn, as an outsider.

Demon observed her, keen and crouched as a hunter. One that must needs eat his prey, for there was even on this first day, hunger. The cruel pull of starvation seeds fear of failure; this was no mere sport.

I had no fear. I knew even then that my fate was written and could not be altered. My divinity was borrowed and the span of it precise. There was tremendous comfort in this. Though I had experienced much contentment as a rabbit, it was a life laced daily with fear: this might do such and such, that might, foxes, dogs and poisons might. Now, I knew already I had many years without those cares. And then I would be gone.

All this I knew. Even then.

For all the many times Demon had run this hunt, had set traps and laid lures to bring in his prey, for all that he would not be here had he ever failed, he was impatient. He had time. Plenty of it. But certainty is best served by haste. So, he set forth, sniffed the air, he sought out the stepping stones, marked the dead-end gullies. He set out to explore her dreams, map her desire. To learn the lay of where this chase would run.

What hopes were trapped inside a soul that he might crack open and release?

She had dreams. I could hear them.

It would take a while to understand what these dreams demanded. But even then I could hear the song of them, the crescendos, the crash and cry, for they were in the form of music.

She heard her music and saw it in shapes all at once
colours, blocks, textures, slabs
a something and a nothing
a holy tussle of absence and presence
a place to be built
a landscape to wander in awe.

Her dreams were pictures and music intertwined. And oh, they were grand. I came to love the landscape of those dreams.

As I spent more time with her, I learned that her passion began with something she could not name, something to do with heft and weight. Sound might lurch through space, through her body, the expression of a mysterious and exhilarating power. She wanted to harness the transporting thrill of it. It was as though it wrapped around and around her, then whipped away, sending her spinning into all the possibilities, the music, it proposed. She felt herself both beholden and wondrously free.

My understanding of Eve came over time. But even on the first day, I caught glimpses, the structure of her mind, and could see the magic of it.

She sat on the bench, a thick tweed gentleman's coat pulled in for warmth by bare hands buried in deep pockets, over the meagre protection of a t-shirt. One eye squinted against the smoke rising up from the corner of her mouth, the other side dragged open for breath. She pulled her shoulders up around her ears. The metal of her earrings was cold against her neck. She resisted retreat, from the cold, into the cosy warmth of home. The chill night, the darkness made a space for her and she did not want to leave the luxury of it yet.

She thought in a wordless, intuitive way about the spell-making of sound, about weight and counter-weight. She measured her ability against her dreams and found herself wanting. And she found her dreams magnificent. The twin binds of her courage and her uncertainty wrapped tighter than the coat.

I understood it was her music that had woken the divine. Demon was excited; here was so vast a yearning, so grandly mysterious a form that even this soon he felt confident of victory. Making a deal was surely a formality.

Well, she had more to her, this awkward girl, than Demon first reckoned with, and she would make him work.

Night had fallen. The model village sat under a net of sour yellow light drooping from a parish street lamp. Still she sat, the sounds and the patterns of music forming a kaleidoscope in her mind. How could she get bored, when there was never an end to all the possibilities? It seemed she could not. But I was curious about the place, my first time somewhere inhabited by humans, and I hopped to the ground to explore.

There was a crossroads at the centre of the model village, two roads of grass mown short. Lawns, I learned, so smooth and tempting to look at, are a disappointment to eat, lacking the sweet and bitter leaves of weed and herb to enliven the taste.

Eventually she stirred, Demon too in response. She stood and stretched, finally conceding to the walk home, the resurgence of everyday demands; chat, help with chores, preparation for the next day's work. Time away from what she cared about. She ambled off on a sigh, bent over a final roll-up, one strand of black hair lolling forward dangerously near the glowing tip. Demon was absorbed, distracted, he nodded to himself, gazing into the distance after her.

And then it was just we two.

Quite a day for me, this first day as a divine.

I had become the companion of a demon.

So much knowledge had been flung into me, then had settled miraculously as though native, into a neat pattern, a web of knowledge. I knew so much. So much that I had not understood I was missing.

I knew Demon's story as though I had always known it. The incredible might, the woes, the anxiety of this anciently divine creature. A creature compelled to undertake work that he no longer understood. He knew only that he must succeed in it or perish in the attempt.

I had come an unfathomably long way, though in distance I had moved only to the village just a few fields from my home. In time it was mere hours.

The last time I saw the dark of night I had not the words for it. I had only the notion to retreat from its vastness into the contained darkness of my own burrow.

Now all was different.

Having no idea of what divine creatures were to do at night I waited. I felt no tiredness, no call to my snug den across the fields. I did not think I would have been able to squeeze into it even if I wanted to. I wondered if my kin would know me if I tried. I feared I might get stuck, not knowing then that divinity let my shape and size shift fluidly with circumstance. I was amused to picture my shimmering body plugging my former family in terror into their chamber.

Sometimes I have missed them.

'What now?' I asked eventually.

'Nothing.' Demon replied. I noticed his impatience. It was to become so familiar. But I dearly wanted to know more than he offered, and so began the dance: my endless questions pushing, as far as I dared, against his thin and brittle tolerance; I already understood his mood must be tested with great gentleness. I tried again.

'How does your deal making begin?'

'I must fully understand her. When I am certain of her desires, I will shape my offer into a pattern aligning with fulfilment. We will stay here, observe, get to know her.'

'We might get to know each other a little more, at the same time,' I offered.

'Yes, yes,' said Demon, but I could see he was not concerned with me at all. I learned soon enough that as long as I was there, with my warm body, my soft fur, my ability to be held for comfort in his arms, the stories that I learned to tell, Demon would make few demands of me. He was not practised in knowing or being known by another. He was poor company, truth be told.

However great the rewards, it was a harsh fate; without asking, Demon had plucked me from my brothers and sisters, for his own comfort. He picked me up a rabbit and set me down a different creature, gave me nothing, no explanation, no kindness, certainly no apology. But I believe now it was this kinship, both of us subject to sudden, harsh realignment, that he valued. As he suffered, so did his companion. Both of us had been pulled without consent away from our homes, the fundamentals of our very being reformed. Only, for him it had happened before.

It had happened many times before. I learned their stories in summary, shaped for the ease of understanding and the reward of listening. Demon learned their entire lives. He learned how they had been washed in dreams and scoured by experience. He learned what had awakened desires of a calibre to command the divine. He learned what terrors and what tragedies had carved through a soul, right to the bone, and he learned how flights of wonder and imagination had been wielded as though wings, raised in the service of reaching for the divine.

He learned it all, from the moment of their birth until the time of his intervention, the time when he, Demon, began to write their ending.

5

Old
tales
once more
unwind, to be
remade and retold

All deaths before time are brutal, changing worlds in an instant. The death of Alan, loving husband to Elaine and doting father of Eve, was no exception.

Eve lay on her bed, school jumper on over her pyjamas, homework open in front of her. She heard a sound, peculiar, unsettling, unrecognisable but clearly her mother. A burglar? A rat in the kitchen? Had she hurt herself? The scatter of homework slid to the floor, she darted to the door. Her breath thickened and shortened. She paused briefly at the top of the stairs; she was afraid to go down. Her mother was not alone. Who were these people? Why was Mum making such strange sounds, looking so wild? Eve was frozen for a moment by her mother's terrible strangeness. But she knew her mother was in pain. Poor girl, she did not know how to help. She could not tell whether to plead for assistance from these other strangers or whether to block them out, make them go away.

She laid a hand so lightly on Elaine's shoulder.

'Mummy?' The naming of young childhood came automatically. And then the terrible consequence of stepping into that room, the unbearable burden of being told, the confusion, the miserable pain, the devastating inability to help crashed over her. This moment cut and charred and broke within her time after time after time.

Later she learned the manner of its happening. On his way home from badminton, her father, Alan, slid sideways on a dual carriage way and into the buttress of an overpass. He received catastrophic injuries, but had made it to hospital. They would go now. Elaine was so wild-eyed that the officer insisted on slowing her. Eve grappled with ugly shards of understanding, confused about what her actions should be. What does catastrophic mean? Shall I bring his pyjamas? Will he die, Mummy? Shhh, where are the car... Quick Eve, get in.

The hospital hummed around the inert body of her father. Eve and Elaine sat on opposite sides. Elaine had stopped crying but her face was red, crumpled. She leaned over her husband, hand cupped softly around his jaw, talking to deaf ears in earnest love.

Eve pulled into herself, her face pale, held still on rigid little shoulders, dressed in pyjamas and a school jumper. She was fourteen and utterly lost. She pinched and pleated a fold of blanket in her hands. She pictured her father. Changing a cassette, fiddling with the radio, saying Oh drat, like he did. She pictured the moment and held it, forever, like a challenge of love, like adoration, like a spell, the incomprehensible shards of what must have happened next, the spin, the whorl, the smashing injury, oh drat. Oh Daddy, please please please don't die.

Her face was guarded, precautionary, carved soap, she tipped her broken heart away from the world, stared at the stars on her pyjamas. She wished. She longed to fall into her mother's lap, to curl along her father's gangly body. She longed but did not move. She begged, pushing all her intention through her white-pressed fingers into the pleats of blanket, please don't let my dad die.

They were there for every day they had. Part of that gentle community of the very sick and their solemn guard of loving sentries. The smells, the blue of the nurses' uniforms, the strange timetable of hospital life soon felt like all they had ever known. It left a chronic sickness in her.

He remained unconscious for a week. And then he died. Eve was fourteen, learning that everything can change, in an instant. Life is uncertain and unkind.

Elaine was destroyed by grief. Eve was destroyed by grief. Their sorrows isolated and separated them. Love was never lost but they did not know how to function. They did not know how to be a family of two. Friends gathered around them, trying to mop up the spilled well of grief, to stop them drowning. But all must drown, in some way, when such a loss comes. Elaine took in the sight of her daughter, knowing how she suffered, how lost she must be and the added weight of it held her down, further, a second grief dragging her below the surface. Eve saw the unravelling of her mother and felt it as a curse on her own head that she could not help.

They learned eventually, over months, to function. It can seem like repair, this treading water, head mostly above the surface, lungs more often clear to breathe. And over time it seems enough of a repair that others began to treat them as though they were no longer in danger. But the needs of grief take their own sweet, sour, ugly, ungainly time.

And truly, there was after a while, nothing anyone else could do, for the task of undrowning is one for the drowned to learn alone.

Eve turned to her acoustic guitar as companion. In her room, with her guitar on her lap, she had an antidote to Elaine's suggestions that she go out, see friends. She began with the conventions of her lessons, though she stopped going to lessons as she stopped much else. She practised chords and scales, pieces set to test a student, to develop learning.

Sometimes she did not practise, she did not do anything, other than listening warily for her mother's soft tread in the hallway. She sat, motionless, in retreat, behind the camouflage of her guitar, ready to project the necessary absorption lest the revelation of her gaping emptiness hurt her mother further.

Mostly she played, picked out tunes from her book, mastered the old and learned the new. The wordless state of music helped her to forget.

She picked up a sheet for an old song. The chords were easy, her hand shaped them without thought. But there was a section where her fingers stumbled awkwardly on a run of notes. She played, back bent, concentrating on her fingers. Perhaps if I can get this, today will be ok, she said to herself. Slowly she mastered it.

It sounded so hollow, the intricate notes, even played well, so drab.

She smacked a hand across the strings. It was boring. Even if she learned to play it brilliantly, it would still be boring. The distraction was slipping. Frustration spilled, smeared her concentration, revealed the meagre limits of her ruse. Frustration rose into anger. Was this all, and forever?

She picked a note as hard, as ugly as she could. The strings twanged under her nails and she plucked it harder. It felt good to risk a bit of harm, to push the strings further than they wanted to go. She could do that. The timbre was so different. She scratched over the strings, then pulled back to her usual soft stroke. Her attention was fully on the sounds once again. What was that difference? Not just volume. She played the tune again, then smacked it out of the guitar, as loud and hard as she could. I like that, what is that, I like that sound, what happens if I... she was drawn into experiments with sound and a whole world opened before her.

She switched on the radio, the latest pop, laced together with brash jingles. She started to play, trying to fit sound into whatever came from the radio. It was thrilling, when the tones meshed, clicked into each other. The songs passed too quick for her to learn, but she felt the excitement of a puzzle, how to make sounds that fitted, however briefly.

What were they doing, these songs? How were they made?

It was too new, she was too young, to make sense of it then, to consider writing music. But she found joy in curiosity, in the experiment, and that was a beginning.

Her ears became thirsty for sound. She listened to music all the time, began by habit to unpick how it was made, working out the constructions and the strategies. Every day she played her guitar, with songs and against them.

Newly found resonances and deliberate dissonances, all as though invented by herself became as thrilling as the records she loved. She scoured the charts and found new favourites. Bands that sounded thrillingly different but readily available through the pop charts and her local WH Smith's.

There was a whole world, an endless realm, inviting her. What happened if this, or this, or this? The sweet interlock of harmonies thrilled her. She could play one note or another, they would fit into a tune equally well. She could play a beat that raced ahead, or slowly followed on. A miraculous array of choices but some felt right, others not. There was an order, so logical and beautiful that, almost of its own volition, became music. Why did not everyone fill the darkness of their days with the light of music?

A simple chord progression filled her, generously gave her both hunger and satiation. Music was edible, visible, it sat within her, she clung to it. A kind of radiant peace filled her; she was just there, floating inside and outside, for a moment. And then it was gone. And she always wanted more.

Music did not come to her as an antidote to her loss, or as a simplistic mode that equated to happiness, but it did present the possibility of a whole new universe, one not moulded only by the circumstances of her grief.

She did not know it, in those first months, but she had become a musician.

She began to open up, a dark and spiky flower. Every night she listened to John Peel. Every day she played her records and CDs, every weekend she searched for new sounds in the town's independent record shop. She was too shy to become friendly with the older, wilder employees but they recognised her intense interest, drawing her attention to new and exciting records.

She found in this music a place to be herself fully. Clamping headphones over her ears, shutting out the world, slipping freely between the sounds and the silence, the gaps in the music, she found a way to let out her aggression, resolve her sorrows. As her mind wove through these hours, wordlessly present, as her connection to music grew, she found that sadness lost its ferocious grip. Within the world of sound she first collected and then built herself, she discovered the means to carry her grief.

Over time, in a combination of accident and through the means of their own partial repair, Eve and Elaine found the means to carry on.

Elaine took long walks, letting the breeze into her, through her. It did not cleanse her of sorrows but during these walks, they were at last more clearly revealed. She came face to face with her grief; she saw the truth of its mighty burden and knew, simply, she must carry it now and forever.

And in that recognition was the beginning of repair. They repaired and remade themselves, each to the best of their ability, and then after a fashion, they remade their little family trio into an awkward but loving duet.

Eve's fascination with music soon eclipsed all else. She bought albums whenever she could, spending hours in record shops, flipping through record stacks to find new thrills. She cut her hair scruffily, badly, to Elaine's horror. Her friend Colleen helped tidy up the rougher bits, but a sweep through of gel brought a sculptural roughness that Eve loved. Elaine watched on, trying not to feel anxious. But acceptance grew from her love. She dug out Alan's shapeless old charcoal tweed coat from a suitcase in the attic. Eve wore it all the time.

As soon as she could she started going to gigs. Getting home from town was hit or miss but Leon, a kid from the village, shared her taste and they were able to wrangle late buses, lifts, secret hitch-hikes and the odd collection by a stroppy parent. There was not a trouble not worth taking, an effort not worth making. Music meant everything to her.

Eve walked into every venue feeling nervous, out of place in the noisy, bolshy confidence of the social melee. Her eyes moved quickly over faces, into corners, slid away from recognition. She slipped into the crowd, stood facing the stage, waiting for the music to begin. As soon as the first sound screamed from the speakers she lost every bind. In the ferocious blast of a packed dark hall, music thumping through the air into her lungs and shimmering through her liquid body, it all made beautiful sense. She was simple – she was light, she was energy and darkness. This was her place. Excitement welled, from her belly, from her feet, along her spine. A marvellous moment of being gone and entirely present. She was not happy exactly; she was complete, blissful, entirely herself.

Leon played bass and Eve played guitar and so they started a band. At first it was an almighty mess, but they found enough to keep them going. They met drummer Mal through a mutual friend. He lived in town, had a car. There was enough of a click between the three of them, enough shared territory for practices to become regular, for vague hopes to become settled ambitions.

Leon became entranced by Eve. Unquestioningly. Her quiet intensity and musicianship, her awkward looks, her spiky style. His recognition of how he might need her.

He could not believe his luck when one night, walking the black road home under pale moonlight, they fell into a verge together, drunk and only half inhibited. They kissed. A spell of dew on his outflung hand, a spell of night air on the warm skin of his back, a spell of half-moon glimpsed through her raven hair. A spell of blinking in the dazzling roar of a speeding motorbike.

They kissed for long enough to cement yearning in Leon. Just long enough for it to seem that they were meant to be together.

He said nothing. He surrendered a part of his heart to her.

She said nothing. Maybe they could just see what happened. They sort of acted like a couple.

Leon soon sensed, with foreboding, that Eve was less committed to him than he was to her. But she did not tell him to go away. They sat on the bench by the model village, she did not push him away when he put his arm around her. Sometimes they kissed. A couple of times when Leon's house was empty, they went to bed. When they talked about music they were close. Not quite close enough for Leon, too close for Eve. But they could fool themselves for a little while.

As his feelings grew, as time went on with nothing changing, it became harder to ignore. She would pull away from him, she was non-committal about meeting outside of practice times. She shut down any talk of what was between them.

Young love is not a softer, easier thing. It is love, as powerful and demanding as all love. Leon was slowly, confusedly, angrily heart-broken.

He hid his hurt, felt himself reduced by the burden of it. The mismatch in their affections, he feared, gave her the upper hand and he resented it. But still he loved her. Perhaps that love had elements of obsession, certainly of self-fulfilment, for it was magnified under the lens of what she could offer, what she could do, what she could be, to him.

And Leon wanted most of all to be a pop star. Not just because he loved music. Certainly not because he wanted to play the bass more than he wanted to do anything else – he loved plenty of things more than that. He wanted to be a pop star so that he would be the person he could admire, some days the person he already believed himself to be. He wanted to be above himself. And he wanted to look down. Sometimes graciously, sometimes with indifference. He did not want to be the one who felt small.

It would be fun, it would be magnificent, it would be a dream come true, to be a star.

He did love music, had exacting taste. He knew that Eve was a better, more inventive musician than himself and so she made the prospect of his own elevation significantly more likely. It was a bitter pill. He longed to fling her off, to dismiss her from his life, to demonstrate his indifference. But ambition had a strong hold.

He set about changing the weather of their connection, first dismissing any idea that they were, or even had been really a couple – no no no; he tried to imply he had never for a moment expected it. Second, he redrew and scrimped on the bounds of their friendship. In this he hoped to mark her, reduce her as he had himself felt reduced.

Quietly, she did very well understand what was happening, and that Leon intended insult with his new, sneering manner. Sometimes he hit the mark and she felt it. She wished it were not so, for it was tiresome as well as sometimes hurtful. But in part she blamed herself for letting confusion occur. She found her own resentment, for his stupid imposition of an unnecessary complication. Usually she let it slide off her, silently mouthing 'prick' at him, his pathetic need to diminish her. But she disliked conflict and usually did not feel the need to retaliate. Perhaps it was her fault, she thought, perhaps his. But that was that. They would get on with it.

Eve's own taste in music took her into unlit corners far from the glare of success. She hooked into a network of experimental musicians. Discs with hand-made covers plopped onto the doormat as she expanded her understanding of what music could be. Some of it was terrible, but the freedom to make long, wordless, textural pieces of music – that felt to her like getting gloriously lost in the wild hinterlands of imagination. She started making music under a pseudonym, eventually sending her own discs out with their own photocopied slip covers, a picture of a planetary landscape from an old library book repeat-copied into grainy black and white. Each new disc a slight variation of that one image, behind the spiky, handwritten track listing.

There was freedom in her un-gendered (let that read presumed male) anonymity. She grew a small circle of followers. Making music on her own, though it lacked the thrill of shared performance, gave her the chance to more deeply search the musical possibilities clamouring for her attention.

Soon she was buying bulk blank discs and envelopes, swapping a little stack of thrillingly earned pounds for new records. The world of music did not make her more than pocket money but what it did offer had no horizon and no boundaries.

6

Come,
Let us parlay,
tell me of your dreams

Now here we sit, many years later, Demon and I, waiting for her; waiting for the conclusion of her time, the conclusion of her music. Waiting for Demon to finally take possession of her soul. This story is almost done. A few hours remain until the deal is complete. A breeze lifts off the sea, breaks over the cliff edge a few feet away. A tang, a taint of salt. We wait. Demon is content, needing nothing more from his time here, only to wait patiently for the conclusion. I am less patient, for there is still so much that could be revealed. Demon has kept his secrets; though I have longed to understand it, I still do not know how he fashioned a dream, so costly yet so perfect that Eve was willing to buy it with her soul.

What I know for certain is that we are nearly done.

Demon will leave. And I will be no more.

We wait on a grassy clifftop for our last meeting with Eve.

I am glad for Demon. This chore, this bondage is hard on him, even the prospect of its imminent conclusion is partial, for this is an always-turning tale.

I tune out of my private thoughts, look up at Demon.

'Do you think you will ever be freed from all of this?'

'I'll never be free of it.' He is cross with me now, scolding me with a sharp hand on my back, for not understanding the weight of what he cannot explain. He is cross with me for reminding him that his bond is eternal.

A handful of people walk the clifftop path, along a gentle curve worn into the grass. Their thoughts drift up to the sky, the wheeling gulls. A woman walks carefully towards the edge, rests her hands for a moment on the dark wire of the slender fence, a mere foot from the crumbled edge. The fence, two skeins of wire between staggering metal poles, is there to inform rather than restrain. She looks to the horizon, lost in the edges of a dream, then retreats back to the path.

I wonder about the one who will bring Demon down next time. How many years or centuries will he sleep until pulled from his own blissful dreams by the urgency of another's? How many brothers, how many turns, how many times must this story of glorious and stupidly prosaic desire be told? I try to soothe him – it is my role, this much I know.

'Maybe they will all be gone. Drowned by glaciers filling up the sea, burnt or starved out of storm-ravaged land. Poisoned by their own tricks. They are doing a bad enough job of ensuring their survival, after all.'

Demon looks at me, pulls me over to him, runs his hand along my back once more. I have mollified him and he is happy again, consoled by the prospect of humans disappearing, freeing him from his bond.

'That may very well be,' he says, stroking my head, as though fondly.

'Let us hope for disaster, it will be easiest for all in the end,' I say, cheerfully.

7

Eve,
make ready
for the fate you called

Music wrapped her. With it she built branching tendrils of possibility. There were vistas, patterns. There were paths and walls, a maze. There was a constant flow between expansion and retraction. It was hard to tell where music ended and Eve began. Her intensity, her focus, the completeness of her absorption was a shield from the scouring of Demon's entreaty.

She, from the many-doored centre sought her way through the maze so that she might fully know it. Demon, from the outside, from a chink in the farthest wall, sought a way in.

They did not come to meet for a long time.

She sat for hours, on the edge of her bed, her acoustic guitar on a crossed thigh. Wandering her idle mind, she would pick out a tune. Something came and then it went. New notes arrived. She shuffled, settled, played the notes again with deliberation, listening now fully.

As she kept playing, and as her imagination filled the spaces around the guitar, the sounds began to sway and stagger. Quiet insistence jostling against imperfect connection. Yes, this was the beginning of something. She sat up straighter, became more focused. So much of her way was plodding patience, wrong turns, flutters that evaporated before they could evolve. But then she would feel the sweet promise of a beginning. Somewhere, she would find the music.

In life she was tentative, uncertain. Seeing no natural place for herself in the world, she painstakingly remade it around herself each time she ventured forth.

But here, in this imperfect in-between, she took her true shape. And it was strong, brave, selfish with quiet certainty.

We studied all that she did to build her dreams in the hope that Demon might find a way to steal the provisioning of them.

He set to whispering, he sent a fog, a smoke signal. He whispered into the chink in the wall. He tapped out tunes, runes, and temptations. He dabbled in many languages to find the one she would understand. He breached the walls but staggered unseen through the maze of her mind.

'Just think what I could do for her. Just think how I could make the world love her,' said Demon. His voice whispered away into greedy longing. 'Think of that soft soul. The prize. Given up and mine to claim. That perfect trophy.'

He was always impatient, but sometimes in those first weeks, he did manage to temper his frustration. He was learning her ways. Once he knew her soul, he could command it, and then could make it his. But she resisted as a rock resists a mountain stream. Even in a storm, even in the full flush of ice melt, the stone parts the onslaught of the water. The rock is unmarked, the water spends its energy and is gone.

But this much I know, water will wear away a stone. Water seeps into the tiniest of fissures, washes away the grains until the ground is gone and the rock is forced to tumble in obedience. Water will roar and wear, and it will creep, settle, freeze, it will push and push at any weakness.

Yes, though he feared failure then, he pushed his way in. He tormented her, over years, with his persistence. He had to work much harder than he could have guessed. She resisted. For so long. And it cost her.

It is not usually a challenge, the marks are so ready to deal. But be it deep in their subconscious, as though hidden from their own hearing, they must say yes. Though Demon shapes his wares from theirs, this is not a honey trap. For there was a gift, granted long before demons were charged with the gathering of souls; the gift of free will. So much made of it and so many troubles. This much I know.

The marks may choose to believe in the glories Demon conjures, to believe that they alone have achieved their elevation. Few who long for greatness are prone to casting another as the engine of their triumph. But whatever tale they tell themselves once high-flying with their dreams, at that moment when they speak to Demon and they make their deal, it is with full knowledge and consent. They give up their souls knowingly, unbeset by confusion or trickery. That some choose to keep such dealings buried in the quiet voice of their subconscious minds is not Demon's concern.

All this I know.

Demon finds it tiresome, the awful moment of clarity at the end, his own work done, his homeward journey secured, when the marks can do nothing but see the deal they have made. The dark depths of the mind, compelled by fate, link to the chattering voice of the everyday. *What have I done?* is the phrase he most despises. Really they know full well what they have done, for they blessed the deal and Demon with the execution of it. Fools. An unblinding that comes too late to be useful.

I ask him as we wait for the conclusion of our years together, what he thinks he will get this time.

'I don't know. I like the ones who say, oh, I did well with those years, didn't I? And they welcome the end, repay the debt without whinging. This curious endgame they play out with me is truly a test of character.'

'Yours or theirs?' I quip. He ignores me.

We return to our wait. And it will soon be done. And Demon hardly sees me now.

All this I know.

8

oh
I see
how wild,
how far and wide.
Let me be your engine,
let me be your beating wings

It is not uncommon for a human to reach beyond their experience, to long for transcendence, for the chance to exceed the limitations of self. Nor is it uncommon (poor Demon, tuned as though only to the frequency of human desire, is plagued by the constant bleating of it) for a human to crave power – in the form that will be best understood by those around them. But to wake a Demon brother, there must be gifts, the promise of the extraordinary. A combination that finds a moment, gets caught on a cosmic incline and is delivered into the ear of a sleeping demon.

It happens, but not so very often. Not so often as a human wishes to be magnificent. Otherwise we would not be able to move on this earth for demons plying their trade, and what would be the point of that?

Eve was one who possessed the key, and I understood why.

For what else does a world built on the frequencies of sound, carved from the cosmos, speak of, if it is not the divine?

She imagined, in wordless pictureless ways, the slender wire of a single silver note hung between the poles of planets.

She imagined, in wordless pictureless ways, a desolate road of ruby and tourmaline running off a burning horizon into the heart of a star.

She imagined, in wordless pictureless ways, gullies cut through rock then zipped shut, sealed by the susurration of an ancient, detuned stringed instrument.

Sometimes a mark will greet Demon with arms outstretched in welcome. He and Eve were cast more as hunter and hunted. He cared for little more than what he needed her to provide. But he felt this affinity with her; there is a grandeur about the place of his provenance that found echoes in her imagination. She made music with her mind's eye and it let him catch glimpses of his home.

All this I know.

Though she was extraordinary enough to wake a Demon, though her yearning was great, though she longed for something more magnificent than she could name, she did not hear him. His voice was a headache, a distraction. She did not want rewards. She did not want adulation or love. She did not want power – at least not for herself. She wanted to find and harness the magic of divinity, not for herself, but for her music. She wanted all that Demon was, not what he could conjure.

As I came to understand this, I began to see why Demon started to become anxious about the deal. Had she even knowingly summoned the divine or was it a quirk of cosmic accident?

Demon had thus far always succeeded. Those who are called have to, for if they fail, they do not return home. If they fail their exile is entire. They are condemned to stay on earth eternally, the shyest, most miserable of wraiths. It is brutal.

He told me once, once only, of the time he saw one such. The most pitiable thing. I shudder at the memory of his horror, even now. That once-brother filled him with revulsion, with horrible contamination. And the rising of a profound pity that kept him momentarily bound. The once-brother was an insipid rag, a face almost comically working soundless expressions of suffering and grief. The once-brother clung to the trunk of a hawthorn tree, silently beseeching, asking Demon to take him back, sending out piercing twists of misery that came with knowing he never could.

Demon was bound between pity and disgust. His companion that time was a snake, she coiled tight around his neck, hid her face away down Demon's back bone. As he told me, I too cowered into him, tucking tighter into his lap, feeling the fear of it, centuries later.

That horrible encounter served as a caution. It was made somehow worse by the ease with which Demon's own trade was concluded on that visit. The comfort of his victory filled him with further contempt for the wretched, beseeching creature, hugging the rough bark of a twisted hillside hawthorn. His pitiable once-brother haunts him still. This much I know.

We sat after in a long silence, never spoke of it again.

I will loose this fear when my time is done. When Demon's time comes around once more, he will awaken to that haunting. It will follow him for eternity.

9

**We,
for now
join two as one,
to make it all come true.
Step closer. Come join me, Eve**

We lolled on the village hall roof, basking in the sunshine. It was summer, a half year and more turned. We had spent (wasted, perhaps, though I never said so) months in that little bedroom. I sat at Eve's side as she explored her music and Demon trudged his dead ends. For several days Demon had been bad-tempered and it had pulled us away from the chore. I was glad, for I relished a change of scene. Without the entertainment of music making the bedroom was an airless, unrewarding place to spend so much time.

Out of nowhere it seemed, with a jolt for me as I tried to adjust to the sudden rush of it, we were airborne. My body still bore some of the weights and measures of my natural form and, in panic, my insides lurched sickly as I tried to catch up. As we sliced through the air Demon told me what had made us move so suddenly. There had been a calling, the soft siren of a rare daydream reaching him, clear and strong, from the convenience store where Eve worked.

Eve did not usually slip into dreaming in this way. But there it all was. An overlay across the shelves of the little supermarket; Eve, alone in an idle moment, daring to dream of her own elevation. Daring to place herself in a fantasy that seemed too much to hope for.

She sat behind the counter of the empty shop, looking over the heads of her conjured, rapt audience at a stage. Banks of electronic equipment covered the newspaper stand. On the right, the chillers were overwhelmed by a posse of cellists and the aerial-like protrusions of strange brass instruments. Along the back wall into the shop next door was a choir, singing the thrum of a wavering drone. The tension rose with the sound, and there, suddenly was Eve, head bent over a bank of effects pedals and a keyboard. Her guitar leaned carelessly against the chair where she sat. I was disappointed that her dreams did not stretch to emboldening her presence, her look, for she wore the black jeans and t-shirts of her everyday. But as we watched the building grew, blond wood furled out over our heads as she guessed at elaborate fluting for sound enhancement. The walls climbed higher, the imaginary geometry shaped itself for the perfect presentation of music. The hall spread wider, the audience grew, the stage elevated, and just for a tiny moment that might have caused Demon's heart to pound, had he the biology of an earth creature, Eve rose up, her hair wilder, glossier, darker, her clothes jet, sculpted black over a white shirt. She unbent, stood taller and took on the adoration of the audience. I could feel Demon's urgency.

He whispered hoarse and hurried in her ear, *I can give you this. All of it. I can give you a collaborator architect to wonder at your precise genius and build a ship for your music. I can give you an audience who will beg you for more. I can give you a stage with any formula of musicians, a residency in the Royal Festival Hall. I can do this! And you have what it costs. You can pay me. You have the fee. You do not need it – not now. You'll barely miss it, so filled with the joy of your waking days will you be. I can do this for you, Eve.*

The door chimed, three school kids walked into the supermarket, comically small in blazers bought for a year of rapid growth. Eve's dream shrunk and slid away, like a silk veil through a wedding ring. She turned to watch the children, though with the owner absent she could not bring herself to care much whether they pocketed the odd Lion Bar or tube of fruit pastilles. A tax for their spending, for they spent a great deal on crisps, drinks, illicit cigarettes.

Eve watched the children, waiting for them to bring their snacks to the counter, thinking about whether to eat dinner before or after band practice later that evening. Demon lay on the floor behind the counter, an arm across his eyes, weakly muttering her name.

'Not exactly wrapping this up, are we?' I said, thinking to tease and cheer him. I regretted it, for it was meant in fond jest but I could tell that Demon was stung at what seemed a rebuke. After all, what did I know of his work only a few months into our time together? But I already had great belief in him – how could I doubt the all-encompassing power of one whose mere touch could transform me so? I believed he would find his way and had thought there was little harm in some light teasing. Demon did not always share my confidence. In the rare moments when I have also feared his failure, I kept it quiet.

Demon, injured by my careless jest flew out of the shop, into the high branches of an elm. He was expecting me to feel sorry. Just then, I did not. I hopped across to a kidney shaped island of grass, studded with the shine of sweet packets, and dozed under the shade of an unpromising sapling. I was content enough.

Later Demon came down from the tree and lay next to me on the grass. We stayed on the oval island into the night. The estate grew quiet, the arcade of shops empty and shuttered until morning. Boys in a battered car screeched out of town, pub-closed-drunk and excited for the speed of the open country roads. A babysitter walked home, her shoulders hunched, looking behind her uneasily, the rough edge of her duffle coat grazing each cheek in turn. Safer in the streets, perhaps, than in the car of the drunken, returned parents. Who can tell? That spectrum of risk and reward is for others.

10

You
are a tepid,
listless creature.
Yet you might condemn me!

But Demon had his own ancient tally of risks and rewards to negotiate. I wanted to help him, I wanted to be a good companion, for that was my divine role. I thought of the stories he had told me, how the memories cheered him.

'Do you remember the wine maker in Turkey?'

'Yes, of course.' Demon showed no interest.

I began retelling what he had not so long before told me, gilding the tale with admiration. I wanted to remind him of his successes and distract him from current failure.

'The wine maker who thought he did not need you. That fat and foolish man who called you down, with dreams, not that time of music but of wine. A taste he dreamed, every sip cherished, every precious drop hymned in praise. That foolish man who thought to waste the attentions of the divine.'

I lowered my voice. I leaned towards Demon, he leaned to me, paying close attention now, and I quietly, intently retold the tale.

'That wine seller had such expectations of his elevation, such imaginings of his might. He fairly screamed at you, what he wanted, what he deserved, what it was he thought the fates owed him.' I widened my eyes, demonstrating my indignant disapproval in the rise of my voice.

'Oh he did. Relentless, demanding. It was unpleasant.'

'He demanded riches, friendship with admiring aristocracy, he wanted all the girls, and a good number of the boys, to fall at his feet – intoxicated by him and by his wine. He wanted so much unimaginative foolishness.'

'Gold, naked bodies, pleasure. At least this one wants better than that.'

'Yes indeed, for this fool wanted what any fool wants. It seemed at first so easy, Demon. And yet it was to be a test of your cunning. For he took fright, that wine maker. He took fright for the loss of his soul.'

'He was scared. So I waited.'

'You waited. And you found the way. You told a tale, wound deep into the heart of his neighbour, you made a lover's pact before he even knew he was the lover. She draped herself before him, she dropped her bare shoulder, lifted her embroidered hem, set the gleam of her skin to lure him in. She found she wanted that fat wine maker more than she wanted anything. You took her to the river and she cast a golden hook. And the wine maker stopped wanting all the bodies, all the beauties of the world. His soul cried, almost piteously, for this woman. Love, the way it does, caught him. She was not the most beautiful, not young. But she dropped her shoulder just so, working in her garden she moved just so, the gleam of her skin, the endless curve of her slow movements. It caught him, just so. No other would do.'

'But she would not give herself to him for nothing.'

'She would not.'

'She baited my trap, Rabbit.'

'For a man cannot have the prize unless he pays the price. She would not give herself to him until he had become wealthy. He forgot to fear for his soul and returned with renewed purpose and ambition to his wines, that they might bring him golden coins, and the coins would bring to him this woman. And desire burned so hot that his mind had not the room to remember the value of his soul. What was the abstract notion of eternity compared to the delicious, impending doom of fulfilment? And so you made a deal, he got his prize. The beautiful neighbour now his bride. And because the wine maker had become foolish with lust, before the marriage bed was even cold on the first day of wedded bliss, before their first breakfast, you took his soul and were gone, bound for deserved sleep. Doubtless she became a very merry widow, that graceful neighbour lady, only one day married. We cannot know if she would thank her husband for forgetting to demand time as well as conquest. But we know that you, dear Demon, were rewarded for your cunning and took a fine prize home with you.'

Demon was pleased with me, flattered that I remembered so much, soothed by my display of admiration. I was in turn puffed up that my telling pleased him so.

At last we settled into the night. I did want to help him, truly. I wanted to be a good companion. And I felt for him, the relentless tremor of fear in the anticipation of failure. It is a thankless, uncertain chore he has been given, without even knowing why. To be so mighty and still so raw.

A thought came to Demon as dawn rose.

'What if I work on not Eve's deepest desires, but her nearest?'

He told me how this might work, a switch to find in the achievable what seemed impossible in the most desirable. There are dreams after all, that are not so bound by unassailable purity as to render them impenetrable. Muckier dreams. The dreams that make Demon pay attention. He told me of such a one.

'There was one, so very long ago. An artist who cast the most refined bronzes. He was a one that could not decide if fame or noble obscurity best suited his vision of himself. A pompous fool, he was. But these mistaken notions of his worth made him slippery. Truth was he did not want to leave his little village, find himself wanting in the employment of the powerful. He did not want the fullness, nor did he want the mighty labour, the work his soul could bring. So I brought him riches and comfort, I brought him local patrons who enriched him absurdly. He was the king of that little hill and never had to test his worth elsewhere. He felt that in clinging to this smallness, he had not sold out. His sense of his own integrity remained intact but his art, of course, did not survive.'

We had been with Eve to her band practices for we had been with her everywhere. We did not always stick around – watching every waking thought of even the most elevated human mind is excessively dull. The construction of rudimentary songs is equally unrewarding. But Demon's new focus changed that.

11

I
who
dealt with
kings and peasants,
ripped away their souls,

They practised in the village hall, and the next time we were ready to join them. We hovered weightless on Eve's shoulders as she went to collect the key from Maureen. She knocked, awaiting with dread the awkwardness that was about to follow. She mumbled a reluctant hello at Maureen who as she opened the door was already chattering; her nervousness in the face of anyone quiet made her fill the silence with sound, pushing both women further into their cartoon forms. Eve shrank, Maureen babbled. She thought how Eve had always been a strange child, even before her father had died. She had been a kind of playmate with her own son, Mark, in the way that all village children are. But they were very different. Mark liked watching videos with his girlfriend and going to the pub with his mates. Maureen still bought most of his clothes without making many mistakes. Eve was silent, odd. She probably could've been a pretty girl but she looked dreadful in those drab and boyish clothes, that ragged black hair, like her head was being attacked by ravens. Maureen shuddered superstitiously.

'If only you knew, Maureen,' I whispered in Demon's ear from our position on Eve's shoulders. He smiled, gleefully, for once seeing the joke.

In a breathless break from thoughts and dislocated chatter, Maureen relented, got the key from a bowl in the kitchen and gratefully shut the door as Eve turned to leave.

Eve unlocked the hall, began dragging amps out of a cupboard stacked with outdated games and gym equipment. Leon arrived through the double doors, a plastic bag of notebooks and fags banging at his side.

'I've nailed the new song and I've got loads of new ideas,' he said.

'Great,' was Eve's flat response, as she bent over her amp to plug in a lead. He talked on about his idea for a song they were struggling with. She did not notice how much he craved her praise, she never did. Sometimes Eve's disinterest, her insularity, was as good as unkind. He stifled his disappointment.

Mal the drummer as usual arrived late, his battered car pulling into the village hall car park with a rattle. He loved making a noise with mates, letting loose on loud, aggressive music, drinking beer. He loved the subtle complexities of rhythm and the pleasure of nailing a beat that powerfully drove a song.

Leon sang and played bass, dreamed of becoming famous, being chummy with other stars and disdainful of interviewers from the NME. He wanted to be the singer in a band more than he wanted to make music. Leon was both insecure and arrogant, driven by expectation of success and fear of failure. He had his reasons; everyone does. It would save Demon and his kind a lot of trouble if those reasons were rendered visible, and thus perhaps, be understood.

The glitchy power of Eve's guitar was perfect. She did not always share her thoughts – nor her disdain, for in truth she accorded limited value to what they produced together. But the music was exciting; it was good for what it was.

She came across to the other two, friendly, non-judgemental Mal and broken-hearted, defensive Leon, as distant, aloof, sometimes arrogant. But lacking the confidence to start out alone, she recognised somewhere that she needed them. And both Mal and Leon knew (though Leon disliked it the more) that they needed her too.

When their time was up, they went to the bench next to the model village, to smoke, to argue about songs. It was entertaining to watch. The most stubborn of games, the most human of games; three people manoeuvring in and around and past each other without any notion of how relentlessly they played. Some always play harder than others. But even passivity is a tactic in the game. We studied them, Demon and I, to find how their progress might become a lure, catching Eve on Demon's hook.

They had been working on a song of Eve's. It was lost, shapeless, adrift somewhere between her intentions and Leon's need to mark the writing of it. For he would not be a placeholder, and if Eve did all the writing, what else would he be?

'It's too long, Eve,' he said, again, roll-up caught in the corner of his mouth. He had a point: most songs of the time were not eleven minutes long.

'But who says? Why should it be short because that's what everyone does now?'

'It's dated.'

'Jesus, it's not a skirt, it's a song. We don't have to be in fashion.' She said this quietly, as she always did; her rare disagreements, those that came to be spoken out loud, were softly worded, if seriously meant.

'We're not fucking Genesis,' said Leon.

'We're not everyone else, though, either. We don't have to get permission, learn the rules.' Eve stared, shook her head, dipped behind her black fringe. She felt utter disdain for Leon's limitations. And though she kept it to herself, somewhere he knew it well enough.

'I'm the last one who wants to follow rules, Eve.' Leon was stung into indignant bluster, and Eve was glad. 'But it's – boring. We're supposed to be doing this together but you're so stubborn and you can't see when things are just not working.'

Quiet anger rippled under Eve's skin. She resented the presumption, the imposition, and somewhere too, she did not want to cause upset. She disliked the sensation of having made enough of herself that she got in the way of another. She had glorious peers but not many girls then led bands, played guitar, made decisions. The ones who knew about music, who really understood it, were apparently boys. She was a trespasser and she attempted to avoid the charge by walking with a slight stoop. Times changed, but Eve was a girl then, in a land of boys. She pulled her anger, as she ever did, back from the perils of expression.

Oh Eve, what a waste.

Part of her could have said, with truth and an indifference that would mortally wound: *Yeah, you're right. I don't give a shit about this song*; a glorious selfish streak whorling out uncensored from her soul, intent on a music she made for herself. The other part would pull away from causing disappointment and conflict. But it was not enough to soothe Leon.

Eve was not giving Demon that much either. Equally without care or malice, she withheld from Demon what he most needed. It brought Leon and Demon into a kind of mucky brotherhood. It was Eve's lack of confidence that gave Demon hope. He was not so different to Leon in that respect.

Sometimes I heard both of them hate her.

She was to Demon and me as she was to Leon and Mal: she did not bend to what would make her most useful because she did not crave anything we four could offer. She would not be so easily shaped. Though I sometimes feared for Demon's peace of mind, I loved her for it. All this I know.

12

to
be now
so thwarted
by a stubborn child?

Eve's finger tapped lightly on the body of her guitar, a comfortable, hollow sound. What was this certainty of hers, about her own music? Was she mad to think about doing it alone? It did not feel extraordinary, to play, to invent, to have dreams of what she could do with sound. It felt as much a part of her as eating and breathing. But to imagine others finding value in it – that was a less comfortable step.

'Ask me!' screamed Demon.

She flicked her head in annoyance, as though in response to a buzzing fly. A fly that would make its way into the crevices and cavities of her skull if she did not pack them out with music. For a long time she was able to hide herself behind a barrier of sound, to protect herself this way from his whining, painful intrusions.

But as soon as she considered how she might fit into the world, how the world might find her, Demon had a way in. Her uncertainty opened a door.

It was too much to do it alone. Being on a stage, alone. No, she could not imagine doing that. But every time she thought about what she wanted, the answer was alway music. Time for music. An audience. You cannot elevate a multitude without a multitude. Yes, she acknowledged she did want an audience. Perhaps it was best to stick with Leon and his three-minute verse-chorus orthodoxies, Leon with his *it's called a middle eight, Eve, not a middle twenty-four.*

It was enough, this raucous, interesting sound they made, to snake through, to wake her soul. It was exciting. The drums and bass pulsed in a jagged drive. She could skip and soar over the top or sink down into the massy bulk of it. It would be a relief not to have to deal with things, meeting people, forced to pursue and persuade on her own.

Demon whispered and seemingly at last, Eve heard. She listened to a voice telling seductive tales of the freedom that comes with success. It sounded like knowledge, like her own wisdom. All she had to do was wise up, accept the easier path. The tension in her temples subsided as Demon's voice became honeyed salve.

Yes, it would be a kind of luxury to be in a successful band. And yes she did believe that this could be such a band.

Demon was frantic with excitement.

Little tendrils were unfurling, reaching out curiously from Eve, to find out at last what Demon offered. And still she thought, as though in defiance, that it could all be so much more.

One day, as Eve played a sinuous thread of mournful distortion and Leon scribbled in his notebook, Mal's car pulled into the gravelled parking space behind the village hall and he hurried, late as usual, through the door. As soon as he came in Leon spoke to them both.

'Listen, I've had an idea for the band name.' All of us turned to listen, as he had asked. Band name had been a big problem. A stumbling block. And all five of us longed for progress.

Leon paused for a moment, both in fear of ridicule and for dramatic capture of the moment.

'What about Never?' he said.

Mal and Eve turned the name over in their minds. It sat well, it fitted. Mal said almost instantly 'I love it. Well done mate, you've cracked it!' Leon beamed. Eve gazed at the word, the name, then she nodded, smiled, 'yeah, it really works. Nice one.'

They were buzzing. Leon was thrilled to have put his personal marker on that aspect of the project, for it is surely the leader's right to name.

Then for Demon and I a scene of joyous comedy unrolled.

'It's really cool too, because it has Eve, right in the middle!' said Mal. The colour drained from Leon's face. How could he roll back on it now? How could he have been so stupid? Eve tutted and smiled, said 'no, it's just a cool word.' Leon started rummaging in his tatty plastic bag, went outside for a smoke. The joy in the room had vanished long before Mal and Eve caught up. The practice passed in mysterious gloom.

But how we laughed!

13

Oh
make up
your mind!

Time idled by.

Demon watched, hoping for inspiration.

Demon did not prevail and so we waited.

Desires have many iterations. Eve's desires and her fears played out in her dreams, in the concoctions of her mind. Yes, it would be cool to fly wild on stage, to ride high on adrenalin and guitars. No, it would be a tragedy to settle for that. Better just to keep working, probably no one would love what she did, she should just do it for herself. It was too big a risk. Was there any point?

She never said that she did not want to lose her soul. This thought, though clear, though held firm, never made it to her worded mind. She just knew that her soul was worth preserving. Yes, she could be famous, but no, so much would be lost. Such were her conversations with a demon. Though it frustrated him, I, having no doubts about his eventual success, was more relaxed. I knew, from that first touch of his hand, what power he had.

She could not hide behind the purity of her devotion forever, this half-made girl.

My time passed in a mixture of idleness, boredom and curiosity. But I always kept a careful eye on Demon, to be ready for my duty, to soothe or boost, whenever it was required. In those early days he kept me busy. These last years I have hardly had to think of him at all.

For Eve, time passed in frustrating confusion. She was host to a silent battle known only in her core. She felt anxious, certainly, but was unable to identify the source. She could not trace these buried workings, the conversation happening in the shadowland of her mind. It takes patience, perfect stillness, to lure out this deepest knowledge. Eve was too young, too solitary, too new to conversing with a demon.

Though she did not recognise what so unsettled her, she felt the impact of it. Stuck in a turbulent river race, there was too much disruption, her musical inventions would not coalesce. She played a listless tune, hearing something in it, a nothing, a scrap. She heard more loudly the nothing in it. What was the point? Boring, predictable chords. She had nothing. She had work in the morning at a mini supermarket a few miles away on the edge of town. What was the point of pretending anything else could be her life? Everything was annoying and uncertain. She went downstairs, stuck her head round the living room door where Elaine was watching TV.

'I'm going to see if Christopher is home.'

'Ok love. See you later.'

She went out, stretched her shoulders, let the cool evening air soothe the nape of her neck where her hair was razored short. She tried to feel the cold as though it were an antidote, freezing away her frustrations. Let thoughts dissipate. Just let there be nothing.

At Christopher's she could soften away the world, with the warmth of a glass of whiskey, with music, with a friend.

We had spent many pleasant hours with Eve and her dear friend Christopher. They were unusual friends as he was many years older than her. He lived in the big house behind the rhododendrons next to the model village.

'I liked Christopher,' I say to Demon, who is lying next to me near the cliff edge, looking up into the sky.

'Christopher?' He says. He really is the most callous being.

14

You
bore
me so…

Their meeting had been slow and awkward, requiring great determination from Christopher. He often noticed Eve sitting on the bench overlooking the model village near his front gate. He remembered her from years ago, she had been visiting the spot since she was a young girl. Now she was a young woman, and clearly, from the way she skipped back and forth, listening on her headphones to the same piece over and over, she was obsessed with music. He was curious.

Christopher was an open-hearted man who liked people, believed all worth knowing. He began to slow his pace as he passed by, on his way to the village shop, or the bus stop, hoping a conversation might begin. But she was too absorbed to notice him.

One day, on a whim of curiosity, he sat down beside her. She stared into the roofs of the miniature houses, embarrassed by this bold and clearly unnecessary intrusion. She continued, listening, re-listening, skipping to different parts. He smiled hopefully at the side of her head for some moments, and though also by now embarrassed himself, felt the need, having come thus far, to persist. She never does make these things easy – it was as awkward a start to a friendship as was possible.

Eventually, feeling no choice in the matter, she removed her headphones and flicked a glance at the man next to her. She was alarmed. Not in fear of harm, but because she did not know what to do, how to react. What could this posh old man want?

'You seem to be listening very intently to your music,' he said. It was a good introduction, good enough. It stopped her from standing, walking away, feigning a realisation of the time as she glanced at the stopped clock on the church tower.

'Yes. It just arrived today, from Germany.'

'Did you buy it from a German music shop?'

'No, we kind of, there's a bunch of people who make the same sort of stuff, we do swaps.'

'Oh how exciting!'

They talked on. Christopher's genuine interest came as a gift to Eve. He asked to listen, which made her, though she hid it, smile. Such an old man would surely not like experimental electronic music. But he surprised her, talking about the dynamism, how the unintelligible spoken word was hypnotic, like an incantation. Yes, she said, yes, it is.

The next time he joined her on the bench, she mentioned her own music. He asked to listen, shyly she agreed to play something to him, some time, always another time. Eve was certain she would never play this man any of her music, but she enjoyed their conversation and felt she had no one else with whom she could talk in this way; she did not trust her peers with her earnestness, her conviction, the scale of her hopes and dreams.

Their paths crossed in the village shop, Christopher hailing her with easy cheer as he put his basket of groceries next to the till. Eve mumbled a hello. He was waiting for her outside.

'I remember you when you were little, sitting next to the model village, where you often sit now.'

'Oh. Right.'

'Yes, Jon used to call you the guardian. He was quite taken with you.' Christopher smiled at Eve. She felt at a disadvantage which did nothing to smooth the path of their friendship. But Christopher did not give in so easily. He saw she was reserved and did not hold it, as some were prone, against her.

After a few months their passing chats became as easy as small talk was for a girl like Eve. It helped that Christopher did not become awkward in the face of her reticence. He did not chatter, or try to fill the silences. But he did ask her, always, how her music was progressing, and listened closely to her gaunt replies. Whenever she made a brief comment, on difficulty with structure, or the mood of a melody, or her frustration with an ending, he was truly interested, and thus she came to learn that music was something Christopher valued as much as she did.

He invited her to the house. Later that evening, waiting under Christopher's orange porch light she hesitated before ringing the bell. She hitched up her jeans, pushed her fingers through the spikes of her hair, huffed out a breath. She looked back over her shoulder at the welcoming anonymous darkness of the village green. Perhaps she should leave? He probably had not meant it. The house was tatty but also bigger and grander than most others in the village and Christopher was kind of posh, and clearly old. She felt sure she had misread the invite, meant only as politeness, and in taking it literally she was intruding, creating embarrassment for them both. Yet he had been so genuinely interested. And he had been so interesting. It was rare for Eve to meet someone who understood the depth of her interest, or shared it. Leon could barely suppress a sneer when she mentioned her own work. She had never directly spoken to any of the people she swapped CDs with. Perhaps this kindly, curious man might, possibly, be just as he seemed – someone who really cared about what drove her.

She hesitated, then pushed the doorbell. Moments later he opened the door with a welcoming smile, leading her into the kitchen. Two enormous hi-fi speakers sat on the kitchen units, wires trailing over the pine cupboard fronts, snaking off into the adjoining room. She saw instantly in this awkward arrangement, the privileging of music, and felt at home. She flicked her eyes over the kitchen, taking in her surroundings surreptitiously, not bold enough for unguarded curiosity. If the kitchen had once been grand it was shabby now. She relaxed, just a little.

He pulled out two glasses, slid a bottle of whisky from behind one of the speakers then, pausing uncertainly, asked whether she'd prefer Sprite. Eve was not much of a drinker, but she did not want lemonade. Christopher filled a small jug with some tap water and put it on the table. She followed his lead for how much to tip into the tumbler. The whisky, barely softened by a slug of water, was harsh but she liked it. She still does.

They talked about how she worked. He was fascinated by the technology; for him rich with the wonder of the new, and for her and her budget, frustratingly limited.

He took the disc she eventually produced from her coat pocket. Her hesitation was almost pantomime. He smiled, kept his hand held out and she reluctantly handed it to him. He followed the wires into the living room, dashed back into the kitchen so as not to miss the start of the CD. Eve sat at an angle, straight legs and back, chin tucked to chest, listening, because she always does and because it laid a barrier between them. The speakers were good. That was something.

Christopher listened too, leaning on his forearms, staring into the floral depths of peeling wallpaper above the speakers. For once he did not hear the ghost of a conversation, wallpaper in the kitchen is absurd Jon. I know but mother loved it and it'll fall off one day and we can replace it then. It was amazing that the wallpaper managed to cling on at all, under the weight of now two generations of sad reminders.

On the first slow rise of the track Eve was instantly filled with regret. She shut her eyes, folded her arms protectively, pulling her shirt across her body, hands clamped to her ribs. She pressed her elbows down tight, as though to trap her hands there. He would think it was rubbish. He had been mistaken about her, and now would not know what to say. Oh god, why did I come? But what would he know anyway? It's not his music. Any minute now he's going to say something really stupid, and at least that will make an end to this.

It lasted around five minutes. Eve leapt from her seat, flew into the living room to turn off the hi-fi, even less happy with what followed than she was by now with what she had so carefully chosen for sharing. She pressed stop just as a blast of distortion kicked off the second track.

'I'd love to hear more!' Christopher called from the kitchen, wanting only to encourage. But she pocketed the CD. She dawdled, preparing for the embarrassment of pretence, ready to be disappointed in him. She expected to be found wanting and expected to find him wanting too. Her frown, drawn in the finest thread, spelled uncertainty and defiance.

Christopher was a man who could read the subtle language of the body as Eve could not. He saw her shrink from this moment, perceived as failure, saw her stand taller to dismiss it. She did not notice the sincerity of his happy surprise. Or, she noticed something, some form of positivity, but was not able to believe in it.

In her slight, shy-bound movements he read the contradiction and the quiet resilience. He felt tenderness and, overwhelmingly, the desire to help her. He admitted to himself that no, perhaps he would not buy it for himself, but there was undoubtedly, thrillingly, something happening here, with this music, with this musician.

Eve left much later, cheeks glowing with whisky and warmth. He had asked such good questions. They had talked for ages, he really was interesting. He played her his favourite music, choosing Schoenberg, Mahler, Berg for her introduction, then moving to more recent compositions. He talked about how new and misunderstood this music had been when it first was performed. She fell into it, curiously and with growing excitement. The soundscape was different, orchestral not electronic. It took an act of will to ignore the singing – too clean and too mannered. And without distortion the music at first sounded thin, until she grew accustomed, tuned in to the rich vibrations of the instruments. And there was a beguiling glitchiness that came from the composition. The structures and dynamics were close to what she sought. She left with two albums under her arm, to return to Christopher when she was ready. They both looked forward to meeting again.

15

**It
could
all be done
so quickly, girl.
Your head would clear
your path set wide and fair –
fairer than you have the wit to dream**

Perhaps it was because I loved Eve's music so much that it came to me with beautiful clarity, as though I shared it with her. I was grateful for what felt like a connection. Demon is a poor companion and he has left me alone many times. I have had no one to talk to. Sometimes I pick up fragments of thoughts from the humans around me, but only Demon hears me speak; only he, if he can be bothered, responds to my words. It has sometimes been lonely.

Envy has made me curious about the way that Demon and Eve talk to each other. It has changed over the years. Back then, when he was trying to find his way, Demon told me that Eve heard him as though his voice was a radio in the background. Her attention was caught, now and then, but she did not respond. Other times she closed herself off, shut him out. He sometimes battered at that door. He harangued and implored to be let in. But she did not open up to him. It was not easy to resist but resist she did. For what seemed the longest time.

I watched her, hands pressed to her face, to her temples. Her eyes closed. She pressed her fingers into her scalp, massaged the muscles of her neck. I wished for her that Demon were not so determined. I wished he would try seduction rather than force.

Sometimes, if he caught her half awake, half dreaming, she might listen. She might slip into a dream of roaring crowds, of trucks filled with amps and roadies, of recording studios with beautiful instruments leaning into corners and mixing desks as wide as two arms could reach. Still she did not signal her wish to make a deal but Demon knew that at least his offer had been heard.

'She knows what I have. She knows what she can have. She just doesn't know yet how to accept it,' he said.

'Or whether to?'

'Do you wish me to fail, Rabbit?'

'No, I do not. Just, I wonder, there must be some who—'

'Luckily for me, there have been none yet.' He glowered at me. He even showed his teeth, like a dog, or a fox. I trembled and bowed my head.

Nothing took hold, nothing was ruled out. Demon had reached a stalemate with his mark. We waited, we were stuck, as though in a sheltered lagoon. Buoyant, safe, reef-protected and sand-barred, the open sea barely a glimmer on the horizon. The sun rose and set. We bobbed in the thick water. The days turned and we paddled, in a mood of whiney torpor.

'You would think it a fair exchange, for all the relentless babble of needs and wants I must listen to, that in return, one stupid girl would heed me.' Demon, with his back to me, was whining, flinging his hands around in exasperation. I felt myself forgiven.

'Why can you not abandon her, leave her to her pathetic obscurity?'

'I cannot. It is a bond only she can break. I am hers,' he said, bleakly. I was moved for I felt we two had that in common; I do not believe I could have left Demon had I wanted to. It astounds me, looking back, that I did not ever think to try.

'Does she not heed you?' I tried to please Demon, to erase the dregs of his frightening ire by sounding cross with her too.

'She does not. She does not, she is cautious.'

'Does she fear the loss of her soul?'

'Yes. But also she is a coward. She fears success. She is unworthy. Unworthy of my presence, unworthy of the might she now has at her disposal!'

I muttered, in theatrical contempt. But why should she not fear losing her soul? Why should she not fear success? Why would a girl who cannot hold a conversation with Tina in the village shop, or Andy at the record exchange, seek out the relentless exposure of fame? And what of the music that had hooked the divine attentions of Demon? Would she not need her soul to make more?

I soon got bored of Demon's whingeing agitation. He was not the only one forced into bondage, and some of us just got on with it. It was feeble to be so easily thwarted. It was undignified. He was a divine creature, it was his role to find what Eve most desired. He had the mystery of divinity, spells to guide and shape the world. He would just have to settle down to it and wheedle out what truly would unlock her.

In his haste, he was trotting out such commonplace staples, such electro-plated dreams. He offered these dreams as though they were something of value. But extravagance and value are not the same. This he would not learn. Such dreams were born to, and borrowed from, a different longing. Not Eve's. They were an intrusion. They were easily spilled, as warm and salty as our lagoon.

She dreamt of tourmaline, slate, the energy of a planet, the cosmic hum of the universe. Demon, cunning though he is, mighty though he is, could not find a way to translate these dreams of hers into the currency of his trade. She dreamed of the grandeur that spawned Demon, the might and power, the wildly ancient storm heralding the creation of all that exists. She dreamed of translating it, sharing it. And here he was, a piece of the oldest, strangest creations of the universe. Mysterious and powerful. All those things were in him, revealed by him, and yet his trade was tamed to serve the narrow, domesticated urges of the human animal.

She wanted space and time, and the joy of absorption. And yes, she wanted to share it. But she did not care enough for the admiration of others, and this, perhaps, in the end was all he had to offer.

I look at him now, and do not imagine he would be chastened by such realisation.

I persuaded Demon that we should leave her for a while. That his prowess would return, his cunning be restored, if he gave himself some time away. The problem was too tight-knotted to find the solution. Distance would give the space for new strategies to emerge. And perhaps she would not like to feel the offer she so uncertainly received might be taken away. I pretended a contempt for Eve that I did not feel. I spoke in a haughty and indignant voice so overdone I feared Demon would see straight through it.

'Let her get used to her failures, then see how she welcomes you!'

But he smiled, and for those moments I joined the mucky brotherhood, waiting for Eve to usefully bend. We left, arcing through the air on indignant little wings of predicted triumph.

'It is the same as the poet. The one who felt fate marked his path so that he had no need to trade.'

'Tell me again of the poet, Rabbit.'

I spun the story of the poet. The words the poet wove to wake a Demon. How he saw himself raised, a sage, an artist. His words already brought him much attention. With that attention came benign certainty. He did not need the magic of Demon, for look, he was already mighty. But spiked, perhaps in cunning, his work caused great offence. He criticised a general, a man with guns and garrisons who feared injury on the soft edge of words. Demon left the poet to languish in prison until he realised his foolishness and turned at last to the help of a divine ally.

Demon's spirits lifted at this reminder of his past success.

'I will get her. One day, I will find the way.' There was once again the certainty and satisfaction of the hunter in his half-closed eyes.

16

See
how you
like me gone

By the time this tale was told we were far away. We went first to a market, teeming with human life. The air was thickened by the voices, calling, bartering, passing the time of day. Demon shut his ears to the incessant roar of human need. I listened to them talk. A stallholder handed over a bag of fat red tomatoes to an old gentleman, asked after his wife's health as he dropped change into an open hand. Two girls talked secretly with each other as they stood in turn to buy sweets. A woman bartered over the price of a second-hand jumper. You want me to give this stuff away and starve? said the stallholder. You want me to buy it and starve? said the customer.

I cannot possibly tell all that we saw. But let me shuffle through the scatter of memories and pick out the bits that shine.

Sea water. To feel the pull, the rise and drop of a jade-coloured wave, the sun breaking into sparkles through flicked up spray. Listening to the clicks of a reef, as teeming with life as the market. To be a rabbit, alive under the sea.

To sleep a week amongst the treasures of an ancient tomb, the weight of human solemnity cooling the air as much as the thick stone walls.

Some human ingenuity – for what do you need the cunning of Demon and his brothers? Bridges, buildings, collaborations, connections. Ways to come together and places to be together. You are more like ants than you know. Seen a certain way, could that not be enough?

And human folly. You will be as gone as the steam that dissipates when glacier and wildfire meet, and for what? Nothing of consequence. Not for your bridges and your meeting halls. Not for the things you have shared but those you covetously accumulated.

I have tasted so many sweet flowers and bitter leaves.

I have seen such beautiful places, such grandeur that I was reminded of Eve's imaginary musical terrain. I tried to keep such thoughts from Demon lest he spoil the pleasure of it by taking us right back into that dank little village hall for another crack at her.

There is so much more. I wish I could share it all. It is the only regret of my dying that this wonder will be lost.

No, of course it will not be lost.

It will be there still, for the wonder of other minds than my own. I am only a rabbit after all, not a library, or a god, or an encyclopaedia of the world's wonders. The joy of it was always meant to be passing. The joy of the world always is.

And I am a divine storyteller waiting on a clifftop for my end.

17

So
is all
eternity
wasted and
so is all at risk

She kept her deepest desires tucked away, off the trade table, even in the dreamscape where she and Demon spoke, where he made his most extravagant offers. She resisted. He was a headache, a buzz of anxiety, he was disquiet. She took painkillers – they did not hinder him. But for a while, music sometimes gave her freedom; when she was lost within music, Demon could be ignored.

And still, without his help, the band grew in popularity. And always, she tested her place in its success, step by step, unable to either turn away or seal her fate in a committed bond.

Their first big gig came supporting a popular band with an angry political stance, angry political songs, a buzz and aggression that Eve loved. She was excited to share a stage with them, even as third support act.

She tried to close herself off before they were due to play, to retreat from the sickness in her belly. It was impossible. It was deathly scary and wondrously exciting. Leon nervously tuned and re-tuned his bass, Mal drove her mad, tapping out beats on the stained foyer-style chairs and the edge of a bin. They drank a couple of beers each, barely speaking.

Hearts thumping, they entered the stage to wide indifference, though a number of their friends, their local fans, cheered. Eve tried to ignore her nerves, tried to ignore the single row of faces looking up from the front of the stage, the black space behind them and the raucous chatter of disinterest at the bar. She fiddled with her amp, took another swig of beer, pushed a hand into the mess of her hair. Her hands were shaking. She thought she was going to be sick on her effects pedals. The shake in her hands was surely going to stop her from playing. The emptiness of the auditorium seemed to grow, the disinterest amplify. Time moved slowly. Mal hit the snare a couple of times, then sat, waiting. He smiled at Eve, and she felt at least there was an ally. Then Leon said: 'We're Never.'

They took off in a frenzy she barely noticed. The opening songs flew flawless into an audience that grew as punters at the bar heard the raucous heft of the music and came to the front of the stage. By the time Eve looked up from her guitar, somewhere in the third song, there was a bigger crowd watching. She looked to the side of the stage where two members of the main act were head-banging along.

By the fourth song she was in a kind of ecstasy. Plastic, liquid. She thrashed out the songs in a loose and miraculously coherent frenzy. It was a blast.

Demon was hollering as though the most ardent fan of all. He swooped through the lighting, above the heads of young wildlings, he saw Eve's joy and could not but predict that of course she would long for more.

And she did. All the way through their set, as the audience grew and the shared spell wrapped around them all.

As she left the stage to the yells of the audience, a last tail of feedback screeching from her amp, she passed the singer of the headline band. 'Amazing, that fucking rocked,' he said. They headed back to the tatty room allocated to them. They were shapeless with excitement.

This is amazing, this is amazing, I want this, she said. And Demon heard.

Eve went back to collect effects pedals from the stage to clear it for the next bands. The side of the stage between acts was in semi-darkness. She held an ungainly pile of pedals and leads.

In the dark of the wings, a voice, a taller body, leaned down, bringing closer shadow. An arm snaked around from behind her, pushed over her arm and down to squeeze her breast.

'It's great having girls in a band. You're not bad.' She flung herself round, dropping a pedal. The singer of the headline band smiled knowingly, held his hands up in mock surrender. 'Steady. No harm done,' he said, sauntering away, grinning. Eve did not tell anyone or say anything.

Demon deflated like a balloon. We spent the night in the lee of a heating duct on the Top Rank roof.

18

I
hate
you Eve

Eve pushed aside what had happened – it was a commonplace, a tax on being a girl in public. But something shifted and her joy was gone. Leon misread her mood – she was being stuck up, good things were never good enough for her. She felt exposed, ridiculed, reminded that to stand before people was to invite their attention – the consequences were on you if it was what you had chosen.

She tried to get over the precise insult of such an act, and those words – how could a dumb bloke in a dumb band have deliberately invented such a killer move to put her in her place? It was just opportunistic, sexist bullshit. Not worth being a killjoy to call it out. So she told herself, but so she did not feel it; the 'got me' knowingness of his chummy retreat spoke of triumph.

But though her joy was deflated, she pushed aside the humiliation, the little reminder that there were always people who wanted you to stay small. She grappled with the dread, the expectation that this was to be her lot; if she asked for attention she should not falter when it came. But resistance was an ordinary condition of life, and though some joy was lost, stubbornness stopped her from giving up.

They collaborated with a local fanzine and their first recording was a freebie taped to the front of the July issue. Most are now resolutely refusing to rot in the landfills of southern England, but lucky those who once were local kids with dyed hair and nose piercings who still have one – they'll be worth even more by the end of the day. Perhaps not a life-changing amount but enough for a treat. Demon is not the only one who will be richer by nightfall. The difference being he can take his riches with him.

Their path was well set, the three members of Never. Their audience grew, they began to talk of record deals. Leon had enough certainty on that score for all of them. Demon feared furiously that Eve would get all he had offered without his help. It does happen, for not all of the successful people in the world have paid with their souls.

A local promoter, Rich, took on the role of manager. Gigs across the country popped up, eventually strung together in tours. Mal bought a van. Leon navigated their growing success as though the heir apparent – impatient, arrogant, certain that the future was his.

Leon never said to himself *I am going to be better than Eve, everyone will know I am the important one.* He never said it, but he played for it in a constant, exhausting buzz of effort. It drove almost everything. He never said aloud *I desire and hate Eve in equal measure.* He said to himself now and then *fucking bitch* without bothering to understand how she could possibly enrage him as much as she did. It was all there, had he ever looked inside himself.

He manoeuvred relentlessly so he might claim ownership of the big decisions. I do not think Eve ever knew how mad her easy indifference made him. How her bursts of opposition made him insecure enough to double down and bluster.

She worked with exclusionary focus, ignored the bulk of his suggestions, accepting those she took with wounding indifference. I could feel him bristle.

In Leon's mind he would soon be too old, too uncool. Insecurity and impatience made time pass like a danger, his dreams were always just ahead and always perilously on the brink of sliding away. It made him resort to tetchy admonishments

– do you want this band to succeed? Do you even care about this song being any good? For fuck's sake, sometimes I wonder why you bother to turn up at all.

Eve and Mal let it wash over them but called him Leon the Prick behind his back. Most of the time they all got on well enough. And they appreciated what they could do together, even when the ease of friendship became stretched. Mal and Eve concentrated on being as good as they could, on getting the gear in and out of the pubs and halls where they played. They let Leon and Rich plan for world domination, sharing sniggering disdain to let off steam every now and then.

As their reputation grew, Leon became insufferable. His entitlement, for all its brashness, was spiked with the fear that it would all be taken away. He perceived himself, in layers, to be both nothing and mighty. It is common enough, this puzzle at the heart of him. The twin poles of arrogance and insecurity create a battery that powers a surprising amount, not all of it bad, of human endeavour.

Eve drew much attention; it caused her little pleasure. A review would sometimes single her out, mark her as the core of the music, the heart and soul of it. It rankled for Leon – and this was apparently a problem that Eve was supposed to resolve. During their first big interview for Melody Maker, after some heavy-handed praise for her playing, the journalist tried to flirt with her in an ineffectual, mildly annoying way that Eve barely registered. But Leon did. When the journalist wrapped up the interview and left the pub, Leon was moved to claim he was glad to have a girl in the band because it gave the journalists something to have wet dreams about.

It was a dark hurt, a betrayal, but Eve could not bring herself to articulate it. She stood up from the table, and went to the loo. She shut the door of the cubicle, clenched her teeth and pushed her hands deep into her pockets, wishing to be unseen and un-judged. Wishing too, somewhere, that she had the courage to smash Leon's head with her pint glass. It was bad enough having anyone dump their dreary sexism at her feet, but to feel so unprotected by a supposed mate was infuriating and hurtful.

But the girl talked herself down. Like so many she took the fault of another man's attention as her own.

Demon whispered black words of revenge. It was not a powerful offer, and Eve took no heed.

He tried a second approach: *Deal with me and you will become untouchable,* he whispered. Eve, tied up with her own disappointments, did not hear.

We left the pub, a wake of Demon's sour anger trailing behind us, mingling with Leon's bitter little victory.

The interview when it came out was short but full of praise. The next few gigs, though still small, were sold out.

I turn now to look at Demon, lolling on the grass, as relaxed as I have ever seen him.

'Did you like Leon?'

'I don't like or dislike. I do my work and then I leave.'

'Sometimes I think you seemed very alike,' I say, tentatively. This stirs a look of such malevolence, I am reminded of his power. I remind myself to be cautious, for even now, so near to my coming death, there is reason to be afraid of Demon.

But much of the time he is a trapped and fretful creature, reduced in years of servitude, his power waned. Maybe he is more domestic beast, in his conduct at least, than divine power. In the might and range of the entire cosmos, he seems strangely bound by the narrow bandwidth occupied by humans.

He certainly does have the power of a mighty malevolence. His stories of past conquests are filled with bad endings for bystanders, enemies, sometimes loved ones, deaths that furthered his cause. True, I did not know for sure that he was the cause of these unhappy fates but there have been many that seem useful to his ends.

Oh, how carelessly I question the mysteries. Approaching death has made me brave, for I feel from here the prickling of Demon's anger at the careless spill of my thoughts.

19

**yet
to you
I am bound**

They got a record deal. And if all Eve wanted was to ramp up the volume and flail with an audience into an electric storm, she had that. And that she did love. Demon could not make it happen for her because it happened by itself. I pitied him. Those same poles of insecurity and wild confidence that drove Leon flashed in Demon too.

It was a restless time. We flapped, strung out like washing in a windstorm.

We just had to wait.
We had to act now.
She was about to hear him.
She'd never hear him.
He would return home triumphant.
He would waste an eternity imploring the void between him and his brothers to change the rules and let him return.

Annoyingly for Demon his prediction in some part proved true, without his intervention. More success did indeed give Eve greater insulation. People respected the band, even the girl in the band. Maybe, she thought, she could handle it. Maybe it would give her the freedom to work as she longed to work. Maybe everything was fine as it was.

The three of them moved to London. Their days between gigs passed in rehearsal rooms and studios. Demon and I spent those years on the lonely rooftops of London's towers. Demon needed to escape, to be above the clamour of dreams, cacophonous at street level, winding in ceaseless sniping pleas around his head.

I thought perhaps that head-pinching clamour might give him cause to pity all that he loaded onto Eve, but I do not think he thought of it.

Occasionally skivers and smokers and sky seekers would join us. We watched one man come up onto a wintery rooftop every day for weeks, a slow trudge from the fire escape that should have been locked, to the roof edge, where he gazed over the parapet, wondering whether he had the courage to jump.

Sometimes I would go over to the man, sit at his feet, lean into his leg, brush my cheek against him. I was small in his presence, close to my natural size. I do not know why I went to him. I do not know if he knew it. But rabbits have compassion, we hate to see each other hurt, we mourn, if briefly, our lost ones. My divinity had not eliminated such feelings.

I wonder if divinity's blessings must eventually end for all, in the callousness of Demon, if it was perhaps only the cynical who could stomach living forever. How many times would Demon have observed such misery? It cannot have been few.

It was a difficult time. Demon glowed with petrol fury, huge and flailing, or sank and shrank for days at a time into damp and lustreless corners. I tried to cheer him. Or I gazed across the city, remembering my distant fields; the smell of the telegraph poles on hot days echoed in the coal tang of city pollution. Little pockets of hardy weed grew in gutters, seed heads blowing against a grey sky. Sometimes, especially when I was unable to help Demon, or it seemed he did not see me anyway, I wished I was still there, already nearing the end of my rabbit life. In that long unhappy stretch of days I felt ready to fall at the field edge on my last natural heartbeat, and be finished up by a fox.

But Eve was still young. There was no greater value in an old soul or a new. There was time for dreams and desires to grow, there was still plenty of time for Demon to win his hand.

As the band grew in popularity and acclaim, Leon became more insufferable with the bliss of it. He was, in his own newly certain mind, simply fulfilling his destiny as though there had never been a moment's doubt, as though there had never been long nights of restless plotting looped by dread fear that no one would ever notice. Of course his band was going to fill venues, to sell records, of course he was going to snort coke with musicians he had loved for years, to sleep with pretty, drunk girls who chose not to see what they would have noticed when he was just a boy with a plastic bag full of lyrics and a gobshite attitude. Though even they asked him about Eve.

Even on the worst of days she lit up the stage. She was beginning to know it. Slowly her confidence was growing. But her doubts did not disappear. Indeed new confidence fed her dissatisfaction. The boredom started to bleed into the disappointment. The dreary patronising comments, the resentment she caused in people, the cack-handed knock-backs meant as a counter to any good she might feel. The choppy orthodoxy of rock songs, of being cool. She resented the feeling of months and years of more of the same, a long road ahead of her, plotted out to the fulfilment of what increasingly seemed to be an agenda best suited to the requirements of the brashly over-confident dudes at the record company. The easy signature on the bottom of a deal that had seemed at the time to be a promissory note for all the freedoms and privileges she could hope for, in reality represented complicated obligations that spilled into every week. No wonder she looked on Demon's offers with such wary caution.

She left it all behind to walk the city streets at night. Places where noise and people made her safe, and where the city, bright with its own business, left her invisible. Close to midnight and Waterloo Bridge was swathed in the steady roar of traffic. The river below flicked with highlights of red, white, orange lights. She pulled her headphones up, over her ears, hit play. The noises of the world were replaced by her own. A sloping plateau of sound falling away into a ripple, like the lights on the choppy water. She walked, waited, listening for what was missing in the piece, what should be cut, what added. This little snip of hours was hers. A snip of time in the tangle of her soul, a few minutes respite to remember its value. Tomorrow she would rehearse again with the band. And tomorrow, Demon would try again.

She longed for the luxury of time to herself, to sit in a space. Not even a recording studio, just a space with decent sound and time to explore her own ideas. She did not have the courage to leave, but operated within a job-like balance, being part of Never. A way of tolerating what for so many would be a dream come true.

Worryingly for Demon she no longer wished for more of the same.

Occasionally she was asked to perform solo work, at festivals, one-off events. There are not many big shake-ups in the disc-swapping world of obscure alternative electronica, but the revelation that Eve was the musician behind those strange, wildly experimental pieces, dragged out of obscurity into wider attention, came close. Some of her old network said she was wasting her time with that mainstream shit (anyone with a record deal is mainstream by some reckonings) and some said they'd always found her work a bit suspect, a bit weak. For others, it gave her credibility as a musician a boost. There are so many tangles a girl can be made into by boys in a boys' club. Arty wank or mainstream shit; somewhere in the middle was Eve, making her music.

Never kept going and Eve kept going with them. They played and succeeded and trundled up the rock 'n' roll hill. And then, just as they neared the top, she pulled it all apart.

Elaine became ill with breast cancer. Demon and I knew of it before she did. He listened to her body, the quiet, wrong pulse of it, the dark burgeoning in her right breast. He listened to the sludgy strum of her heart. He read her pallor. And he sifted through these clues with greedy pleasure, savouring the glint of opportunity it afforded him.

Me, I did not like watching over Elaine, like vultures on the settee back, waiting for her to become ill enough for it to be useful. I sat with her, on the sofa watching tv, or on the counterpane as she massaged her body, trying to measure changes she would not find. We were there in the doctor's consulting room as the likely course of her disease was laid out for her. I sat under her chair, wanting to be a comfort – what was Demon's need, in comparison? He was listening only for what he might use. I was listening to her frightened heart.

It was an instance that for once did not fill me with curiosity; I did not wish to know if Demon had caused this sickness, or whether it was the useful work of chancer Fate. I did not wish to know all.

A slot to appear on a popular television show she never watched had kept Eve from being with Elaine for the diagnosis. Unwilling to face the seriousness of Elaine's condition she had been glad to avoid a visit to a hospital, knowing that simply walking through the doors would bring nausea, faintness, a physical residue left in her the week her father died. Later, she berated herself for this cowardice, angry and ashamed that she had allowed herself to be wheedled by the record company and by Leon. The next day, when Eve went back to see Elaine, she decided in an instant that she would stay. She could not bear to think of her mother dealing with serious illness alone.

Elaine protested, wanting to save her daughter the tedium of care, wanting to reassure her, however falsely, that she would be fine, she would have the odd visit from Eve, the rest of the time her friend Colleen and the surgery would take care of her.

But Elaine also knew enough of Eve to guess there was something welcome in retreat. Without too much protest she let go of guilt and embraced the new proposal with relief and quiet joy.

20

and
for you
I must wait

I'm leaving the band was never going to be an easy conversation; it meant the end of so much – work, hope, determination, cherished songs that may never be played again. Leon had his heart broken, by Eve, for the second time. But he hid it behind pinch and swagger. Fucking hell Eve, you owe me more than that. Fuck you, I'll start another band – one where everyone is committed. Yeah, who cares? Why not just visit your mum? We can gig less, record back home somewhere? Please!

It was sad, seeing him come to terms with his world falling apart. Eve felt it too. He had not always been her most loyal friend, but having shared so much, he was deeply bound up in her life. In spite of their differences they worked well together, sometimes brilliantly well, and even as it felt like a limitation, Eve had needed the company. She had needed, she knew it somewhere, Leon's confidence and determination. She had needed not to be alone.

She was sorry. She told him she was sorry. Leon did not take it well, one moment determinedly whipping up the bravado to call a bluff on it all. The next, the barbs and tethers of his younger fears rose up from their hiding place, gleefully revealing they had never truly gone. I felt sorry for him. I alone was paying attention to him, for Demon was on Eve's shoulder, whispering (with such inept a clue for timing) about the prospects for her solo career. I almost felt I should advise caution but my divinity is recent and borrowed – who am I to coach a demon?

However great the hope, whatever marvels wrought in dreams, most must accept limitations. Leon dreaded failure, dreaded a retreat into a life, like so many others, lived not under the heat and glare of acclaim, but beneath the dimmer days and nights, the suns and moons of the ordinary. Just a life, one of billions.

21

these
changes,
may they serve,
bring us at last together

Eve packed up her flat, and several years after leaving, returned to her childhood home. She was twenty-seven, more experienced, she was successful by several measures. She had toured Europe, made two albums, signed posters and watched a sea of ecstatic youth thrash out their hopes and hates and beautiful joys, transported by the scream of her guitar.

Though she had grown, settled, become more comfortable in herself, she felt as shy and awkward as she did when she left. But to others, she had stamped her spot and had been lauded for it. She had power to them that she did not feel within herself. She was a little bit famous in a small world, and she was willingly giving up the expectation that there would be more.

It was a big step. Was it, as Leon sniped, hubris to think she could do any better alone? She took comfort from knowing that at least she was not leaving the band to follow her own path, however many times she had longed for that freedom. She was leaving because her mother was ill. Music she would come back to. She could not think anything else possible. Then she would see, then she would have time, then she would let something come.

Eve settled back into her bedroom, overlaying the left behind and old with new belongings. The only thing that mattered was her mum, was being here. Everything else could wait. She felt purposeful without really knowing what her purpose was.

Elaine was downstairs putting dishes away. Eve left her clothes half-spilled from the holdall on the bed, and went down. She did not know what to do when she got there. She leaned in the kitchen doorway watching Elaine, then reached for the staple, the glue of awkward kitchen moments and asked if Elaine would like tea.

It took a bit of time for Elaine and Eve to learn how to live together again, in this unexpected way. They were a re-aligned household, not the same as before. Finding new ways that neither of them yet fully understood. Two adults living together.

Then Elaine began the treatment. Eve did not know how to help. She hovered, watching her mother closely even as she did the simplest thing – folding laundry, making tea; she wondered whether she should take over, force her mother to relax. But how relaxing would that be? Offering assistance was, in these early stages, with little but fear preventing Elaine from living as she always had, more an expression of loving concern than it was any real help.

Eve was unused to the intimacy of care. What did her mother want? From her? At all? She did not know. She did not resent it, just did not know how to do it. And it made Elaine nervous. Eve kept watching her, uncertainly, half getting up when Elaine did, not sure whether her mother required her to fetch and carry, or whether she wanted everything to keep going as normal. It drove Elaine, who could read her daughter as well as any mother can, a little crazy. She did not have the heart to say she need not be so present, in case, having given up so much to be there, she was hurt. Two people drifting in strange awkwardness, all for the love of the other. Neither wanted to get in the way, or put the other out. Both wanted to be helpful, understanding. Is it even that selfless, taking a pat on the back for not allowing themselves to be the one to cause hurt or inconvenience? Or just another way of reaching for a reward.

I have observed much of love. For all the convolutions it is a wondrous thing. This much I know. Rabbits too love, in our own way. Everything is simpler for us. I see in Demon all the complexities of emotions that taint and tint and scent the lives of humans; perhaps the bond between human and demon is based on a deep understanding that comes from being so similarly made – a kind of kinship.

I turn to Demon, who lies with his back to me, gazing across the water, stifling his impatience to be gone.

'Demon?'

'What?'

'Have you ever loved?' There is a pause. I see a little shift along his bumpy spine, imagine the lithe form of Puppy, leaping joyfully in autumn leaves. I feel again the tug of his yearning to be home amongst his brothers.

'What a stupid question,' he says. That's Demon all over. Never knowingly admitting to joy of any kind. Sour old git. Still, were I not to die when he leaves, I think I would miss him.

I wonder how my field is. How my kin have fared. There are none to know me now. All of them gone.

I have been back to that little pocket of the world, during the times when Demon was so listless with failure that he cared not if we were up a tree, down a gulley, or stuck in the under-stairs cupboard of some unknown house half way round the world. I had to cajole, but a couple of times, we went back.

When we did go to my old home, I felt myself soothed in an instant. A wonderful familiarity, a sense of being somewhere good. The smells, the hedges, the trees that gave cover for our burrows – though I did keep away from the burrows. Animals sometimes have enough of the old craft to sense our presence and I did not want to frighten them.

We lay instead in the long grass a few fields over, and there I had some of my best dreams.

After some weeks of sloping round, offering cups of tea, putting laundry in the wrong place and sweeping most of the kitchen floor, Eve, after much insistence from Elaine, finally went to visit

Christopher. They rarely spoke via the telephone and had never formally arranged her visits and it felt awkward to start now. After so long, nearly seven years in which she had only seen Christopher a handful of times, she was worried she might be intruding. She regretted allowing distance to grow and dearly hoped that this had been a pause in their friendship, not an end to it. She stopped before she got to the house, at the bench overlooking the model village. Here we three were again! Eve smoked, Demon whispered, irritating to my ear and unheard by Eve's, though she did massage her temples. Why would he not try harder to make her like him? I hopped away along the lawn between the houses, nibbling at the speedwell and longer grass that had evaded the latest mowing.

Eve dallied, putting off the time when she would know if she was still welcome in that beloved old kitchen. She got out her iPod and we knew we would be there for some time. She listened and replayed, listened and replayed, gazed into her wild and malleable geography. I hunkered down next to the little church just past the crossroads and dozed off to the lull of Eve's music and the intrusion of Demon's crude enticements.

She wondered if she should prepare an excuse as to why she was calling. But there was none. She wanted to see her friend and would just have to hope that he still wanted to see her. We accompanied her to the house. She hesitated before knocking. But as soon as Christopher opened the door her worries disappeared. He was delighted to see her, breaking into a big smile and warm greeting and the easy connection between them was instantly restored. Eve felt strengthened by the rekindling of his friendship, and was glad of temporary respite from her worries about Elaine.

In the kitchen once again we sat in our usual places, I under the table, Demon behind the backs of Eve and Christopher, impatient for the chatter of catching up to be over.

Christopher asked about Elaine. Eve found it helped to talk to him, simple talk, outlining the shape of her days, the fears of her nights. But an outline was enough, she did not dwell on it. He asked her about the concerts she had played. She smiled at his use of the word concerts when everyone in her world called them gigs. She relaxed, her thoughts drifting back into the joyful memory. She tried to explain, the energy flowing between the band and the crowd, the uplift, the ferocity. She could not find the words but she remembered a kind of shimmer, from all those bodies, how it lifted them. It was a form of union, some kind of rite. But she could not express these feelings, could not find words that did not sound ridiculous. Her body language revealed enough for Christopher to become grave, presuming a great sadness in the sacrifice of it all.

But then, so matter-of-fact, she said she was glad it was over. Working with other people was tedious. Her easy dismissal of what had moments before seemed such a wonder surprised Christopher, but he always was more romantic than Eve.

Christopher was delighted to have Eve back in the village. She, in finding him again, felt a little less lost.

She went home early enough to check on Elaine and found her dozing on the sofa. She sat in the armchair for a while, unsure whether to wake her mother or leave her.

Demon scowled, flew out to the branches outside, perched like an angry crow, chucking and cussing.

'I'm so bored of this! I'm so bored of her, of them all. Stupid, lazy, ignorant girl. Idiot girl. Stupid blind girl. How dare she call down my might so easily, waste my time so carelessly?' Demon chuntered on with his curses. I waited silently in cold autumn fronds of dewy grass. Demon cussed like a demented parrot. Honestly, I was pretty bored of him too. But I was his companion and had a job to do. This much I know.

I tucked myself under the overgrowth of a shrub, left Demon to spill his temper and his twigs. The garden was unkempt and Demon's scatter of angry sticks disappeared into the grass, seemingly the work of boisterous magpies. Hooligan birds. No need for Elaine or Eve to fear an uncanny presence causing disturbance in the night.

In the morning light we went out to the village green.

'I can't bear to just sit there for yet another of their insufferable breakfasts,' said Demon, his voice tetchy, pettish. Unnecessarily so, as we had only been back for a few weeks and had not been around for more than a handful of perfectly ordinary breakfasts. He's so over-dramatic sometimes.

It was wonderfully pretty on the village green. The low and slow-rising sun shone weakly through a hazy veil that thickened, as though in folds, across the grass. The model village was in mist, the actual village was warm, inviting, in pale sunshine. It was time to mollify.

'This turn of events will give you options, won't it? Maybe not as quickly as you would like, but certainly there will be opportunities.' I began my seduction, to bring Demon to a better frame of mind.

Demon sighed in grudging assent. I resumed, calmly, admiringly.

'It's like that time, many years many visits ago, the boy called you down, then forgot all about his dreams because he fell in love. You had to be patient that time too, did you not? You had to wait, and wait you did. Until love had soured and he was an old man who wanted other compensations.'

Demon looked at me, encouraging me to tell more.

'That boy found simple truth in love. But you saw through it, you knew how to make simple truth serve you just as well as mucky fantasy – you just had to wait, to shape the viewing, to find the chink. Demon, that is your power, you hear so much, the endless babble, the torrents of need that would sweep another away. You rake it all in and you find tools, coins, gold, hidden in the trash. You spy a little handle, or a golden key, or a crowbar, or a sledgehammer, to open the door, spring the lock, jimmy the lid, break open the case. You find it because you take it all in. And you are strong enough to bear it. You are not buried in the weight of it.'

'That is the miracle, Rabbit, for there is so much confounded want and need and so much clamour for my service. And here am I, bound to this coward of a girl.'

'You will give her the courage she needs, the courage you need. For you are wise and brave, and you always find the way.'

Demon smiled at last, nodded gracious assent.

Even as he tormented her, his attentions would protect Eve from accident, disease, untimely death. Only he would command her ending. He had as many heartbeats of time as she was born with. Maybe three score years or more, from the time of our arrival, to unlock the door to his deal. The years since he had arrived and gathered me into his service were but a fraction of the allotted span. The deal they made would dictate how much time she would have at the peak of her dreams but by then Demon's work would be done. He lay back in the pale sunshine, slid into divine rest. I shut my eyes, the low sun glowed gold through my lids and soon I too was drifting.

22

**Did
you not
want more?
I thought you brave.
I thought you bold as lightning.**

Elaine had an operation that removed the cancer and most of her breast. Eve felt a hollow sickness seeing her mother so weakened, so vulnerable. The shock created her transition from awkward bystander to practical carer. Personal boundaries were erased by necessity and there was less confusion over what was welcome, and what was intrusion. Her mother for a while needed assistance with most things and their previous awkward decorum was soon dissolved.

There was now three of them – daughter, mother, disease. Days were made awkward, unshapely, by the ravages of the treatment. The disease brought upset and quiet resilience. It brought love, marbled with fear. Eve and Elaine settled, however they could, into the bearing of it. They dusted off their residual memories and repurposed them, once again sharing the uninvited terrors of life.

Elaine woke often in the nights, somewhere sleepless between fear and discomfort, and crept downstairs to make tea. Eve, who took to leaving her bedroom door open, woke up. She knew how fears can slide in, take over, in the darkness and loneliness of night-time. She wanted Elaine to be spared that. When she heard the careful sounds of slippered feet on the stairs as Elaine tried not to wake her daughter, she waited a little, so she could pretend she had woken independently, and followed her mother down to the kitchen. Though fully awake in her watchfulness, she mimed a yawning hello, oh, you couldn't sleep too?

After Elaine wore out her protests about Eve missing sleep they would sit in the kitchen, in the soft synthetic halo of under-unit tube lights, drinking hot sugary tea. These were peaceful moments. Elaine's fears were gently pushed out, into the garden to be squabbled over by the magpies. She was grateful for her daughter, for her presence, for her clumsy ruse. It was all that Elaine really needed from Eve, it was tonic.

I was grateful to Demon that at these times he knew enough not to pursue Eve; for a change he just let her be.

She woke each morning with a buzzing behind her eyes and tiredness that she took care to hide from Elaine. Still in pyjamas, she picked up her guitar, strumming absent-mindedly, with the light touch of habit. A platitude. A distraction. And that was precious; the buzzing subsided, Demon quieted. But it wasn't music, not as she had dreamed it, a soaring expression of freedom and potential. The habit comforted, but musically, the rewards were meagre. At least she felt more fully herself. One day she would be able to concentrate. When Elaine was better and when things had settled down. Then it would come. Now was not the time to think about it. Now was the time for relief that one pressure had ended, and acceptance that another took all of her.

But in the gaps, in the small moments she had to herself, Eve became afraid that music had left her for good.

23

You are all so disappointing

Some months after Eve's departure, a couple of replacement guitarists come and swiftly gone, Mal finally had enough of being treated as though he were a part of Leon's staff. He gave up paid music for doing up vintage bikes and playing drums for pleasure. Leon tried to keep going with new members, a supposed fresh start. And for a while, it went along well enough.

He kept it going but felt bitterly that his time had gone. In terms he had so often and so carelessly used himself about those no older than he was now, he was an old fuck, undignified, mate. Give it up.

Leon had wanted to be famous, and though he loved music, he had never much cared about making it. He had no plan and no defence to the charge of irrelevance. The level of fame he had reached had sufficed, when hot out of the oven. But it was not enough to feed him for the rest of his days. The worst feeling of all slunk down upon him; no one cared.

24

I
will
get you, girl

After a few months back in the village, it was as though we had not left. But it was different. Endings cobwebbed Eve's dreams when they used to spark with beginnings. Those eerie abstractions, the landscapes shaped by music, were shrouded in an acrid cloud of Demon's frantic offerings. Oh, I longed to hold him back, to slow him down, but so wedded was he to the completion of the deal that he could not see he was overwhelming her. He just turned up the volume, turned up the grandeur, turned up the persistence. I wished he would understand that more is not always better. Though in the end he clearly did not need that advice from me; Demon knows his trade, for here we are, waiting for her to arrive, waiting for Demon to take possession of her soul.

But back then, before he found his way, the outcome was uncertain and success seemed far away. A deal was eluding Demon just as the magic of music was beginning to elude Eve.

As she had done so many times, she set out, as if in search of clouded promises. She set out in search of the divine stream in subtle and infinite waves. An idea sparked by a fragment, something on an old recording that had caught her attention on a track that had never quite worked. She had listened to it that morning, heard in a new way. Curiosity about a reframing, a way to pull out the original intention. She replayed the recording, listening intently, trying out ideas in her head. It was so nearly, tantalisingly there, she was certain. If she tried it this way. She played a variant on the keyboard, borrowed a sound from another piece, if she countered it with... *let me take you Eve, you are wasting your time here when you could take your pick of studios, of musicians, when you could be on posters across the land!*

She yelled her frustration, kicked a box, scattering the blank disks under the bed in a plastic clatter. She left the bedroom.

We two interlopers were sitting later that evening under the table in Christopher's kitchen, where we had followed Eve. Demon was in a huff. Christopher was playing different recordings of a much loved concerto. He was attuned to the subtle differences, and Eve was trying to understand them, following his prompts, finding variations between the works. He was enthusiastic about the prospect of a new musical discovery for Eve. But she was listless. The lack of her own output, the headaches, left her sluggish, under-exercised, starchy.

'I just can't get anything done. I don't know why. I used to be fine, with that room,' Eve told him.

'You've probably got used to better things, it's no wonder that it feels a bit constraining.'

'Is it, though? Better?'

'Why not? More space, more options, more ways to expand and explore. Of course it's better. You must have more resources now too.'

'It just feels so lame. I'm wondering if I've actually got what it takes to make music on my own. Because I'm not managing to do it now.'

'You do, you already have done. What about those discs you used to send out?'

'Exactly – I feel like I should be able to go back to what I had then and make it work now.'

'Only if you feel you have something to prove. Surely, somewhere between the four tracks of your first experiments, and the 48 or whatever of your last album, there's a place that suits you as you are now?'

Demon leapt with a suddenness that startled me. I may no longer be invariably scared of cars and foxes but a divine being flying past your head at enormous speed would make anyone jump. He sprang onto Christopher's shoulder, wrapped his arms caressingly around his head, even stroked his hair. He whispered. There was a moment's pause, both Christopher and Eve stared into the bottom of their whisky tumblers.

'Eve,' Christopher began excitedly, 'I've had an idea. Why don't we build a studio for you here? Maybe not a proper one, but a space you can use, spread out into. There's a kitchen and bathroom,' he gestured behind him to the glass doors, 'and a whole garden to, I don't know, relax in. You can come when I'm here, it won't bother me. Or when I'm out. Whichever you prefer. I won't want to get in the way.'

'Oh no, thanks, that's kind. But no.'

'Why on earth not?'

'Because, it would be, I'd get in your way.'

'Have you not noticed how stupidly big this house is for one person? I barely go into two thirds of it.'

'Yes, but –'

'Yes, but you don't like being beholden to people, you don't want to owe me anything.' Eve tried to shake her head in denial but Christopher continued '– and I get that. I don't much like that either. But you'd be doing me a favour. I so often feel like I should leave, how little use it gets, but I like being close to – well, to my memories. So if you were using a room, I wouldn't feel like it was such a waste.'

Eve was silent, thoughtful.

'How about if I paid you some rent?'

'Are you earning any money?'

'No.'

'Then how about you pay me out of royalties on a future album!' He smiled triumphantly, as though the logic was undeniable. And so it seemed, it was to Eve too. She smiled, her half smile tipped under the crow's wings of her black hair. Demon beamed from Christopher's shoulder.

They toasted, another whisky, then Christopher led her around the house, showing her the empty rooms. There were four bedrooms in the main house, three entirely unused. There was a small extension, a room on each floor, built onto the back of the house. Christopher muttered, dashed back into the kitchen, leaving Eve in a hallway. He came back moments later with a key.

'This bit has its own door! I don't think I've unlocked it for years, let's have a look.'

They went out into the garden, round to the far side of the house. The door opened to a tiny hall that gave onto a room used for storage, next to that a loo. There was a staircase. Upstairs was one bigger bedroom with an old bed, a wardrobe, drawers.

'This would be perfect! I mean, would it? Could this work for you? I never come here. You could just let yourself in whenever you liked.'

Eve could not find the words between gratitude and wonder. She shook her head slowly but smiled at the pictures forming, the potential already stirring. She made some token protests – she is built that way. But she trusted Christopher. He would not make an offer he did not want her to accept.

'It would be – amazing,' she finally managed.

Demon bounced on the bed, repeating over and over *once I get her making music then I get her dreams.*

Christopher had checked everything in the bedroom and the room downstairs, had taken a few bits into the main house, the rest could go to the dump. He was caught in awkward enthusiasm, wanting both to help out and not get in the way.

Eve kept a chest of drawers and a faded watercolour landscape painting. Later, they brought up a kitchen chair and small table from the room below, and an armchair which she covered with a tartan blanket.

Mal came over with his van. They heaved everything that was not wanted off to the dump. Soon the two rooms were almost empty. By the end of the day, Eve had moved in her musical equipment. Mal gave her a hug and left. She began to organise the space.

Extension cables and leads ran one from one another connecting a network of grilled and buttoned boxes. Her three guitars were lined up against the wall. She moved discs from shoe boxes into one drawer, sorting as she went, a section for revisiting, a section for archiving. She coiled spare leads in another drawer. She sat in both of the chairs, letting herself become familiar with the room, the view from the window, the rhododendron hedge lit in small glints by the house lights, the glow of the street lamp over the model village beyond. She listened to the sound of her feet, a tap on the bare floor that bounced almost mutely from the walls, the soft reverberation native to the room. These small actions spoke of the luxury she had longed for – space and time for her own music.

Christopher was torn between going up to offer her a whisky and demonstrating that he had meant it when he said he would not interfere. He was not surprised, though he was disappointed, that she did not come down to the kitchen to share his celebratory mood. Demon however, was ready to raise a glass with Christopher, for he could see the path opening up ahead of him, just as Christopher hoped it might open up ahead of Eve.

Later, she popped her head round the kitchen door, thanked Christopher inarticulately but truly from the depths of her heart, and went home to bed.

25

I
will
secure
your soul

Without discussion they kept social visits separate from work visits. When she was there to make music she let herself in, and eventually left again often without speaking to Christopher. A couple of evenings a week, she came to the front door, knocked, and if he was home they spent the evening together at the kitchen table, listening to music, talking about music, drinking whisky. Christopher worked hard to stifle his urge to enquire about her progress. For a long time, Eve did not mention it. She worked like a ghost in the back corner of his house and he heard only faint passes, shy and shadowy hints.

Though still unwell, Elaine was able to look after herself. She asked often if Eve would like to get on with her life, now she was almost better, whether she felt trapped. But Eve was content. And though she did not voice it, she was afraid of leaving Elaine. Long-buried instability that came with the death of her father crept around her, upsetting in subtle and profound ways. Elaine's frailty after the operation had been a shock. She feared being absent if the grim history of loss were to be repeated.

Elaine was grateful. And she recognised that in some ways she needed Eve's help less than Eve needed to be there with her.

It was a quiet stretch of time. Eve was content, a little bored, but she lacked the impetus to make changes. She could not pin down what it was she sought, what had for so long haunted the edges of her mind. All should be possible, in the space and time afforded by this quiet life, this gift of a room in which to work. Yet she felt she was marooned, miles and years from what her dreams were made of.

That she had chosen it was the sigh in her acceptance. But she feared, a terrible, dark fear, that the music she had so long dreamed of making might be gone for good; she had taken a fatal wrong turn with Never and had somehow been rendered untrustworthy, unworthy, by their briefly sparking fame.

She missed playing live. To feel herself lifted by the noise, shaken by the rip tide, sweat pouring from the sheer effort of keeping up. Oh those were glorious moments. She dared not think about it too much. And if she did, Demon would leap in, promising all could come back. She felt the nagging in her head, the unsettling harassment. The wheedling. She just had to want it enough and she could have it.

But she was older, the weight of her fascination with music, so long carried, so long cherished, demanded more than the particular, narrow spectrum of playing gigs with a rock band. If that meant it came to nothing, that was how it had to be.

She thought she was being grown up, accepting all these dead-end, might-have-been analyses. But Demon had other plans. Christopher too had his hopes and plans for Eve, though driven by other engines than Demon. He felt almost paternal, perhaps grandfatherly, love for this awkward girl, and a music lover's thrill at her potential and only ever wanted for her what she would want for herself. It meant he had to school himself, often, not to let his enthusiasm and belief spill over to embarrass or annoy her. Giving her space and time was truly his gift.

Eve tried putting some of her older work together, with the aim of releasing it under the old pseudonym. But it felt wrong. It was as though she had tricked people, for many now judged her for her gender and her fame – both, for those of a certain mindset, signifiers of a light-weight commitment or some kind of stupid luck above talent. She had real allies, real fans, who cherished those early discs but she learned with its absence that anonymity had given her courage, allowed instinct to flourish. She struggled to find anything in those first months back in the village. Instinct, by itself, does not serve forever. It is fire starter, not fuel.

Perhaps she needed anonymity, or the shelter of a band. Perhaps she needed Leon's brash certainty as a camouflage.

Perhaps she needed courage.

Demon was beside himself with her uncertain ramblings.

Though she was not creating anything that felt valuable, she did still explore. Eve had at first found the human voice in Christopher's twentieth-century classical recommendations too clean, almost indecently so. But via the swell of much older multi-part sacred music, her interest in singing was evolving. She came to understand the primal power of the voice. It was after all the first instrument. The vibrations of sound created by movement within the tissue of the human body.

At first it was the voice as a wordless drone, a meshed harmonic, that made its way into her compositions. The mystery of blended voices stretched back into ancient history, connecting it to the present. She could slide into the thick wall of sound created by choral music as she had once discovered she could slip between the harmonics of distortion and feedback.

Christopher lent her a recording of Thomas Tallis, *Spem in Alium*. She listened for days. She sat in the village church, listening on headphones, imagining the multitude of voices coming from bodies, moving through air in the cool stone echo of the building. Reverb for real, created by the path of soundwaves in space, against walls, in emptiness and architecture rather than bent through the channels of an electrical set up. That would be something, she thought, to work with voices set to such dense harmonies they become a sea to ebb and flow, a sea to lift or drown.

In the church, first checking that no one was near, she took off the headphones and tried a self conscious note, listening to the sound bounce back to her. She wondered at all the voices that had cut through that cool space, picturing a fine geometry of waves sketched on the air, as though time and the cool temperature gave it body enough to hold the traces.

She began experimentally recording her own voice, which was not particularly strong but able to hold a tune. The results were poor quality but listening, noticing, in different locations helped her understand more about the dynamics of vocal sound. She bounced notes off bathroom tiles and mirrors, muffled them with curtains. When she did not feel self-conscious or overlooked, she sang and recorded refrains in big and empty spaces, under bridges, in alleyways. Soon, reformed by the spaghetti of electronics (for she was loath to be mistaken for a singer) little snippets of her own voice made its way into scratch compositions.

There was always something new to learn, something new to weave and warp. New sounds to hammer, stretch and bend, new gems to set, smith and cast. There was always the joy of play, even when there was no progress.

Christopher, with his absolute faith in Eve, was pleased to feel he had been able to help. He enjoyed being included, even when it stretched beyond his own tastes. She was glad to have Christopher there to talk with, to test out ideas. She was glad to have an audience of even one, because without an ear to hear it, what meaning does music have?

And here once again was Demon's hope.

She made music the way she did to please herself, but music is communication and so needs an audience to make that true; the listener completed what she made. *Yes Eve, the rapture of their listening, can you feel it? Can you for all that matters, just let it bear you up? LISTEN TO ME!*

And sometimes, even I could hear that she did listen. She listened, but warily. For she knew she did not want to go back to the shallow bounty of playing in a successful rock band. She knew she did not want an audience at that cost. She listened and then she turned away.

You bitch.

26
oh
you
fickle,
fearful
creature!

The three of us sat on the bench overlooking the model village, all lost in the same thoughts; Eve's. She took a break from this strange burden, rolled another cigarette, watched blue smoke rising from the tip. She shut one eye, lined the cigarette end up with a chimney, imagined a fire in the miniature house. This spot, sitting on the bench overlooking the model village seemed a foil, an orderly counterpoint for the elusive grandeur she sought and could not at that moment find. It was so familiar, so easily contained in a single view.

Since childhood bereavement had forced her to understand the way that grief had marked her out, she had found comfort in the rows of little houses. No judgement behind the doors, no awkward conversations, no sense of being the one that was out of place. It had been as though a harbour, a safe and familiar place where she could tame thoughts that left her feeling unsure of where she belonged.

Her choices weighed upon her. She felt herself as uncertain as she had ever been. She wondered if she had thrown her dreams away.

The model village was a knowable counterpoint to the wild unknown of all that might be possible. The model village was the weight at the bottom of the metronome. Understandable, safe, a refuge from wilder dreams and an antidote to the chaos of life.

Though, this model village also spoke of a dream.

A dream of the domestic. Dreams that natural rabbits know just by feeling the sun on our pelts in a field of daisies. Dreams that many humans take just as fore-granted. Dreams that because they may be barred to some are just as wild and distant as Eve's own. And then Christopher opened it all up, lifted the lid so she could see the simple yearning from which it had been so carefully, so lovingly built.

27
Jon

It was hard for men like Christopher, and his lover Jon, to break free of the restrictions and persecutions of their youth, when homosexuality was still a crime. Society may have become, to a greater or lesser degree, more accepting, but individuals within society do not always keep pace. Individuals can cling to old prejudices and be far from kind.

At many times and places, society expressed such unkindness as its collective, indignantly spiteful right.

Christopher and Jon had grown up in such a society, subject to the expectation of shame, guilt, approbation. Their true selves remained hidden, though disguise is often partial and, seeing what was meant to be concealed, people knowingly muttered and sniggered behind their backs. Both had been injured in the many gross and subtle ways that societies have of turning on whoever is deemed outsider.

Jon had, as a young man, been arrested and fined. He was told by his father, with absolute certainty, that this shame, not her long-standing heart disease, was responsible for the ill health and subsequent death of his mother.

The death of his father a few years later came almost as a relief. He had loved his parents deeply, and they him. But Jon was the embodiment of a rift, a schism, that as he left the hiding innocence of childhood, could only serve to drive them slowly and certainly apart.

Returning to the house he inherited on his father's death had felt like a necessary defeat for Jon. A burden that he must take up. The ghosts of his disappointed parents sighed from the skirting boards. Flickers of his innocent youth, when their love sprung vivaciously around him, as yet untwisted by disappointment, caught at the corner of his eye.

Jon felt defeated by his first vain attempts to live a different life, be elsewhere, out in the world. Defeated by the skew of who and what he was. He believed he could neither bring nor find happiness, so he accepted the strictures of his loneliness and the house drifted into solemn decline around him.

With the house and the remnants of family wealth he needed little. He worked half the week in the town library and spent his evenings reading. One day, he went up to the attic, searching for a beloved childhood encyclopaedia. Tucked behind some boxes was a doll's house, an old toy of his mother's. He remembered her plans to bring it out, spruce it up, should they ever be blessed with a daughter. It was her sadness that no daughter of hers had ever got to enjoy that favourite toy. But secretly, Jon had come up to the attic and played with the doll's house. Now in early middle age, he remembered those quiet afternoons, the space cleared before the opening front, books beside him as cover for his activity in the attic, should he hear the warning creak of the attic ladder.

Those early playtimes were not what caused a little pulse in his heart when he came across the house again. That had been the simple, curious play of a child, for all the strange complexity of having been told that it was not a toy for boys. What caused that small skip was the house it had suggested to his imagination.

It had begun on lonely nights when he was away at university, free for the first time and still as ever constrained. He longed for intimacy, for love. Before he found it he dreamed it – into the doll's house. It seemed ludicrous to imagine his terrible secret in the real world. The doll's house was a make-believe stage set for what he knew could only ever be make-believe happiness. So the doll's house became in his imagination the setting of his dreams.

He imagined coming home to the pretty little house, opening the door to find the latest young man, in real life entirely unaware of Jon's longing, sitting, impatient with love, on the bottom stair. He imagined him leaping up, taking Jon's hand, leading them both up to one of the bedrooms.

He found himself too extraordinary to imagine he could ever be in the arms of another man, in an ordinary house, living an ordinary life. The doll's house had provided a setting that made at least the dream of love possible. Now, as he saw it once again up in the attic, he was moved by the memories it stirred. The flat front, the four glassless windows, open to the world, the painted ivy around the door speaking of time and settlement all sang in his memory and his heart. He took the doll's house down to the dining room table.

He began to picture what might exist around the little house. A garden, a neighbouring cottage, a winding lane. Could his dreams not occupy more than a house? He found he could at least imagine a village.

As a child he had been steered from practical, manual work into indifferent academic pursuits more suitable for the son of a country solicitor. But he had enjoyed the bit of woodcraft allowed as a hobby, whittling and such. That the doll's house had been made, his mother told him, by her uncle, was another reason he had been drawn to it. He was entranced by the notion of actually building, constructing something new where there had been nothing. He had on a couple of precious occasions persuaded his father to help him make some of his own toys; a box for his farm animals, a little horse on wheels that lacked beauty or refinement, but they had made it well and he had been very proud. That too was in the attic, kept safely amongst other relics of family lore and more preciously, the embodiment of rare success – the harmonious working of father and son, unburdened by later disappointments.

One day, reading a book that bored him, frustration caught, souring his mood. Books were not enough, reading alone was not enough. He realised he needed more, he needed something to do. He needed occupation. He left the armchair and the fading garden light, the book draped like a pitch roof over the chair arm and went into the dining room. Why not make his own model house? In his late thirties, with an indifferent degree in English, a small income and lots of space, he realised he could revive the happy pleasure of making, the satisfaction of sawing, planing, fitting wood together and seeing it become an actual object, something occupying a space. There was nothing or no one to harm in such a gentle experiment. No one need know if he succeeded or failed.

The next morning he left the house for the library in town. Books were the natural place to start. His colleagues were surprised to see him on a day when he was not working. He found a book on model railway making and a book on woodworking.

Rushing back into the house, he passed the tennis court. The sad drape of the net across the mossy, unkempt grass always annoyed him, feeling as it always did like a scold. His mother had been unnecessarily proud of that tennis court; such a small achievement for a family with that much money and space to use for their own devices, but something about it had made her feel as though she had reached elegantly beyond her limitations.

He had noticed a section in the model railway book about creating outdoor set-ups. What a perfect elision, to turn the court into something he would tend after all. There was also plenty of space – more than would fit on the forbidding shine of the dining room table. He would build his houses outdoors.

This would take further planning, more careful building. He had no idea about the durability of materials, holding only vague notions about tar pitch for wood preservation. Did cement make small things too? How would he build? Would they need foundations? As these complications grew, so did his excitement. This really was a project and it really would be something to fill his empty days.

He cleared out the room where the gardening equipment was stored. He fixed a clamp onto the work surface. There were hooks *and pegs that once held bags of twine or nets lumpy with bulbs. He hung some brand new tools and a few salvaged from the box kept since he could remember working with his father. The sawmill made a substantial delivery.*

It was daunting and a thrill to lay out what he would need to work and he felt more excited than he had done for years. In the study, a collection of books and model-making magazines grew. He sketched out ideas, quick and hand-drawn, firmed up using a ruler and set square. They never looked right but he knew how they were meant to look. His first efforts in the new wood from the mill were already close to his imagined pictures.

He worked diligently, carefully following the examples in a woodworking manual. He so wanted to get it all right. The houses must be well made, carefully constructed to keep out the weather, but a little bit of roughness to the joints could be hidden by paint and render.

Over time he learned how to build, how to combine materials, how to create effects with paints, how to shore up against the weather. Experiments sat in the garden, a hamlet of half-formed or crudely impersonated houses, beginning the durational process of testing by wind and rain. Only when he had learned how to make a house to his satisfaction did he take it out to the tennis court.

A sketchbook lay open on his desk, filled with layouts, both rough drawn and to scale. It felt like courage, when so many possibilities remained, to decide finally on a design. The almost-village had residents, lurking loosely in his mind, waiting to be housed. One house, similar in appearance to the dolls' house, destined for the crossroads at the heart of the village, was to be his.

Jon kept all of his note making and drawing, his planning, securely in the realms of the practical. He measured, wrote up experiments, drew floor plans and laid out plots. As he worked, stories of the idyllic lives led by the invented inhabitants of the village sent out soft and hopeful tendrils. Friendly encounters, kind neighbours. A lover even. A happy life where he would not be rejected, outlandish, repulsive. He felt it daring to even imagine such possibilities. But these fleeting fantasies were kept from the imperfect security of a page. It was foolish enough to have become a man, a bachelor, with no real purpose and no real welcome in the world, who made models of houses. He could not bear the idea of that more secret layer exposed to the scorn of others.

So the residents stayed in his imagination. They waited in the wings, sometimes loosely swapping their future place in the village, sometimes changing names, forgetfully or on a whim, as the tiny world grew in detail and began to form in actuality. He built stories about them as he built their homes, changing little things here and there. It did not matter so much if Mrs Inkhorn suddenly became Miss Wellington and moved from the cottage with the garden well into the house with attic windows. The point of Mrs Inkhorn, a kindly older woman, sometimes a widow, was that she would smile, benevolently, welcomingly, at Jon from her garden gate, whoever he had on his arm as he went for an evening stroll.

He built outwards from the crossroads, two roads, four corners, making first a church, the vicarage, a pub, and his own pretty house. The four buildings looked lonely on their own, and he hurried to build more houses and cottages, adding garden fences and paths. He made a churchyard wall and some gravestones, enjoying the careful application of an ageing process that in the real world required centuries. Painted lichen, mosses, the uneven dishevelment of age.

He laboured in frustration over the tiny lettering on two gravestones, making repeated attempts with an ever-smaller brush, and finally the rigging of a magnifying glass over his table. He lettered the names of his parents. He wanted them to look old, as though they had always been there. Anciently part of the village, forgiving at last.

Soon there was a cluster of buildings, still too small to have a population that would keep a pub and a shop in business, but customers would come – as fast as he could build the houses for them to inhabit.

Over time, the people living in the real village took an interest in Jon's project. He doesn't mean any harm. Nothing wrong with a bachelor, it's when they flaunt it that I can't stand it. He's alright, really, when you get to know him. He's not doing a bad job. So the casual cruelty of what they offered as though generosity seeped through the hedges, across the gravel drive. But Jon was grateful all the same and soon was talking to villagers about the project; he talked with Graham, the publican at The Plough Horse who had lost a son in Normandy about the best place to put a war memorial; Mrs Wickes who ran the village shop had some thoughts about the necessity of including decent storage space at the back of the model version.

Jon was moved by the interest of his neighbours. A tender wish to keep pleasing them drove him to greater efforts. But leaning over the gate to talk was an awkwardly intrusive manoeuvre for shy villagers so he had the tennis court fencing removed and the front hedge cut down to waist height. He hoped it was an invitation to look, and perhaps, if he were at work, an invitation to chat.

In time, the main layout of the village was complete. Lanes connected the two main roads, knitting the body of the village together. It was possible to imagine the pub jolly with customers, and the shop, in an age before supermarkets circled every town, sucking the customers and their cars away from the older businesses, busy enough to survive.

Eventually Jon removed the hedge entirely, planting a new one further back, behind the tennis court, so that the model village now was in an open space on the edge of the village green. Jon was still a private and cautious man. But a bridge had been built and he felt himself blessed by the gentle affirmation of his neighbours' goodwill, though it never quite blossomed into friendship, the connection was valuable and through the model village Jon was gently brought into the collective. It was acceptance, it was how it felt to be a part of village life.

It took years to complete. And it took all the years after to repair, improve and refine. Sometimes there were nods, little references to reality – the colour of a painted door and the arch of yellow roses around it, the setting of the church clock. Little ties that linked to the real world. He did not have the courage to believe in any kind of manifestation, but still he threw out ropes that might better tether his dream to the shore.

Painted detail, brickwork and roof tiles, door frames, letter boxes, became ever more elaborate and precise. He bought a scroll saw, cut and carved tiny end gables by hand for some roofs. He made trips to other villages, seeking out interesting or enchanting details in the vernacular architecture, taking photographs or making sketches of anything that caught his eye. He strayed briefly into the modern – he built a small place on the outskirts of the village that began life as a Bauhaus pavilion for an imagined opera singer but it drifted into a new role as the village library, the daring modern design seemed calmed by a role in civic life.

The village grew outward in scale and inward in detail. There seemed to be no end to how the project could occupy his time and his invention. Jon was content, happy even. His loneliness was not gone, but the howling of it receded to a whisper behind a closed door.

At work in the library, Jon began to notice one of the regulars, a man who came to borrow music books every few weeks, and to read some of the subscription magazines. He was younger than Jon. He was easygoing, friendly, as he requested to see old copies and subscriptions of music journals held in the library store. Jon presumed he was studying, though he never made notes and did not seem particularly focused on what he asked for.

Months later, to Jon's delight, the man confessed that he had but little interest in the magazines, reading them mostly in order to extend the time he might legitimately be in the library, and close to Jon himself. This man was Christopher.

Their friendship emerged slowly, as friendships between people taught raw lessons in the dangers of hope often do. Christopher was younger, and braver, than Jon. But he too had his share of betrayals, risks that suddenly became perils.

It was the model village that gave the two men the means to connect. Though Christopher's interest was concocted so he might get to know Jon, it did bloom over their years together into something close to genuine passion; never quite a match, but happy companion to Jon's own.

Christopher had worked hard at that early enthusiasm. It was one of the staple jokes in their love story, transformed into a comforting and fond tale, a binding element of their lasting devotion.

After some awkward chats and weeks of Christopher making little progress in the library, Jon had finally understood that an invitation to see the model village was desired. He had in glimmers thought it possible, but dared not believe it. How many times must a man say I'd love to see it, smiling openly, warmly, before the prompt is understood? Many more than once, it seemed. Christopher would mutter with inward exasperation, at the blank, slightly alarmed look Jon gave him in response. Had Jon not been so attracted to Christopher, had Christopher been a woman, an elderly gentleman, anyone other than someone desirable and showing signs (could it be true?) of interest in Jon himself, the invitation would have come at the first hint. But eventually his courage took him by the hand and led him to ask if Christopher would like to come and help him with some of the ongoing chores of maintenance.

Christopher was delighted and aghast. He had not a clue about actually making things and feared he had overdone this angle of his interest. He had hoped he might be invited for a glass of sherry and a closer inspection. But he accepted and in the same breath tried to mitigate for his pretence, gushing awkwardly that it had been a while since he had done much actual making and hoped he would not be too rusty, probably could not remember one end of the hammer from the other ha ha ha.

So, Christopher visited and Jon showed him methods of woodworking and render mixing as he repaired and replaced roofs, added stone walls, remade houses with new, more durable techniques. He was at first, until the ruses of lovers became confessions under the bed covers, confused by Christopher's ineptitude, even as Christopher kept up the pretence of remembering how it worked the instant he had been shown.

But using the cover of working on the upkeep of the models, their friendship bloomed. Truth, it was love that bloomed, leaving friendship to follow, building bonds in service of love, once the choice had been made.

28

Eve,
I curse
your luck

Eve went out one night to see a band. They worked with a combination of electronic sounds and classical instrumentation, something that Eve had been experimenting with herself. There was a cello, drums, a singer who also played a flute and an accordion. The varied sounds meshed and pulled richly behind the drone of a keyboard.

She slipped in quietly to the gig. People did not invariably bother her, but many knew her from Never. She would be told which track was their best and why they should have done something, this or that, to improve another. Sometimes a bloke she did not know would want to educate her about her own playing, in case she had got there by strange instincts she could not possibly understand. Her blankly cool response (she was not able to muster the forced friendliness that might manoeuvre an easy exit) often lead to belligerence from half-pissed aficionados of the scene. Most often though, she was approached with gluey good intention, by someone blind to the signals of her disinterest. They meant no harm but she had no desire to become pals. She did not really mind being labelled a stuck-up cow, all she really wanted was to be left alone.

As she was getting herself a drink a man ambled over, all 'Hey Eve, what are you up to these days? Never were a bit shit. Cheers!' He kept on, leaning at her, beery breathing in her face. One arm stretched to the bar behind her, his body square in front. He sneered down at her. 'Hey don't be all fucking high and mighty, you're just a punter now.' Little clicks of the ratchet sounded; the threat, the potential for threat, built around her, just from this one man-boy, as he pursued his baiting. Eve felt the edge of his aggression and the careful disinterest of all those around her. 'Hey,' he said, 'hey, stuck up bitch, got nothing to say?' She tried to assess her best response, but would have to physically push him aside to leave. It felt a risk. The singer from the band came and stood next to the man, she came up to his shoulder, as slender as a French bean in her green dress.

'Fuck off, leave her alone.'

There was an outbreak of disharmony, watched from side-eyes and over shoulders; no one wanted trouble and so no one stopped the man from causing it. But the bouncers noticed eventually. Strolling over in their own time, picking on the man for being the loudest and the drunkest, if indifferent to his role as protagonist, they at last threw him out.

It was an imperfect but useful introduction. The singer, Kim, brought Eve back to a table where the other band members sat.

Demon pounced on a little spark, a frequency, a blur in the air that flew between Eve and the cellist, Danny. We knew right away that he would become part of the story.

Maybe Eve, with her useless integrity, would become unwound, rewind-able, in the pursuit, at long last, of love.

But it did not work out that way.

It was too easy.

The two of them fell into harmonious connection, both musically and personally, without hitches. They met, they fell, they worked. They still do.

Good fortune conspired against Demon. He cursed Eve and cursed her luck with a bitterness that made me shrink.

Maybe that luck is where the angels hide.

I got used to and then bored of his fearsome, impotent spells, against all that went well for her. Somehow, through the luck of angels or the desire to keep possession of her soul, she remained unharnessed.

Danny and Eve's relationship, though on steady feet, wound a careful path. They kept their separate accommodations for a long time. Eve was too cautious for sudden changes and though Elaine was mended, her frailties were raw in Eve's mind. She was in no hurry to leave her mother. She had come to value being back in the village, loved the room at Christopher's, the nearness and ease of it. Though Eve and Danny were soon committed at heart, their lives took longer to mesh.

They fell into musical collaboration as easily as they had fallen in love. He kept working with his own band where he had more autonomy, but he loved working with Eve. He had liked Never well enough but could see something truly precious in her solo work. He could see through the frustrations she was experiencing, and believed from both completed older work and the new, disjointed, incomplete beginnings that she was a musician of great originality. She had more intense expectations and made more rigorous demands than any other musician he knew. In the sudden switches, the wild ideas that went into the unfinished experiments of her current work, he heard music to believe in.

'No, not like that, again,' she would say.

'That doesn't work,' she would say

'No, again,' she would say. To the point of Danny's tightly held irritation. But each time they persisted, each time they reached a point where she beamed at him, each time they got to the point she had been searching for, he knew the music was better. He knew it had been worth the chase.

They played different instruments, tried things out together, for the sheer enjoyment of playing music. It existed on a level that was not Eve's own work, but it fed into it. And that freed her, in a way I do not think anyone but I noticed; for all the intensity of her curt instruction, so light was Eve's heart during this musical play that Demon barely noticed its passing. Thus, when working with others, Eve was often free from his destructive attentions. I was careful not to make this observation to Demon for I could see that she needed this, if she were to be allowed to remain whole.

Eve did not want to share her old bedroom and the single bed and its childhood tints with her lover. It was too squeamish a mix. They spent nights together at Danny's, and she tried not to resent the time that getting there took away from the studio. She held out against moving in with him.

But she was certain of her love for him long before her actions showed it. She knew in a few short weeks, by a soft weight in her heart, by a smile that warmed her from within, that she loved Danny. Shyly she examined her feelings for him, keeping them tucked away lest exposure leave her foolishly mistaken, recklessly vulnerable. At the beginning, love felt more like a private pleasure than something shared. The joy she took in a frown of concentration as he played a new piece, the warmth of his skin, the unbelievable sense of belonging and security that eventually bound them together.

In return, it took time for him to learn how to tally the evidence of her love. He was a wise and sanguine man, but Eve took some getting to know. It took the effort of confronting his own insecurity in the face of what sometimes seemed her indifference. Luckily Danny too was stubborn and he loved Eve enough to hope, and soon enough he understood her, protected her caution, accepted her undemonstrative way. He was able to trust her, took her presence as affirmation that she wanted to be there. He was not jealous of her music, or the island that, inhabiting it, she sometimes became. He understood that her tetchiness, when she was troubled by a headache, or frustrated with her work, was not aimed at him. He understood her terse and unromantic nature, knowing that feelings can also be strong when slenderly expressed. He understood, and cared enough to take the lesson of it; to be with Eve was only possible in the acceptance of how she was. She would never swamp him with affection or praise him with declarations, but he came to learn that her love for him was deep and true.

29
do
not
waste
this chance

With and without Danny, Eve's path became wider. Opportunities were offered, collaborations with those who stepped onto the path to walk with her. People had not known what to do with her. But she did not go away. And as she did not die or give up, the rough corners of youth were knocked off. Her solo work, music with the power to call down the divine, the music of her dreams evaded her, but her skill and understanding evolved and grew.

Eve joined Kim on a longstanding project setting poetry to music. The two became close friends. Kim's background in a Gospel church choir had trained her voice from a young age. Eve loved working with her, helping fill out what Kim had already done, and all the while discovering the power and range of tone a skilled singer offered. The voice, for Eve, remained simply another instrument, one of many options, not by default the centre of the music. A simple keyboard line, or abstract site-specific percussion could be as much of a focal point as the singer. But she was excited by the discovery of a new musical palette.

She had an idea, a splinter of an idea. She listened for the shape and the voice of it. Something was there, voices layered in startling geographies, dividing and massing around the beginnings of a melody. She longed to pull it into being. But the more she chased, the further it fled. The harder she tried, the more her ideas disintegrated. The more she was drawn, in longing, to create a piece of music, the harder Demon tried to pirate her desires, transposing them into a commodity he could supply. She cried *I want to harness the divine!* And in this summoning he heard not the words, but only the yearning. And yearning he thought he knew, he thought he understood it well, for he had done much trade on its satisfaction. But I could see, if Demon could not, that Eve's longing and his understanding were not the same. This much I know.

She had achieved the long-sought blessing of her own space, the freedom of her cherished ideas, and come to the bleak truth that music still eluded her. The more she worked the more of a grind it became.

A wavering drone from a looped and distorted keyboard spilled across the room, filling the space. Eve fiddled with it, creating variations in the pulses of sound. She had a picture of water, a body of water, rock surfaces shaped by water. A body of water and sound wavering the cube of space bounded by the room.

And as her fascination grew, Demon of course, began whispering his silent, ferocious assault, into the private darkness of her mind.

She gritted her teeth. She refused to hear Demon, she was not listening. But nor could she evade him. Inside her head, in the vast darkness, a relentless scouring echoed, shaping choppy cross-tides of fear and seduction; it was intense and unwelcome. The vision, the water and the rocks, the wavering energy and above all, the possibility of music was wiped like words from a whiteboard. The vital secret darkness of her mind was overwhelmed, flooded by the harsh light of Demon, demanding that she respond.

Eve slumped back into the chair.

30

some
would die
for what you
careless spurn

Leon, still in London, however furious still with Eve, was finally getting over his disappointment at the end of the band and was discovering his own new path. He had always been a good writer, his lyrics were the best part of his contribution to Never. He had assiduously collected contacts – including those alienated at the peak of his success. He made the most of those connections, calling up any journalist who might help, and made a connection with a music magazine. He began writing reviews, arch, smart and stinging. Sometimes he interviewed up-and-coming bands but his affectation of world-weary cynicism worked less well in the face of a fresh and hopeful newcomer, disinclined to believe, however hard he insisted, that Leon's story presaged their own. He could not get his subjects to sparkle in the same way as his reviews, for though he could heap praise on a record, it was harder to admire its makers to their face. It felt too much like an admission of defeat.

He was getting by. No need to dust off his A levels and rejoin the dull monotony of the real world. Writing for the music papers gave him a place in the familiar sphere of hope and longing. He retained some influence and that is a kind of power. In a frustratingly faint echo of the thrill of his days of fame, he was noticed, if only by the members of the band, when he came through the door to a gig. Sometimes the meagreness of the comparison was hard to take. They were not all that, the fresh-faced little shits.

Leon and Eve did not stay in contact; the bonds of their friendship lost all shape in the stretching of band politics. But he always watched out for her, gratified that for a while, he heard or saw nothing. But after a year or so, as various collaborations brought new interest and some success, she began once again to appear in the public realm. She cropped up on a late-night arts show, a languorous piece with her on keyboards and Danny on cello, backing a newly lauded singer. She was, he heard, signed up to write the score for a small but relevant independent film. She was making grown-up work, no longer needed to be young, and he was stuck with teenage brats.

Somehow the equation became one in which Eve's accomplishments lessened the value of his own. In this new reckoning, writing reviews elevating or dashing the work of other artists became insignificant and boring. Her work had moved on so far that it was not even reviewed in the paper he worked for so he could not even relish the prospect of a delicious dismantling, a sharp put-down of her efforts.

He was dissatisfied, sick of going to gigs and feeling like the oldest person in the room. He rarely was, but so in tune to the power of youth was he, so harsh had he been about those only a few years older than himself, that it stung to feel old. He was thirty, nearly thirty-one, an age he had confidently claimed in one early interview, was well past it. He had predicted in the same interview that he would be dead by forty, that there was little of value to expect from age.

It felt like time to move on, grow up. The music of his youth no longer felt serious. He needed a new way to be seen. He was frustrated, burdened by the sense that his good fortune, his right, had been taken away, and by the nagging fear that he had not been up to it. He needed to reclaim lost ground.

The notebooks of lyrics were full of unfinished or unlinked sentences, thoughts that meandered, too complicated to pin into a song. He reached into his writing, trying to find his way.

After a couple of years of reasonably successful journalism, Leon stopped writing reviews, told people he was working on serious stuff now. He was going to write a novel.

He broke up with his girlfriend, blaming her for the creeping unrest that grew within him. He blamed her, vaguely and destructively for not insulating him against the perils of his own soul. She was broken-hearted. And angry. She painted WANKER in yellow nail varnish across the grooves of Never's first album and propped it up on the pillow on his side of the bed. She felt a sour burst of triumph at her childish revenge.

Time passed and Leon spent days on his own. He took drugs, uppers mainly, dabbling in little foils of heroin now and then but staying clear of a habit. And he worked hard, indiscriminately, greedily, on the book he thought would salvage him. Loosely based on his experiences, carelessly constructed and spiced with crude invention, it was a tale of a cynic, a misanthrope, a musician.

Little piles of rollie dog-ends grew on the corners of tables, sometimes to be swept into his hand, dropped inaccurately into an ashtray or takeaway box. He drank red wine from the afternoon into the evening. There was a sourness to his body that came out in his words.

Leon's novel grew, fattening the pages of a series of notebooks, the day's progress slowly typed up late, with wine-clumsy fingers, curses and typos clamouring.

Eight months after he started writing, he came to the end. He showed it to a friend with contacts in publishing.

'Look, it needs some work' is all that she said.

It was not what Leon needed.

He took to the new platforms of social media, writing long and rambling posts about other people's stupidity couched in loosely cultural terms.

31

**this
gift you
so stubbornly
so foolishly are wasting**

Happiness is achieved when there is enough, and for Eve and Danny, there almost was. But for the absence of her own compositions, Eve was happy. She and Danny found a little house to share, with a scruffy garden and distance from neighbours so that music would cause no disturbance. It was near enough for Eve to keep working at Christopher's and to keep an eye on Elaine. Everything, almost, fitted. The two of them worked together and apart and spent quiet evenings in each other's company, talking about music, already written and yet to come.

Everything had evolved: her skill, her desire, the shape and tone of the sounds that enthralled her. Those wonderful landscapes built of sound had been refined as by the weather of her experience. She could see them still, just, but as though from a great distance. She had lost her way into them. Frustration evolved into sorrow at what felt to her like exclusion from home.

She created little rags of music, strange and beautiful instrumental pieces. Yet none made it to completion. The thrill of invention swept her along only so far. Everything remained as fragments. Nothing coalesced. The more she worried at it, the more she tried to resolve a piece, the more her head ached, and her anxiety grew.

The headaches were seeded by Demon's ardent breath, his despicable, relentless, tawdry offers. The effort of resistance disrupted her invention, her ability to finish a piece. I could not have told him for I never would want his fury turned on me, but being fond of Eve, and hoping she would not concede her soul, I wished she might find a better way; better for her perhaps, for then I remembered the wraith clinging to the hawthorn and felt something like love in my hope that Demon not be meant for such a fate.

He had not chosen this any more than she. How could I hold it against him that he wished to prosper from the deal, even at the expense of knocking off some of her artistic brilliance?

32

So
many
dreams
have faltered

Poor Leon, it was not a good time for him. He spat his late-night thoughts, ground through wine-stained teeth, onto new, open access pages of social media. The praise of a few old fans kept him going. They could sense the sweet, rank smell of alcohol breath, the dishevelled murk of an unloved body through the pristine screen, and loved it that he just doesn't care, dude. It did him few favours. A one-man band of bitterness. Perhaps all the one-man bands of bitterness could meet up and form an orchestra, for it is not an uncommon thing.

He scribbled and muttered. His teeth became dark with wine, his hair lank and long. Rambling opinions typed into the ether. Fragments of words on paper, a poorly stacked pile of sheets that kept sliding from the small table, unlatched from each other. Girls in shops held back from the damp and unloved smell of him – it was his coat but they were not to know that.

Here he was, long past the youth he had so sneeringly cherished, leaning on the third floor walkway of the flat he had lived in for years, the door behind him still mustard yellow, the 6 of 26 still missing. Smoking a rollie, tapping ash, finding fault with the young people and their brash, track-suited style, finding fault with the fatness of old ladies, finding fault with the blokey camaraderie of the road workers. They don't know, he sneers. They don't know and I do. But what do you know, Leon? What's the big secret? That it's all fucked? That's it?

Here he was, an unhealthy-looking man in a secondhand overcoat, a plastic bag with a notebook and newspaper, a few pens trying not to fall through the holes in the bottom. He dragged the bag along the railings at the edge of the park.

We would see more of Leon, though so broken, so incomplete was he that I did not guess it at the time.

33

cut
loose
and lost

The headphones covered her ears, sound filling the small space within. Demon was trying, as he ever did, to insinuate himself into that privileged chamber. He could not find the opening and his frustration glowered a threatening halo. She was shaped by the cost of keeping him out. Tension wedged her shoulder blades against her spine. For all the ease he promised, his offerings landed not as a gift but as pain, as an upset to her hard-found equilibrium. Anxiety threaded her limbs and organs, pulled her body into constant low tension. Now and then, as he grew more insistent, or more desperate, it flared, bringing headaches, anxiety, fear.

In her resistance, she suffered. That she could no longer properly write music was the most terrible feeling of all.

She knew, somewhere in the wordless depths of her mind, that the malign influence of the divine was the cause. But she did not choose or did not know how to acknowledge it. Times were hard, she was blocked. It would probably come back. With dread she feared it might last forever.

She kept trying. She kept resisting – whatever it was that she understood Demon to be. She turned inwards, her armour the scraps and beginnings, the shreds of music she could find. Sometimes it was enough; insulation against the jagged drag of his threats and pleadings. Demon's eyes flashed with malevolent anger. I pretended not to see. I pretended carefully, lest he read my inattention as a deliberate slight.

Though unable to complete a piece she kept working with what she had. Sometimes I could understand the wordless mesh of Eve's thoughts, why this part was too much, that part too thin. Why a change here needed greater – what? Hit? Weight? Power? What kind of sound was missing? Words offer mere interpretation and only meagrely describe the subtle shifts in the process. And I could understand her frustration; the answers did not come, lost as they were in the babble of a divine interloper.

I was fascinated by it all. I began to see, as I observed her struggling with compositions that had once come so easily, that much as with a story, the listener must give themselves up to the music. The lifts and the drops and the inclines of it do not, like a ride at a funfair, co-opt the might of gravity to make their impact on a body. But a body surrendered to music may be altered by it. Just as a body that listens to a well told tale may find it is changed by fear, by compassion, by joy, a spell created in the tale but made complete within the interior, the realm of pulses, chemical signals, the ticks and trickles of life. Yes, perhaps it is life itself that is affected thus.

Demon might know how this is so, if he had the curiosity to explore the great wonder of who and what he is and how it came to be. He is, in his ancient provenance, something from the beginning of it all. It is a great sadness to me that he does not have this curiosity. For what a tale that would be to tell. And what a magnificent offer to make to one such as Eve.

The composition, though filled with sparks of promise, would not coalesce. She pulled the headphones from her ears, slapped them down. It was no good. Her head ached, her eyes and shoulders were bunched in pointless, painful tension. She closed her eyes. It was no good.

In her mind's eye, scraps of her landscapes, her cosmic shapes still danced, floated, slid in and out of view. She could see them, she carried them everywhere with her. But she could not pull them close enough, could not make them whole. A shimmer of sorrow slipped down her arms, into the palms of her hands. Something wonderful was, perhaps, gone. The sadness wrapped her so well it even quieted Demon.

There was other music. And perhaps her own would come back one day. Perhaps she just needed to be patient. She shook off the gloom. No point in feeling sorry for herself. She was working on a project with a film maker, writing the score for a movie. Music harnessed to the enhancement of another art form was not as thrilling as music written simply for the requirement that it exist, but it was a good project. She was glad to be involved. *Would you not like to be at the top of your profession? To be flown around the world, to be known and rewarded as the best? The best of the best? The most celebrated? Would you not like...*

Eve plugged her headphones into the stereo, flicked the needle onto the vinyl, turned up the volume. Someone else's music roared into her head. She shut her eyes, her shoulders relaxed, her hands resting on her thighs. Demon shrieked, a worn out story of future success. She pulled the headphones off, batted a lock of hair away from her face, an unexpected flash of irritation as though she shoved him away. And she left the room.

Of course, he did find a way to reach her or we would not be here now, on this clifftop, waiting for Eve to arrive, waiting for this telling of a strange tale to reach an end. For Demon's sake, I hope the next time will be long hence.

34

gone,
unheard,
silent in the
drag of years

Leon could not keep despair at bay. He felt he was on the brink of something terrible, waiting for a natural disaster.

In the past, whenever bad feelings welled too close to the surface, he had mounted an emphatic multi-pronged defence, anticipating the change of mood just before he was forced to acknowledge it. A rash of wine and drugs, heady nights out, sex with new women. Drugs and alcohol still had their place, but the high of anything was gone, and he no longer had the knack of picking up women. He had never been an ace but he was not bad looking, he had swagger, and the early ease of a little fame gave him the advantage of expecting success; it had sometimes hit the mark.

Now, people held back, kept their distance from him.

He was lost. So brash he had been, so certain that for a time, it had given him the world he desired. But worlds made that way are flimsy, not built for endurance.

Now, for protection, he had no more than his forced habits of cynicism and indifference. But the crust was worn so thin it served to keep off only the most passing glance of strangers, where once he had not even seen through it himself.

Leon had run out of bravado. He curled into himself, brittle, dry as autumn leaf-fall.

He stopped telling people he was writing now, he had ditched music, all of that puerile shit. He stopped because mostly he did not see anyone. It had come to a point of diminishing returns anyway. The last time he had told someone, a kid in a pub, that he had given up music because it was shit, but he used to be in a band called Never, who played a kind of music that was true to something, lost now, the kid had said 'Yeah, it does sound shit, man.' The kid had drifted away as Leon tried to scrabble back the ground and explain that it was not shit at all. He remembered the joy as well as the success, the sense of pulling off a marvellous feat. He remembered catching sight of Eve, mid song, lost and wonderfully present. That, all by itself, was something. He felt as though he had wasted a beautiful chance.

Sadness curled out like a mould in the dim channels of his body. The soot and grime of the city curled inwards. He felt himself dissolving into the vast disarray of London.

Oh, Leon. I came to have compassion for him, even to care about him. What a stupid mess he had made, what pointless misunderstanding of himself, his place in the world.

And Demon was keeping an eye on Leon for his own reasons. I noticed that, as time passed, Demon was holding more of his thoughts to himself. When first we met he would bang on about it all so relentlessly. Not even really speaking to me but somehow expecting that I would listen anyway. *Yes, Demon, no, Demon, three bags of magnificent wisdom full, Demon.*

I often wonder what difference it would make if he knew how much of a part I have played to humour him. But equally I wonder what difference it would make if he knew that something in me loves something in him.

35

Do

you

disavow

your dreams

and all my many gifts?

Eve's mouth was dry. She sipped her beer, but dared not quench her thirst. She did not want the sludge of alcohol blurring her senses, nor the need for a visit to the loo when she was on stage. Someone talked to her. She half-smiled in response, without interest. Her thoughts flicked over preparations, all completed, the details become bald with handling. Nothing needed to be done.

She would leave, any minute, shut out these people. But they were owed something of her time for now, their commissioning and hosting of her work gave them that. They were excited, wanting to congratulate, willing Eve to share in their eager anticipation.

You can have this forever, hissed Demon.

I hate backstage more than anything, she thought at that moment, as another beaming face ready for the thrill of a new performance came over, expecting her to be a mirror.

Yes, she was excited to share the piece, she said, dully. Yes, a bit nervous. Ha ha, yes, no doubt. She looked at her watch, said 'well, I've got to, you know' and abruptly left the group to their wine and their anticipation.

She walked down a backstage corridor into a small room with a bowl of crisps and a few beers. What a relief to find it empty. She sat in the silence, let the words disappear. And with them, slowly, went worry, the expectations of others. *I am just a body in a room. And I wrote some music for a film.*

Demon had learned by now that of all the ways he wasted his efforts with Eve, these moments, when she was fully in retreat were perhaps the most unprofitable. I was glad for them both that he had, for he achieved nothing useful – an unintelligible, formless buzz of anxiety, a clamour snuck into the corners of Eve's mind, distracting, upsetting, and achieving nothing.

Finding a way through this stalemate was beginning to seem hopeless and secretly I too began to worry that Demon might fail.

What would happen to me? Would I be doomed, like him, to eternity, never to be part of the dark earth, the unknowing nothing? This I did not dare ask, and, happily, I never needed to know.

Eve changed into a suit, kingfisher blue with a pale box check. She looked in the mirror, re-plaited her black hair. She removed some of her silver rings, tucked them into her jacket pocket.

She took a quick and quiet sip from her bottle of water, listening from her dark section of the stage to the cello, the brass, the recorded track. Lights would come back to her in the next passage. She checked settings, notebooks, keyboard, laptop. She had a few minutes. She could see, just, faces looking up at the stage and knew they had been won. She had done a job, for someone else. A good job, that was true. And for now that was precious. But it felt almost like a cheat.

After the performance she was more relaxed. Whilst still not enjoying the clamour of attention, she had less desire to run away. It had gone well. The film producers and the audience were delighted with her work. She had successfully fulfilled the brief and that was worth something.

She gazed over the shoulder of the percussionist's partner, who was telling a story about being snowed in. She was astonished to see Leon, in conversation with Christopher. She mumbled an exit and went over. Eve and Leon gave each other an awkward hug, the bristles on his cheek grazed her face. She put her hand on the front of his shoulder, a barrier to too much proximity.

They exchanged a conventional greeting, congratulations from him, thanks from her. She was waiting for the sting. But it did not come. Instead, with a sincerity she had never seen in Leon, he told her again how great her work was.

'It's a great film Eve, really good to see you doing so well.'

'Thank you, yeah, thanks. What about you?'

'Me? God, nothing, who knows? I don't really know what I'm doing.'

As they said goodbye a few moments later, Eve briefly caught a defeated look in Leon she had never seen before. She turned to leave, casting a look over her shoulder. He watched her walk away. She went to join a group of the musicians toasting each other near the bar, and soon forgot about him.

There were many congratulations. As the night wore thin so did the balm of a successful performance. She sat with Christopher and Danny. Both noticed the drag in her response to their enthusiasm.

'What's up?' asked Danny.

'I don't know really. I'm being a jerk. It's great, I've been really lucky to do this film. They've been great to work with.'

'But?' asked Christopher.

'It's – it's kind of easy, it's kind of easy to do.'

'Isn't that a good thing? Not many people would find it easy.'

'I guess. But the hard part, the proper stuff, I can't – it's gone.'

'Give it time.' Christopher tried to console, and encourage, as he always did. 'I was talking to Leon, he would work with you again at the drop of a hat. He's by no means the only one. You will have work, people to work with, and somewhere you will find what it is you have been searching for.'

Eve nodded, grateful that he wanted to help but without any belief in his prediction.

'You're still young, Eve, you have a lifetime. I know you will find what you want.' Christopher leaned towards her, willing her to feel cheered, to feel hopeful.

Demon started hissing in her ear. In her frustration she left the table, left the care of Danny and Christopher unacknowledged. She went to the bar for three whiskies and three beers. Might as well slip under a fog. Alcohol would push the messy clamour, the frustration away and for that she would be grateful.

We two were still there when the harsh overhead lights had been flicked on, and our players, indeed all guests, had long departed. I watched the bar staff clear glasses and wipe tables, the manager check the till, lock away the cash, note the stock levels.

Demon lay under a bench seat, his back to the room. The manager finished his preparations, turned the lights off and left. We were in darkness.

'Demon?'

'Mm?'

'Give it time. It will be alright.' I wanted him to feel better, but I was afraid that I was wrong. The night grew old. Demon and I lay on the floor in the dark. I feared this could be our eternity. Ghost shadows under a formica table, a buzz of something, once another thing, on the faded lino. A forgotten, inert smear of the divine.

36

**I
am
a demon,
divine and ancient,
in fear of dread eternity.**

We finally left the bar when the morning shift came in to open up the next day. We skittered aimlessly across the city, alighting randomly on a tower block. The pebbly tarred surface and low wall was similar to the roof we had haunted in the years when Eve still lived in London.

I thought of the man who had unwittingly accompanied us back then, hoping he had won his battle with the edge. So many, near and far, would not find a way out of that darkness. Why could not a fleet of Demons be sent for them, built as they were, in some strange way, to provide a kind of happiness? The value of a soul must be too high for such a simple thing as an end to misery. Perhaps the soul must be retained if a true cure is to be found.

Demon gazed across the city skyline and held me close. I felt the breath of a sigh graze my ear. Fearfully I considered the possibility of his failure, and then, deliberately, turned to his success and what that would mean. Success for Demon, yes. I felt a chill for Eve, regretting what she would lose. Such a soul, to see into the divine, to make music that echoed the beauty of the cosmos, played upon the hearts of listeners as though they had been strung for just such a tune.

Demon's offer would not take that away, surely? It was meant to make her happier. But what was the happiness that Demon offered? It is better described as something else, when one finds oneself seen and rewarded by the world in a way that fulfils the wish to be seen and rewarded.

What is a soul?

All these years later, I still do not know. For all that I know its absence is dreadful, eternal nothingness. But the absence of a thing, like a reflection in pewter, only smokily describes its presence. Eve, I was worried for you that long and lonely night, and I am sorry that we wait for you, here on this grassy cliff edge now.

These feelings of mine are less than a footnote, not even a mark in the margin, in this ancient story. I tell the tale, and may, in the telling, shape the sense of it here and there. But I could not then, now, or ever, change what happens, what remains to be told. This much I know.

There was nowhere Demon needed to go, no thread to follow, no fiendish plan to finesse. We were adrift. We languished for days in the most unpromising corners. On civic rooftops. Behind the recycling bins in a town car park. I do not know how long in the garage next door to Elaine's house. I lost track of time, tried not to imagine this state as one eternal.

Now and then, Demon would mutter about Eve or another of the players in our story. It was as though he needed to confirm that pessimism was still the safest option. *Pathetic, she guards her soul, buries her head in her damned music. Why am I saddled with one who has such a damnable lack of ambition?*

I did not think it fair or wise to blame his predicament on such an assessment, for I knew by some measures she had the grandest ambitions of all. Demon should perhaps have saved his ire for the fates that cast him, ask them that he be given better tools, that he be granted the cunning, or the power, or the right, to bring true magic to dreams. He would win her soul if he offered to open up the wonders of the divine, granting her access to other realms; that he could merely offer embellishments in this one was not Eve's fault. Perhaps other brothers have learned these subtle arts, but they were beyond Demon and he seemed to have run out of ideas.

Out of loyalty I tried to stop thinking about it, but around this time I often found myself wondering how banishment on earth, denied divine repose, would work. I found myself fearful I would be forced to share it, spend all eternity, with him. Nowhere and nothing together. Just at this time, I hoped very much this would not be the case. I wished I had never been made other than as I first was.

An ordinary creature is not such a bad thing.

We were lying under a spare-room bed. I felt the cold of an unused exercise machine against my rump. I do not even know whose house it was. Demon roused me listlessly.

'Rabbit, come. We may as well see what we can see.'

I felt heavy, as though I had been called from deep sleep. I wished it were the case, for I had not been blessed with absence, with unconsciousness for many days. Demon was pale and bleary as though dusted in a bloom of mould. Markings that in better times flickered magnificently across the surface of him seemed to pool in his joints, stirring only to a listless waver. Flotsam on a tide turn.

We took a turn, found Eve in her studio. She hummed a tune alongside the track playing in her headphones. For once Demon kept quiet, and she knew not that we were there.

'There must be something.' Demon muttered as we finally left her. My head was foggy, I could not even summon the performance of a good companion, and made no attempt to reassure.

Downstairs, Christopher was snoozing in an armchair, a newspaper across his knees. Demon leapt onto the chair back and grimaced furiously down at him as though all his woes could be blamed on this harmless sleeping man. Christopher frowned and for a horrible moment, he seemed to stop breathing.

At last he muttered a breath into his cluttered chest, closed his mouth. He did not wake. I hoped he did not have a bad dream.

We dragged slowly, as though for the bitter pleasure of confirming our exclusion, through all the lives touching Eve's. Elaine, redecorating her bedroom, a spell of renewal against her time of illness. Mal in the park with his two young children, keeping an eye on a bike auction on his phone. Kim, Mick, Lorraine, Ellen, all the musicians she had worked with.

Danny was at home reading a novel. Demon muttered, casting Danny as a lever – his death, or running off to find new love and spurning Eve, creating space in which Demon might flourish – *no no no for she would just close up, in, turn away*. Demon snarled at Danny, furious with how unhelpful he unwittingly was. I do think he knew something of Demon's spite, his plans verging on a death wish, for in a sudden rustle of anxiety he picked up his phone and messaged Eve, asking that she drive carefully on the weather-washed roads. She probably would not see or respond; Danny's peace of mind would have to wait for her return.

We went next to Leon.

Shortly after he had left the family home for London, his mother and father had sold up and moved to a bungalow by the sea, then both quietly, undramatically died. He had never liked the place, or felt at home there. He had visited them only rarely. But London had become too big, too strung out, too overwhelming. He realised he missed his parents, their uncomplicated lives, their simple love. With a bag that contained a few clothes and his notebooks, he had boarded a train to the coast.

The damp of long absence had muted the house. He threw his bags down on the kitchen floor, flicked a light switch, filled the kettle. There were still teabags, from his last visit nearly two years before, in a jar tucked against the wall. Luckily, for he had forgotten to buy them. No milk, but some indestructible sugar in a bowl.

Sweet black tea steaming in a mug, he sat with his coat on as he waited for the radiators to dislodge the chill.

He thought about his mum, making the tea, the way she peered down into the mugs as she stirred the teabags as though a precise alchemy was required. How she would turn and shout towards the kitchen door 'there's a tea with your name on it here, Ian love.' How his dad would ho ho, rubbing his hands in anticipation of the excellent treat as he made his way to the kitchen.

He thought about the simple acceptance of their lot in life, their ordinary lives and absence of grander ambitions, at last without scorn. The remembrance of his scorn pained him; the ungenerous presumption of it.

He had been loved, simply, by Ian and Veronica. They were not impressed by his time in an up-and-coming band. They would not have been impressed after that when younger bands wanted him to favour them, to write good reviews. But nor were they, as he had been, scornful of choices they did not understand.

Simple love had never been enough for Leon. He craved admiration, and the little heft of power it accorded the admired. How were Ian and Veronica to understand that, as they so carefully lived and loved in their uncomplicated, accepting way?

They did not scorn Leon's choices, but he did make them sigh.

He missed them now more than he ever had.

We arrived at the bungalow on our dreary tour. He had been living there in a half-hearted way for a few months. Leon, of course was oblivious to our arrival. He sat at the table, turned a leaf of the notebook, for the shroud of an empty page. He wrote a line or two, scribbled out some word. He turned the page again, began writing again. Scraps that coalesced and fell apart, asked to be remade. Cobwebs. Moths. Bright motes flickering in a ghost ship of solitude. He wrote little filaments of a lonely man's tale, the voice of a soul immured.

Something in these loose skeins spun a fine thread – the promise of a mooring. No one would know how, just yet, least of all him, but these words marked the beginning of a change for him.

Demon sat on the table, gazing down at the page as though trying to make sense of it where Leon could not.

There was something, maybe. But no clarity came. Night fell bleak and we left.

37

**I
am
losing
all hope**

We came to rest next to the sea, as moonlight climbed to catch the waves. Demon sat with his knees pulled up, his head tipped into the shelter of his arms. His back stretched over the bumps of his spine. I wondered, for an unsettling moment, about demon bones.

This cursed curiosity.

'I am worried, Rabbit.' Demon's voice was muffled, his hands wrapping the back of his head. 'I cannot find a new way. I do not know how to shape my offer,' he said. 'She will not let me in, and I begin to fear she never will.'

It has always felt presumptuous, to imagine I could help Demon but I felt compelled to try. 'Demon, you must not give up!'

'I will not, no. That is impossible. Until she draws her last natural breath, I will keep trying.' He slumped down next to me and I edged into him, rubbing my head against his arm.

'Do not be afraid. Let us remember instead all the times you have won. I only need to remind you, so well you know the tales. The wine seller, the metal smith. The one who carved wood in the mountains and ended his life a resident in the cathedral palaces. All had their challenges and there must have been times you feared failure – I know this is true because you told me of dark times and I told the tales back to you.'

'You are right. I must try to hope. We should perhaps go and see my work, seek inspiration that way?'

I was surprised and deeply honoured to be asked for an opinion, even such a trifling one; it seemed as clear a mark of his uncertainty as I had ever seen. I think it was the only time, in all our years together, that it happened.

It was wise for him to remember his successes and I was always curious about all he had done before, the wild stories he had created, but I was startled as I had thought those he had encountered in the past were long dead.

'They will never be dead, exactly,' he reminded me, 'but neither are they still living. What they made however, sometimes that survives.'

'And when we see what survived, you will remember all your successes and find a way to add Eve to their number.'

'I truly hope so Rabbit.'

Our first stop was a mansion in London, its former glory now lost in subdivision and commercial use that is the lot of grand buildings in an ever-growing city. It was built for a girl, a poor girl born within planked walls, gaps stuffed with canvas and rags, in a part of the city that slid into marshlands. A girl with muddy feet and a voice that caused those who heard her sing to dissolve in tears.

Her singing brought Demon. With her charm and their combined cunning, she built the house. She spent her happiest hours with the architect, planning the five-storey mansion. She had wanted colours. Colours to line her walls, to plate up her table, to cover her body. Colours picked out with jewels. Colours that did not appear in more than the tiny heads of wild flowers in her dun and muddy home. She was the city's jewel herself – for a long while, for she made a canny deal.

She sang the favourite songs of the day and became the favourite of the rich, of royalty. Her generous nature and foresight kept her free from entanglements that may have brought her down. She did not lack attentions from men, but rejected them quietly, kindly, saving love for a discrete and long-lived connection with a woman.

As she aged, her purse grew fat, her performances dwindled, but she never lost the happiness singing to others gave her. She gave her final performance, her voice soft with age but still beautiful, the night before Demon came to claim her. She was one who accepted their final encounter with a grace that still earns his respect.

I wondered where eternity was spent.

Would she warn others not to trade with my difficult friend or would the brightly jewelled beauty, the good she did with it for others, the wonderful invention of her life make it all worthwhile?

Sometimes I am glad we cannot know.

We next stopped in a national art gallery where the works of a painter hung on permanent display. Demon had not the means to make the paintings greater than they already were but had guided the right feet, opened the right eyes to their curious beauty and the subtle flex of ideas peeking from behind the layers of paint. The artist found his form and Demon helped the world to want it.

So often Demon's gift is in the priming and opening of the eyes of others. Is that then what so many want? Attention? Certainly it is the lack of attention that keeps ordinary the lives of those who could by rights have been extraordinary.

Next we were on a hillside, above a deep ravine. A river pulled through rock walls, steady and powerful. An ancient route for mountain rain to head back to the sea. Little drops of water, become a stream, then this slow-moving body. Gravity making a whole out of many, the sun's boundless energy freeing the many from the whole. It pleased me to think of that cycle, the endless repetition. The slow clock of water.

Just off the narrow road a natural widening in the rock had become a parking place for coaches. The indestructible bright anoraks of tourists and holidaymakers dotted the way down to the ravine and across the bridge. On the bridge, reached on both sides by a slender causeway suspended on wondrously graceful stone arches was a chapel. The whole structure seemed miraculously poised above the gulley.

We went down to mingle with the sightseers. It was a special place, and I could understand why it drew visitors. Some came for faith, others for the beauty of both the scenery and the invention that graced it. A display board told the story of how the chapel bridge came to be built but I had a wonderful first-hand, and less glossily pious, account from Demon.

The ravine was once crossed by a rope and timber bridge. It was subject to wear, storm damage, and sabotage in times of conflict. A travelling priest came to the town just east of the river and settled long enough to learn the cycle of need, damage, repair that the uncertain river crossing told.

His gift had been to speak to people, to their hearts, creating both understanding and drama, turning uncertainty into conviction. He could set a spell with his words over a congregation. It gave them much, but in the end it gave him more. It gave him Demon.

Demon found a man restless with the limits of his small sphere of influence. The town was not important. Though his rhetoric had given him power within it, the bounds of that power were set small. He wanted more. Oh, he wanted very much more.

His desired elevation came in the form of holiness. He did not wish to know that he was conjuring the reverence that came to him. He did not wish to be a showman. He wished to be elevated and equal to the power of his god. He wished to believe this was so and for others to believe it too.

For god-given might felt more complete, more immutable than mere human influence.

But after all, this is still only the usual tawdry desire for power. He no longer needed to hear the divine, only for others to believe that divinity spoke to him.

He had a vision of building a crossing of stone that would last forever, with a chapel where all could praise god, where all could thank god, where all would see the miracle he (which he? Our priest hoped there would at least be some confusion) had wrought.

And Demon brought a stonemason to the town.

And Demon brought a builder to the town.

And Demon inspired the men and boys of the town with courage so they followed the priest into the ravine, to swing on pulleys and ropes, cantilevered on stout timbers to build the bridge. Three drowned. One broke his leg and his wrist in a fall, was saved from the river, but died later of his injuries. Another was crushed. But the zeal of the priest, the whispers of Demon, made them martyrs and the grief of their families was burnt off by the townsfolk in this elevation.

And the priest was saved from the charge of recklessly endangering lives for his vanity.

The people were proud of their bridge and their chapel, proud of the masterful ingenuity of the craftsmen, proud of the faith that brought the miraculous bridge into being. They were proud, as local people still are, of the beauty of this impossible structure.

Does it make it any less a thing of wonder that Demon had a hand? I think not, for he worked no magic on the stones, he did not make the drawing, test it against his own slowly-gathered knowledge. He arranged the passage of the man who could do all that. He made fate from coincidence.

The priest grew in stature, became more important, more powerful, was honoured as though chosen, as though it was his god who elevated him.

There are many like this priest, tucked in amongst the well wishers and healers and helpful hopers, their zeal a fateful tell;

with or without the intervention of a demon brother, they make a helpmeet, a butler, a cheat sheet, a demon of their god. They are nothing but showmen. They promise to tell the people what their god is thinking. I give you god's wrath, god's love, god's fearful vengeance, god's just and mighty reward, they say. And tucked silently into this promise are other words; because then you will give me power.

So the world is shaped. What has any god to do with it in the end?

38

Jon

Even as deep and enduring love bound Christopher and Jon together, it was a relationship perpetually hindered by the stubborn bruising of experience. So attuned was Jon to the opinion of the village, so careful of his new acceptance, however qualified, that he feared any upset. So raw and close was his parents' humiliation and his disgrace, that when Christopher stayed for the night, Jon made him leave through the front door, banged shut after a loud Cheerio, the signal crunch of feet on gravel, then walk out of the village as though heading for his own home some three miles away. Down the lane he would slip a loop through the woods and return quietly back into the house, through the door now used by Eve to access the studio. In the morning, he left by the same route, to re-enter as a platonic, model-making guest through the front door, where Jon enacted a hearty hello, too loud and too surprised. Christopher felt demeaned by such pernickety pretence but he complied with good grace and tender care for the anxieties of the older man.

Though this charade was eventually allowed to fade, they never properly lived together, because of Jon's anxiety, his yearning to protect his bachelor-passing. They would come into each other's houses and stay hidden away for a few days. Christopher could never decide if that inconvenience were more tiresome than the theatrical ruse of leaving and sneaking back. But he understood there were some in that village, as in all such places, who would take spiteful delight in noticing whether a visit had lasted nightlong or not and find in that observation something that might still be turned to ill will, and not so far in the past, legal harm.

So much scrambled meaning in so many scrambled arrangements. For of course it was not foolish for Jon to care what people noticed or said of him. When others have the power to imprison you for being what you are, it is natural to be wary. It is wise to fear what has in the past caused harm. And so though the unkind, untidy law that made Jon and Christopher's love illegal was revoked, the danger remained. Prejudice may have been put on a leash but it was still an angry dog.

It was friendly Mr Edgar, who lived in a sweet, ivy-covered cottage on the other side of the village green, who noticed a young Jon, back for the holidays from university, climbing over a garden wall one summer dawning. He felt it his duty to the father of the house to tell him what he had seen. Kindly Mr Edgar, who loved his grandchildren and his dogs to distraction, who nursed nest-fall baby birds back into the wild. Mr Edgar who fell prey to a dark and nameless threat from the sudden understanding of what the wall climb must mean, for all in the neighbourhood had marked the sweet and languorous son of the house behind the wall as 'one of those'. Nice Mr Edgar whose concern for the family made it his business to tell the father of the house. And so on to other adults, able to cause harm to young men and women in the name of protection. It resulted in young Jon spending time in the police cells, the contempt of the jailers roaring into his soul and poisoning for good the last bonds with his parents. Strange it is that love, the greatest of protections, can be reshaped by some into an insidious, contagious peril.

But years later, at last, love for Christopher and Jon was ascendent; their love described their lives more fully than the hostility of neighbours. And, Jon being a reasonably wealthy man, they were able to take trips, blissfully free weeks in places that were less inclined to notice the touching of hands and the sleeping arrangements of two likeable, ordinary men.

And so to one evening. Dusk in falling made a darkening pool of the garden. It was time to retrieve the electric heaters from the attic. Christopher and Jon huddled on the sofa for warmth. Melancholy music drifted from the speakers, slow and dreamy they sank in the autumn evening. It was a mournful time of the year. Christopher's thoughts stirred as was his habit when unsettled, to the contrast of their private happiness and their public pretence. He said as he had so many times that it was unfair that they had to keep their love secret, that they should be able to go to the convivial warmth of the pub. Sometimes, in lover's insecurity, he spied rejection in Jon's obsessive caution. How could he truly be loved when that love was so easily and thoroughly disavowed? How could Jon be so supine? Why did their love not make him braver? They were not doing anything wrong. They should be able to live as any married couple and why on earth could Jon not accept or understand that? Did he just want a dalliance?

They were used to rows, they fought as any couple ever did; Jon was primed for indignant hurt and Christopher for rash anger. But Christopher was surprised to see Jon go quiet, then stand, hold out his hand for Christopher, and lead him outside.

They stood side by side, looking down at the model village.

'It's all I've ever wanted,' said Jon. 'You are all I've ever wanted. I didn't know it at the time, but I dreamt you, and you are all I've ever wanted.'

39
I
ask
so little

Years later, a similarly autumnal evening, seated at the kitchen table, Christopher and Eve were listening to that same music, a piano piece by Ravel. They talked easily, as they always did, Christopher opening her eyes to the musical past, showing her points of interest with practiced eloquence. He told her some of the story behind the music, its difficulty, the mysterious tale that it drew upon. She responded less directly, by drawing Christopher's attention to what was for her good, or bad, the elements that shaped her experience of the music. She gestured wonder, an appreciation of the movement by a subtle sweep of her hand or made a face of boredom, a little curl of the lip. She exclaimed now and then, amazing, oh yeah nice. Christopher had many more words. It astounded her how he could do that, for she understood what he said and often agreed – yeah, exactly. They fell into contemplative silence as the music unfolded, a gentle, mournful swell drifted around them. Until Christopher dropped his head and Eve recognised with awkward horror that he was feeling sad.

Her embarrassment was saved by Christopher leaping into action as he abruptly stood and rummaged in a kitchen draw, then went out to the hall, exclaiming and banging doors and drawers. When he came back he was holding a torch.

'Come with me, I want to show you something.'

Eve followed him, first to the workshop, where he picked up a screwdriver, then on to the model village. Christopher stood, a little uncertainly, looking around in the darkness.

He gave Eve the torch then knelt at the crossroads. There was a moment of stillness as though at prayer. He leant over to undo a screw in each side of the house. He beckoned Eve over, then lifted off the roof.

Inside the box, sealed against the weather, windowless and invisible to the outsider was a beautifully decorated room, a hushed secret. The walls were papered in tiny patterns, a felt oval rug lay on carefully painted floorboards. There was an exquisitely made miniature dresser, a wardrobe, a double bed.

'Look,' said Christopher, pointing at the bed. There was a square of satin and a square of cotton, both edged in tiny stitches. He lifted them from the bed and carefully picked up the carved figures of two men, embracing in the dark and sealed room, at the heart of the village.

Back at home later that evening, Eve turned the story over, thought about the model village with tender, new insight. She felt she understood Jon, his experience of knowing he was an outsider, even if she had not endured the same collective cruelty as he had. She understood Christopher's sadness when he spoke of Jon and she understood the pain of loss. She understood how such gentle dreams could be so wild, and so distant.

Until she met Danny, she had always been overwhelmed, eventually, by the attentions of the few lovers in her life. What did they want from her? How was she supposed to give them whatever it was they did want? It was not that she had rejected love, or sex, or close connections, just that never having found a version that did not seem to be a fetter, she had chosen for most of her life, until Danny was part of it, to do without.

But what of the loneliness that must be endured because love is forbidden? What was it like for Jon, and for her dear friend Christopher, to be a misfit, to have been scorned? She thought of gay friends now, able to be themselves, and yet some of them still kept it hidden from parents for fear of their disappointment. She had always been protected by Elaine, she saw, suddenly.

Elaine might regret her daughter's lack of conventionality, her insecure path through life, but she had always been there. Eve felt an awakening, of gratitude, a realisation of the blessings that had also surrounded her. She could define herself in many ways, and was free to escape any of them. Though some kept their distance, confused by her spikiness and insular demeanour, no one in the village thought she should be imprisoned. She had no desires that required the close guarding of secrets, away from the spite of those who presumed to define what was acceptable.

In her vague and abstract way, she thought about secrets, about things buried in walls, about where we keep our dreams. What is within. What is kept hidden. Tombs and secret rooms. It seeped into her work, threading out into new and unexpected shapes like ink from a pen dipped in clean water. And still the music never gathered into more than fragments.

40

**A
soul
to take
me home**

I feel the warmth of the sun on my back. My fur shimmers, the lustre of divinity played by the sea breeze. I am so close to the end and still I am not done with the wonder of it all.

I would not stay. We have our time and we must be content with that. This much I know.

I turn to Demon who is sitting up, legs crossed. He beckons me to his lap. It feels nice, my ears flattened back by his long-fingered hand.

We have talked, a little, of his life, his sleeping life, out there. But what of it I really understood, I do not know. We have visited some of the near reaches of the mighty cosmos. Oh, that wondrous place, the ferocious peal of it, the painless mighty roar, the soothing rush, like black-light-infused water, bearing us along. But Demon comes from so far away we never got near his home. Only a soul can take him back.

'Demon, tell me again of what you long for?'

Demon sighs, his hand slows, his voice is flavoured by pleasure brought in the telling.

'It is belonging. It is seeming to be eternally safe and blessed. It is like forgetting that sometimes we do not feel so. It is the deepest, most enduring pleasure, without a source, without fearing the termination of the source. And around me, my brothers, lost too in the very same blessing.'

'I am glad that is what you are going back to.' I feel a little bubble of sentiment I am more used to noticing in our human subjects than I am to feeling myself. Maybe rabbits and humans are closer than we are used to thinking.

'Yes,' replies Demon, 'I am glad too.'

It is not exactly a return of his earlier fondness, but he holds me close and continues the lovely lulling stroke along my back.

I risk Demon's impatience by asking how long we will be waiting here, but now the deal is made and the end so near, he is sanguine.

'It will be soon. Any kind of soon.'

41

**I
miss
my brothers**

The next time they met, Eve and Christopher talked into the night, the long shadow of Christopher's grief woken by the music and the telling of Jon's secret.

'I can't bear to think of him doing such a thing and believing it might never be known. He thought it would remain hidden until he had died, until the place was ripped up. It's so sad. And I know that we were happy, really happy, and that was precious. But to think of him before that, alone and imagining he was always going to be alone, I just want to go back in time and tell him he must only wait a little.'

Eve nodded. The death of her father when she was young had first lead her and Elaine into separation, part of the disaster of grief. It felt for a time to each as though they were immured, eternally alone. In this solitude, she began to imagine music.

She felt tenderness for Jon. She too had presumed herself marked out – not in her case by her very being, but by her misfortune. The distinction had felt like burden enough at the time, like ejection from the safe centre of shared experience. Her few vaguely remembered encounters with Jon, when she was a child in the village, had not lead to connection, to kindness, to welcome and she regretted it. She had sat so many times, gazing across the miniature rooftops, comforted by resting her thoughts in the imaginary. An escape from the grazings of the real world. She was given solace by a place built from the loneliness of a man she had barely even noticed. Now, she felt that she must be connected to him. She wished she had known he felt his relationship with the people of the village existed on such a perilous footing. She wished she could make it up to him.

The revelation settled in the core of Eve. Those little fragments persisted, and can be heard today. I feel a sense of great wonder that I was there to mark the invention. Fragments that eventually became music with the power to make people weep.

42

I
must
keep searching

Our trip seemed to have done Demon some good. Visiting the scenes of old victories had recharged his sense of purpose, and though still lacking an answer, his intensity for the hunt had returned. He began again his close study, his mutterings, his dissecting of dreams.

One of our first stops was once again with Leon. There was about him a puzzle, a disclosure, something useful to find. Leon fidgeted, flicked through the pages of a notebook. Demon watched him closely. Leon stopped on a slew of words scrawled diagonally, sliding free of the fine blue lines of the page. Ended days, loneliness, welled up within him. The tenderness of a lost being, exposed, raw, visible on the page, hidden from the view of the world. This experiment with exposure, being kept so close, had brought little change.

We watched him. He gazed again at the little wedge of sea visible between the neighbouring bungalows, he paced the room. I saw a murky Leon, reflected in the dark gleam of the television screen and saw Demon cross the floor to land on his shoulder, his hands cupped around Leon's head.

'Why are we here?' I asked, once Demon had ceased the caressing whisper in Leon's ear.

'Maybe he is going to find Eve again,' Demon replied.

'Why? What are you saying to him?' I asked.

'That together we can trap her,' Demon replied

Yes, Leon would surely wish to trap Eve, almost as much as Demon.

Had she not done enough carrying for these two? But perhaps having summoned a demon I should not wish her exempt from the bearing of such a load.

43

the
scraps
you leave

Eve was working on a score for a dance performance for an arts festival. It had been nationally funded and was well paid, and she had begun the project with enthusiasm. The performance was to be community-based, with musicians and dancers coming from a local secondary school and college. But the funding had also brought in the services of an overambitious curator who wanted changes that Eve knew would be too hard for the musicians. She came out of the studio to smoke on the bench. She needed a break. A slip of time to calm her irritation.

Her thoughts drifted over the model village, what she had learned about Jon, the two secret figures tucked so lovingly inside the house at the crossroads. The image was, as though loosely tethered, never far from her attention. She imagined the two men, embracing secretly in the darkness of the little house. What of the rest of their lives? The hours each day when they were working, busy in the house, or in the village. They could be making some lunch now. Deciding what they needed to get for dinner. Any minute they might open the front door and go to the pub. That would be more likely these days than when Jon had made them. She thought of Jon's vigilance, his anxiety grown in the ugly glare of experience.

A tune, a sound, a theme came to her mind. Double layered. Reality and unreality. The world and the dream tucked away inside. She turned it over, caught by the perfect, simple device of the two melodic layers. But back in the studio, she did not follow further. Her faith had wavered. And, she had a job to do.

She was being paid to make music for a festival. She let the idea slip away and turned back to the problem of fulfilling what the director desired and what the children might achieve.

As her mind wandered half-heartedly across the problem, Demon stirred a vision, an alternative. Eve getting good money for her work, free to do what she wanted. No need to accommodate the misguided input of directors. Just rewards, ample rewards, for whatever she produced. Demon was trying but it was a hackneyed effort, greeted with indifference by Eve. Why would she want rewards for work that had not earned them?

Later that afternoon, Christopher knocked on the studio door, quietly, as he always did on the rare occasions he came up to see her.

'Hey, come in. How you doing?' said Eve, glad to have a distraction.

'Good, good, but I – look, I hope you don't mind but I've invited Leon over, for the night I think, and am really hoping you will be around for a bit of the evening?' Christopher was anxious, both about Eve's response and the possibility of being left with Leon for a whole evening on his own.

'Leon? How come?'

'We spoke at that performance, and he seemed so lost, I gave him my number. We've spoken a few times since then, and, well, and...'

Eve's eyebrows formed a question, but she waited for Christopher to continue.

'I know you didn't always get on brilliantly, but you did get on fantastically sometimes, and he's come up with rather an interesting idea.'

'Ok, what?'

'We spoke a couple of days ago, it was rather late, and I was a bit drunk, actually. I ended up telling him about the figures Jon carved in the model village. He got quite excited by it, saying it sounded like a film, or a tragedy, and, then he said it would make a fantastic opera.' Christopher stopped, looking at Eve as if expecting her to take up the thread. She did not oblige, so he continued. 'Er, as I say, it was quite late and I was a bit drunk, and we talked for quite a while about this. And the upshot is that he suggested that he could write the libretto, you could write the music, and it could be an opera about Jon or about the village, about the secret and the hiding. All of that.' Eve looked at Christopher in astonishment. But she did not, as he had feared she might, reject him out of hand. She was interested enough to agree to meet Leon when he came.

Christopher suggested they start in the pub; he thought an ice-breaker pint or two might be useful. As Christopher waited at the bar for the first round, Eve and Leon talked awkwardly about what was new in their lives. Eve noticed a change in Leon, a new uncertainty. It was a subtle yet profound change; certainty had always been one of Leon's most unchallengeable characteristics.

With their pints before them, they chatted about life in the village, Leon's move to the coast. Then Leon began his pitch, that he and Eve create an opera, about the model village.

'Do you mean, like, a rock opera?' said Eve, with a curl of her lip.

'No. No!' said Leon, horrified. 'No, look, I mean like the music you make now. I mean, I don't know much about operas, and it doesn't need to be like an opera even. But a story, with your music and my words, the story of Jon's secret and the model village.'

Enchanting an idea as it was, for Leon it was not the draw. The draw was working with Eve again. He could not put her away. I looked sidelong at Demon as we watched their exchange, at his greedy grin, and presumed he had helped Leon shape the lure, so suited was it to catch her interest. But both knew her well enough to understand how a musical project about her beloved model village might do that. And still somehow I did not doubt Leon's sincerity.

She sipped her pint, letting her thoughts drift over the proposal. She remembered the pitfalls of working with Leon, but could see also that he had changed. His brash intensity was dulled, his tedious swagger gone. She believed that he truly wanted to do this. Her own work, beyond the few commissions, was taking up time but producing nothing. Here was an opportunity to get something worthwhile happening. Collaboration, work following a set brief, was easier for her now than solo work. She remembered how thrilling it had been, in the band, when it had all gone well; how close they had felt then. She remembered that she had been, in some important way, able to hide behind Leon's confidence. And that had given her something, for all that there had been many pitfalls.

She did not forget how she had longed to leave the band. But that was seven years ago. They had both changed. She would not let herself be swamped this time. And Leon, reduced as he was, looked less capable of doing the swamping.

Christopher watched Eve anxiously but held himself in check. The whole idea was a delight to him. A way to honour Jon's beautiful, careful, shy work, a way to undo the stain of his loneliness. It would be simply marvellous. But he would only trust such a project to work if Eve were a part of it. There was no knowing what Leon might bring to it left to his own devices. And, it having been his idea, there would be no way to prevent him from taking it on in some other form. He did not know that Jon would be safe in Leon's hands. Christopher tried not to stare at Eve as she fidgeted, thinking it over, trying to see the angles, trying to evaluate.

Eventually she conceded it would be interesting, but she needed to think about it before making a commitment.

Christopher knew Eve well, and tried to restrain his enthusiasm, but he was hopeful, bought doubles for all of them, then promised he understood that nothing had been agreed yet, but wouldn't it be wonderful? Wasn't it such marvellous fun anyway?

44

eyes
unseeing
must open wide,
find new and other ways

Demon warped the nights, sweet-souring Eve's dreams. She slept badly, worn ragged by night scenes of death, riches and savagery, a throne of snakes. She woke with a headache, her mouth parched dry. She gulped half a glass of water, reached for trays of ibuprofen and paracetamol and downed two of each with the rest of the glass. Pressing her temples, she wondered briefly whether the doctor could help. But she knew somewhere enough of what ailed her to ignore that pointless path. She lay in bed, carving up her worry.

Should she embark on this new project, the opera, with Leon? It had so much promise. But perhaps it would mean only frustration, a return to what she had been so glad to escape. But older and at a greater distance, it might be easier than when they were young, crammed together, the heat of Leon's ambition scouring the air.

Eve thought he had really changed, that he seemed now to appreciate her, had maybe even learned from the first time he drove her away.

But her natural caution could not be ignored. It is true, there was underneath the surface a fondness, and a kind of love between them, but also, beneath the same surface lurked Leon's desire for what would serve him best; even reduced, hollowed out by the breaking down of his many certainties, he still wanted so very much. And he still understood Eve as his most tangible pathway to achieving it.

He had always genuinely admired her work. He would not have spent so much youthful effort in diminishing it, had he not known it to be of value, and had he not been so jealous.

When Eve sent him an idea, sketched in a few layers of keyboard sounds, a loose attempt to see how they might be able to proceed, he was thrilled. He was more thrilled than she was. Too easily delighted.

She could not escape the feeling that she would be winging it, failing to create something that reached its full potential, failing to create work worthy of all the hard-found meaning, the weight of real lives that made the story.

45

**In
odd
corners
scraps and
chances gather**

At long last Christopher decided it was time to get rid of the gloomy kitchen wallpaper. He had always hated it and finally he set about it with a scraper and a sponge. It lay in bedraggled shreds over the sideboard, sweepings in a corner by the door. They had talked about brightening the kitchen up, several times but in the end Jon had always insisted on keeping it; his mother had loved it because it was expensive, once daringly fashionable, so it stayed, in loyalty to her, who in her life had shown him none.

He was tired from the work. But he took to it in small doses, soaking and scraping and pulling down the dark green floral sheets. He was excited to bring brightness into the room. Jon was safe within his heart and soul, he did not need to keep him in the decor as well.

Danny came over, helped him finish the job. Christopher was glad of it, someone to go on the step ladder, reach the high bits, in fact someone to do most of the work. By evening and whisky time, the old wallpaper was stuffed in rubbish bags by the front door. The kitchen walls looked tender, plaster pale. Danny offered to paint for him over the weekend.

Next morning, Christopher sat for a moment to admire the progress, the room flooded with low morning sun. He felt pleased that these walls at last offered the chance for something new. Things had been wonderful, at so many points in his life.

He had been blessed and was now blessed again by this small renewal. A bright colour to cheer up the kitchen instead of the dark green floral wallpaper he had always disliked. He thought about the houses in the model village, how only one had an interior, a home for the two wooden figures. He thought it was time to bring the figures in to the house.

Fifteen minutes later, the roof was skewed on the grass, next to the house at the crossroads and the dark interior was open to the sunshine. Christopher picked up the two wooden men, shaped for an eternal embrace, one in each hand. He took them into the house and placed them on the kitchen table in a shaft of sunlight. He imagined a shelf on the wall, newly painted, perhaps buttery yellow, or pale apricot, where they could be part of life in the kitchen, watching over the small goings on. Danny would help him put up the shelf.

He sat with his back in the sunshine, for a rest.

Danny arrived an hour later, paint trays and rollers under his arm. There was no answer when he knocked. He went round to the back studio door. Calling Christopher's name, he made his way through the house to the kitchen.

Christopher's head lay on the table, his hand at rest next to the two carved wooden figures.

Danny touched his fingers to Christophers neck, laid a hand gently on his shoulder, warm still from the sunshine, and felt with deep sorrow the burden of having to tell Eve that their beloved friend Christopher had died.

46

deaths and dealings

It had been a quiet and gentle life. Christopher had no close family. He had many people who loved him, but they were friends collected over years, and did not live near by. Eve and Danny, realising that no one was going to appear and take control of the situation, found themselves in the daunting roles of administrators. Though at first baffled by what might be expected, what one did with a dearly beloved, dead friend, they had loved him enough to accept the role with a sense of anxious honour.

Danny began with a search for any instructions Christopher might have left. In his writing desk, he found an envelope with the words *After I have died* written on the outside.

He brought it down to the kitchen where Eve sat at the table, fiddling with a teaspoon.

'You open it,' she asked Danny. He pulled out a sheet of note paper, then handed it over to Eve.

'It's addressed to you, love.'

Eve's jaw clenched, her eyes shut briefly as she steeled herself to read. The letter was short. It said that his will was with a solicitor, followed by the name and contact details. He said he wanted to have a service in the village church if at all possible. He thanked Eve for her friendship, for the joy it had given him, how glad he was that she had been there.

For the first time, Eve cried. Danny hugged her. She felt slight in his arms. She pulled away, walked into the garden. Danny stood, holding his own grief, and the letter.

I felt deep sorrow for Eve and Danny. On my own account too, I was sad that Christopher had died for I liked him a great deal. It is strange to experience these one-sided friendships. He did not even know of my existence – but my existence is such an extraordinary thing I think I can forgive him that. I cared for him and he knew not a thing about me. But people cry all the time for characters who die on stage or screen. And we surely had more connection with our little cast and crew than viewers of TV dramas have with theirs, so perhaps it is not so odd of me to care as I did.

Though I was forlorn, Demon was showing signs of his old determination. The dull pallor was burning off in patches of dark radiation, coal-glitter riches that found a lesser echo in my own renewing splendour. As I did not like to see him so worn down by his fear of failure, I found it a welcome change, but I wished he understood me better, enough to set his pace a little to match and perhaps lift my own. I hope I don't presume but with little cost to himself, he could have tried to ease my sadness. I doubt he would have done it well, but I would have appreciated the effort. And there was no other being to reach me. However close I imagined I was to our players, however invested I became in their joys and sorrows, without Demon I was alone.

Demon did seem to notice once, for a little moment, that I was not myself. He bid me come to him, stroked the back of my head a little while, muttering 'there there' in mechanical tones. But then he said, 'well, I must get on.' And so he did. He left me at the edge of the model village and I did not see him for some days.

I was afraid that the death of Christopher might be an upset in his plans, that Eve might falter, be held back by the weight of her sadness. But Demon was recharged with purpose and I began to fear the opposite – that he had wrought this outcome to suit their shared ends.

How careless this stupid game can be, and though I say it quietly, how very pointless. But there are hoops, and we must jump. Welcome to the show.

As I was alone, abandoned even, I went everywhere with Eve. I thought that in a subtle way, I might represent an undiagnosed waft of goodwill, I might be of some comfort to her. And I felt better, perhaps foolishly, tucked into her shadow.

Christopher's death unmoored Eve. He had been her ally, her true friend. He had created and maintained belief in her, a supply from which she had been able to borrow when her own had dwindled to nothing. She had much for which she was grateful – Danny, Elaine well and happy, collaborations that were nearly marvellous. But without her own music, without the cheerleading loan of belief from Christopher, the magic she had so yearned for seemed rinsed from the world.

A few hours into the first night of grief, something of her old self rose in her. It could have been a guide through her sorrow, had she been able to hold it. But the thread slipped through her fingers, and floated away, out of reach. Not away, for she was always aware it was there. I could hear it too, faintly, a melody, soon after she had begun to hear it herself.

Such melancholy and such uplift.

It looped ceaselessly, distantly, tucked away behind the many disruptions that a death will bring. Waiting for the time to demand proper consideration.

It coiled, like mist, within the territory of her imagination, and escaped, to wrap around her. She was not yet ready, not able to form it into the music that would be a salve to her grief.

We went to the solicitor's office, just a few streets from the supermarket where Eve had worked all those years before. The solicitor was brisk, bored, distracted. She performed the odd caring look that reminded me somewhat of Demon's poor attempts at joviality – the mastery so faint and the authenticity so partial. But she was a woman doing her job in the middle of an ordinary day. And when she told Eve that Christopher had left her the house, it did not matter so much what she did, for Eve's wide-eyed astonishment would not have taken in the sight of her with a pencil up each nostril and the wastepaper bin on her head. Danny might have noticed, but barely. I wished I had the cunning to make it happen, for a foolish moment of my own enjoyment.

She told them, though they did not fully take it in, that the land where the model village stood, which had still officially been part of the garden, was now held in a trust, separating it from the house and the rest of the garden. She had a right to be a part of that trust, if she wanted (there was, thoughtful as he ever was, not a single burden of administration attached to this) but the model village now belonged, in effect, to the whole village. She read out several stipulations or clauses, or instructions – by this time I was losing my own ability to concentrate.

Eve and Danny went back home. They sat in dumb silence. They felt as though they were interlopers in their own good fortune. A day later, a letter arrived from the solicitors; inside was another, handwritten and addressed to Eve.

My dear Eve

I am sure that you will find it strange, or awkward, that I want you to have the house. I write this to reassure you it is entirely unnecessary for you to feel that way. (I had the same when it passed from my darling Jon to me, so I do understand!) I lived here in part for the connection to Jon and because I was always afraid that someone new would flatten the model village and reclaim the ground it is on and that would be too bad. But I hope I have now secured the village fate (who will run the tombola?!) and if you do decide to stay in the area, I will be so glad to think of you casting an eye over the rooftops every now and then. But I want to be clear, this is in no way an obligation. And it is something I decided long ago. I hope it will be a while until you get this letter, but it is not a decision I have made rashly.

All of my other friends are well set up, they need nothing. All of my family are dead or too distant for me to know them.

It has been such a pleasure for me to have shared the house with you these last years, to hear some of what has come from that room you have made your studio. Now you may be able to do more with the space. You are such a talented composer and it has been an honour to be, in a small way, a part of your work.

I hope it will not feel like a burden – the house, as you know, is a bit of an old hulk and I do not know that you and Danny will want to live here. But if you want to sell and move somewhere else, please know you have my blessing.

I could not bear to think of you having nowhere to work. Not that you would be unable to secure an alternative – they're scratching each other's eyes out by now to give you space, after all! But *you seem happily settled. You seem, in a way, a part of the place, and so it is now yours.*

Thank you Eve, you have been a true and dear friend to me.

With love always,

Christopher.

Had Demon known of this letter? Even had a hand in its writing? Surely Eve could not have wished for this. Perhaps she made a better fit with Demon than I had thought.

Eve passed the letter over to Danny. They looked at each other, in silence, still trying to assemble the right response. Eve could not speak.

'Shall we, shall we just go there for a visit, see what happens?' Danny said eventually.

'Yeah,' said Eve.

'I mean, it wouldn't be bad, would it? Living there.'

'No,' said Eve. They picked up keys, jackets, went to the car and did not speak the rest of the way.

The two carved wooden figures were still on the kitchen table where Christopher had left them. Eve sat in her usual chair, held one in each hand.

'Jon and Christopher,' she said to no one in particular. She thought about the people whose wealth had secured the house, and whose uptight views (the commonest of views) had in a roundabout way created the two figures, perhaps the whole model village. She ran a finger lightly across a shoulder of one of the wooden men then picked them both up. There was a photograph of Jon's parents on the dresser in the unused dining room. She took the two figures in and laid them next to the half dozen photographs of Jons family that Christopher had, like the wallpaper, never quite had the heart to remove.

Eve wondered at this, if the house had ever felt entirely his. If he had been truly at home. And then she remembered how he would run back to the kitchen from the living room where the big stereo was, to not miss the beginning of a record, or one of Eve's compositions. Every now and then he would kick the speaker wires back to the side of the doorway, saying one day he would get it done properly. She remembered his smile, an inviting flicker of eyebrows as he offered a slug of whisky. He always seemed so warm and relaxed, and in this room, she knew he had been happily at home. This comfortable, scruffy kitchen with its big old speakers, its large selections of single malts, gifted by people who never knew what else to buy him for his birthday (there were unopened bottles going back decades, still tucked in the top of a hall cupboard.) The freshly peeled walls, waiting for colour, once acceptance of all that had changed allowed him to unhook that little claw from the past.

His chair, the pine faded along the backrest where the sun bleached it. She would miss him terribly, sitting opposite her, his excitement, enthusiasm, his interest and kindness.

She noticed that Danny had gone from the kitchen. She found him out in the model village, reattaching the roof of the house at the crossroads.

'It looked wrong with the roof off. I thought we should keep the figures in the house, it seems he wanted that. But we can always put them, or something, back later?'

'Yeah. Good. Thanks Danny.'

He tightened the last screw then sat next to her on the bench. They held hands, looking down at the familiar pattern of the painted rooftops.

'I think we could live here. What do you think?'

'Yeah, I think we could too,' he replied.

'But not now. I can't face it yet.'

A few days later she got another message, from Leon. A postcard of a cheery seaside view. All it said was *Eve, so sorry, I know you loved him, L x.*

I hoped that the death of Christopher was not a part of Demon's plan. For it certainly gave something to Eve. I had not thought her to be one who wanted riches, but she had dreams of certainty, security. Is that so different? Wealth is often sought that it might become safety. There is little security in poverty after all.

I sincerely hoped that if an uplift in her fortunes was what she wished for, Eve had not accidentally bought it at the cost of Christopher's life. But would Demon make such a terrible move merely to prepare the ground for his offerings? It seemed unlikely. He could not have been foolish enough to think that the death of her dear friend would make Eve greedy for the other delights Demon offered. I was ignorant, I had no real idea what Demon might do or what he might see that I could not. This much I know.

Christopher was not young. He had lived long and well. And within all I knew of Eve, there never was covetousness or greed. There was certainly no glee at their new circumstance. There was gratitude and wonder, and deep sadness, and I do not believe Christopher would be unhappy with that.

When Demon came back, much later, I asked him. But he said nothing as usual. I almost wished that he would start whinging again – at least it was someone to talk to.

I truly hope that in this last meeting, all will be revealed. I resist the temptation to ask him one more time for he has said often enough in this last period of our time together, 'you will see.'

And when she arrives, I hope I will see. I hope I will be allowed to understand how Demon framed his offer at last, and made it something that was worth her soul.

I will be sad to say goodbye. I had not thought it would be so. I am resigned to death but sadness, I see now, may come with goodbye. I edge closer to Demon and am glad to feel his hand come to rest on my back again.

47

is
it all
set now
for me to win?

Weeks passed in the quiet tumult that follows a death. Sorrow and surprise undid any sense of what a normal day should be. Eve and Danny did not discuss the prospect of moving to the house again though Eve already knew that she wanted to live there. It was a place where she had been made so welcome, a place she associated with belonging, with having the freedom to express her musical self. But in the raw aftermath of grief there was no sense of a future, or a plan.

It was impossible; moving in meant accepting the indisputable fact of Christopher's absence. If they moved in she could no longer picture the front door, under the orange light, awaiting her knock and his answer.

She had lost an anchor as well as a dear friend. Though never analysed, Christopher's warmth and his belief in her was the basis of a connection she had rarely found elsewhere in life. Early bereavement had cast in Eve a sense of loneliness that restricted her capacity for the bonds of friendship and trust. Friendships had always remained guarded, and in some way dispensable. She came to believe that this was a choice, that future disappointments in people, or their departure and absence, was inevitable, that what she felt was complicated and could not be trusted to the clumsy hands of others.

This belief was cast as protection over her heart, thus fulfilling the conditions for its truth.

There where only three who had not been kept out by the spell: Elaine, Danny, and Christopher.

Eve's grief continued to rise, like a spring tide, dragging the bulky remnants, the storm damage of other fears back onto the shore; the death of her father, her mother's recent illness, the desertion of her dreams. And the dabbling of a demon unsettling her mind.

Eve was overwhelmed. Some days, groggy from sleeplessness, she did not get up. Danny brought them both up a coffee. If she was asleep, he left it to cool on the bedside table. If she was awake, he sat on the edge of the bed, sipping his, reminding her that the mug on the bedside was getting cold. Sometimes he tried to talk her, hoped for a response that might ease his worries. But she didn't have much to say.

'How are you feeling?'

'Ok.'

'But you're not, Eve, you're not ok.'

'As ok as yesterday.'

'Do you think it's time to get some help, go to the doctor?'

'The doctor won't help.'

'They might.'

'Please leave it Danny. They won't. It's fine.'

'I'm worried. I'm worried about you.'

'It's fine, I'll – I don't know, right now. I'm tired.'

Danny left, not wanting to impose too much of his worry and frustration. She was so bloody stubborn. He hoped that eventually the passage of time would at least ease the rawness of her grief.

What could he have done, dear Danny, if he had known all that assailed her? Nothing. And what would he have done if he knew she were coming to meet us, to meet her end, just these few years later? What will he do, poor, dear man, tomorrow, when she is gone? I feel terribly sad for him, for the goodness of his love, and the waste of it.

In his unexpected role as a guardian of Christopher's death, Danny took on the chores of organising the funeral, contacting friends, discovering the layers of admin that fall from a death, paper scraps, clogging the machinery of the lives that remained.

Eve came downstairs. Danny did not hear her arrive in the kitchen. She watched him, bent over bills and letters and lists. He sighed in frustration, searching for the piece of paper in the pile that might untangle the puzzle of the one before him. Here was this man, taking care of her and her dear friend. She stood behind him and placed her hands on his shoulders, dropping her forehead to the top of his head. He reached his own hand up to cover hers for a moment, then exclaimed the win as he pulled the right page from the pile.

Eve felt the shift of muscle and bone in his shoulders as he reshuffled and resorted, thought of the movement, demanded by the cello, the modification of a body in the service of that sound. He has played himself into this body, she thought. Though the modifications were small, music had a part in the creation of strength, flexibility, tension, sometimes pain. She watched his hands as he scrawled a note.

Christopher had never seriously played music but he had been shaped by it. The choices in his life, the passions. He believed music was important, foundational, in the way Eve did. He had been an enthusiastic concert goer, a collector of records, a fundraiser for musical venues, a supporter of ensembles.

Danny was deeply touched by a handful of cards and letters that came addressed to the house, many from those he had helped, expressing sadness at the loss of a man who had done so much to support others. In the pile was a letter sent to Christopher's house, addressed to Eve. Danny gave it to her to open. She read the handwritten page on her blanketed lap, her head bent, one had pushing through the mess of her black hair.

'It's from Gordon, Christopher's friend from way back. He visited a couple of years ago. They went to university together.

He's in the US, and won't be able to come to the funeral so wants to know whether a memorial some time would be a nice thing to do.'

'I think that would be great.'

'He's involved with an event in a couple of years in London. Suggested it might be a good time.'

I cast a glance at Demon who was watching intently, but not giving anything away.

'Well that sounds perfect.'

'He asks if I might be able to play something, or write something for it.'

'You should. You definitely should.'

'Yeah. Well, I'd have plenty of time, so-'

Eve's thoughts were woven with the ribbons of music, the slender thread that hung in her mind, waiting for attention she could not give. She knew it would be a piece that belonged to Christopher. If only she could pull herself together.

Each hour each day, it was there, waiting, unformed. But like dust motes in the eye, as soon as she turned for a closer look, it slid away. Seventeen notes. Shades of light and dark. A miasma. None of it whole, none of it would hold still. Then, eventually, the music faded away. She felt it as another abandonment.

Since the moment we first met, Eve had been the land under two weathers – her music and Demon. For many years, music had held the territory, and in so doing, had kept Demon at bay. But now it seemed that Demon was in the ascendancy; he was the coming storm.

48

now
must be
the proper time

That afternoon, Danny was readying himself to go to Christopher's, to take meter readings and check the mail.

'I'll come with you. Maybe stay and work for a bit?'

'Great. We can spin it out, I should go through some of the papers in the filing cabinet which will take a while,' said Danny.

Eve was worried about all the work falling on Danny's shoulders, but she did not offer to help; she did not know how at the time and accepted her incompetence for the task. But other failings were harder to pass by. She wanted desperately to find a way back to music. To write the piece for Christopher. If she could not reach this one piece, could not find a way to bring it into the world, then what did any of the rest of it matter? It was the only thought she had room for.

Eve was nervous on the drive over, trying not to think about the emptiness of the house, the absence of that familiar warm welcome. Danny talked carefully about neutral subjects. Demon strained, leaned between them, his eyes vivid with urgency, waiting for any sign of slippage in the masking small talk. I sat on one of Danny's jumpers, abandoned some days ago on the back seat, letting myself be lulled by the journey. It did not seem to me to be a time when Demon would find his key. How could he think she would swap this piece for anything? But he knew his job better than me, and was not fond of advice, so I settled back and drifted.

Danny unlocked the front door. There was a scatter of mail on the mat. Demon picked me up and whisked us up to the studio. I made my way to the armchair, settled into the lumpy cushion.

We were waiting for Eve. Demon paced the floor, he rose sometimes into the air, he spun a new kind of energy into the room. I watched the walls waver through the thickening of the air. I felt it through the fibre of my body, I heard crackling, a vibrancy, as Demon claimed the emptiness.

She finally came. She paused on the threshold, alert to an intangible difference. I did not know if she could feel what I did, or whether she felt a strangeness she believed was her own. But she was hesitant, anxious. She crossed the room to her chair, twisted away from the table and reached for her electric guitar, flicking on the amp next to her. She frowned. She hummed the tune that had come to her soon after hearing of Christopher's death. She played a few notes, then stopped, put down her guitar.

'Eve, listen to me.' The room was flickering with tension. There were no empty spaces. Eve's eyes darted, she turned her head.

'You could end this struggle right now. Let me elevate you. Let me make you great! They will speak your name for centuries.'

And then, to my astonishment, she spoke.

'Just – give me this tune. Give me this one piece of music. Give me this.'

Demon scowled, bared his teeth, then pulled himself back to the floor, softened, sat at Eve's feet, a sickly simulacrum of loving attendance.

'I cannot give you music, but I do not need to – you have music, you can have as much music as you want, what is already within you. Without you, from your skin to the edges of the world, I can make you beloved. I can make it a perfect world.' He stood, moved behind and laid a hand on her shoulder. 'You have your music. I can give you everything else. You just need to name it.'

Eve bent over her lap, her hands massaging her temples.

'It will all stop Eve, the minute we trade. I will be silent and you will be free.'

She wrenched her shoulders away from him, picked up her guitar.

'Eve –'

She plucked a few drab notes. Demon leaned in and hissed. 'Eve!'

She bashed a series of discords, hitting the strings, slowly at first but boiling into a pulse. Demon shrieked her name. The room seemed fit to burst with the clashing energies sloshing dangerously in the air. It made me feel nauseous. Eve banged her guitar down with unusual roughness and pressed her hands to her head.

'My god! This pain! I can't do anything.'

Demon was immediately emollient once again. 'Let me end it for you darling girl, let me soothe your way, let me make the place where you will be safe, free, happy, beloved.'

'But what good would that be? I feel so empty. There's nothing there.' Eve sank, utterly deflated, back into the wooden chair. The sickly vibrancy of the room dissipated, Demon grabbed a hold of me and we were gone in a boiling hiss of frustration and fury.

We span and soared and Demon shrieked. We screeched down a chimney, ripped through branches, hurtled up and up and up to the edges of the sky. I huddled into Demon, shut my eyes. The reckless violence of our trajectory was terrifying. I shrank as small as I could.

We left the last shreds of earth's atmosphere. The chill black of the cosmos soon soothed Demon. He loosened his grip on me and, more slowly, I loosened my grip on myself. We hung, our bodies slowly finding out-flung passivity, adrift on the inclines of other gravities. After what felt like a long and relieving rest, Demon spoke.

'I am afraid.'

I waited to speak, not knowing what to say, but knowing that Demon needed me to comfort him. If he could not find his comfort, where was I to seek it out? I searched my cache of stories for the right one.

'There was once a scholar, living in a small town in Germany,' I began.

49

for
me to
take command

We did not return for several days. When we did, Eve was in bed and it seemed she had been the whole time we were away. We had gone away so Demon could gather his resources but clearly hers were depleting. I dreaded to think what might happen to Eve, with her once easy defiance, the protective carapace of her music, her soul's work, gone. I did not like her chances in the next round of this wearing, years-long battle.

Christopher's funeral was near. Danny had liaised with a distant cousin of Christopher's and some old friends. They had between them put together a funeral that they thought Christopher would have wanted. Eve did not know how to help; it seemed a presumption, to guess at what Christopher would want. But she did insist that the Ravel piano piece was included as a way to bring Jon into the service.

Demon spent these days muttering and poking around, jabbing here and there in what seemed a random fashion. I did at last venture that it might not be the best time for a seduction. Ruefully he agreed, but he could not entirely leave her be. I was worried about Eve, for the twin burdens of a needy divine in her head and the weight of grief in her heart were wearing her down terribly.

We were sitting on their bed. Danny was out shopping. Eve was sleeping, her back turned towards us. I edged over, tucked myself into the small of her back. I could feel the raggedness of her breath and blood, the jagged pulse of her restless sleep. I was worried. Demon, facing the window, tutted and muttered.

'She doesn't seem to be doing very well. Can we, can you make it easier at all?'

'Yes.'

'Then, will you?'

'Yes, if she gives me what I want. It is up to her. I cannot help it if she chooses not to take my offer. The consequences are not mine to manage.'

'But is it not the burden of your offer that costs her so much?'

'Oh Rabbit, how do I know? I cannot be responsible for all of it, all these damn marks and their dreary needs and wants. How should I manage if I were to consider them more than I already must?' Demon left in indignant temper and I was alone with Eve.

I had foolishly thought Demon might ease my worries. Had I taken even a moment to think about it, I would not have bothered. I tried to press myself into Eve's back, tried to soothe, at least, her present sleep. But I do not think it helped.

The funeral came and went. It was very sad. Eve met Christopher's friends, and the few distant family members. None, as she had feared might happen, made reference to his leaving her the house. They were all lovely. Danny was thanked for all of his work in managing it with so much care. Eve felt overwhelming love for Danny, felt lucky to have him by her side.

Afterwards, she sat on the bench by the model village for a long time. She had no answers but she made a solemn promise that one day, she would write the piece for Christopher. And soon, sometime, because he had loved the idea so much, she would think again about the opera. How very big, and how daunting a promise it felt to her in that moment.

50

**soon
it will be
too late, Eve,
for uncertainty**

The funeral done, Danny hoped it would mean a return to better health for Eve. Each morning he took a mental tally, checking her over, trying not to let on that he was examining her progress. Each morning she was dull, powerless, insipid and sad, just as she had been the day before. He wanted her to go to the doctor, to find out why she was getting the headaches, why, even before Christopher's death she had been so tired and sad. He was afraid that she was seriously ill. But she would not; she kept making excuses, putting it off. She knew enough already. It would not help. She knew, somewhere, more than Danny, about what ailed her. It was knowledge that did not require words, or complete understanding. Knowledge that is akin to instinct. In the depths of her mind she understood the cause of her malaise was not body-born; a scan would not find Demon, nor an aspirin banish him.

She knew she was not faring well and feared it might be lifelong, but she knew too a doctor could not heal her. Somewhere, in that dark and secret place of reckoning, she understood that if she met Demon's demands it would all be done. But in that same place, she was in horror of the cost. Trapped there, in her own weary darkness, she feared she had already lost.

But she kept trying, to resist, to stay afloat. The unmade strains, the floating patterns of an unborn melody, fragmentary and unformed as they were, gave enough for her to lose herself in the music they promised.

She was in bed, staring at the ceiling. Shapes formed around the sounds she was imagining. A path, dropping into grit and mist on each steep side, wound a single note towards the infinite possibilities awaiting discovery. She stepped onto the path, and knew it was the beginning. She almost wept in joyful recognition, to be back in this wonderland. She walked on, towards the slabs and swirls, the structures forming in the distance. And for a moment, I walked with the Eve I had first encountered; older, if possible even more serious, testing now her music on the sharp edges of experience, yes; but certainly that same girl, filled with ferocious intent and private wonder.

I felt the jolt of panic as her head began to pulse with pain. I looked up and there was Demon, crouched on her pillow, bent to her ear, hunched over his urgent message, her hair grasped in his fingers. I felt a sickly stab of revulsion and had to turn away.

Moments later Eve threw off the covers and went downstairs, joining Danny in the kitchen. She was pale, worn, nearly defeated; surely Demon was soon to win.

She sat opposite Danny, fidgeted with an old envelope on the table. She wished with all her heart that she could find a way to cling onto those little fragments, to insist on that music, to bring it into being.

'Maybe if we moved in to Christopher's I could work better.'
'Do you reckon you can face the move now?'
'I've got to do something. Maybe being there will help.'
'It wouldn't be a bad idea, we'd be able to stop paying rent.'

They were getting by financially, Danny taught cello and Eve had a little money from royalties. But it was a scrabble. The rent was due to go up and the odd token fee for a film score or dance collaboration would not cover it. If things did not change she would be back working in a supermarket. Not paying rent would make everything easier. Later that day they gave notice on the house.

The two months notice period passed, with little change, until they began to pack up in a panic in the last few days of their tenancy. While they were boxing up their belongings I spent the time in the scruffy little garden, listening to the quiet rumble of distant traffic, soft as a lullaby. Demon had been absent for a while. He had been distant with me, with everything, it seemed, since I had turned from him in the bedroom. I had tried, often, to recross the ground between us, sidling up to him, not asking annoying questions, but he had paid me little mind. I did not think myself truly abandoned, but I was anxious.

Eve and Danny regretted that they had not made more decisions about what they should keep and where things might belong before carting all of their stuff in supermarket carrier bags, boxes, and suitcases into Christopher's house. There was still a whole house full of not only Christopher's, but Jon's belongings. And because Christopher was loyal, and Jon weighted by debts to parents who had themselves so easily cast aside their debts to him, Jon's parents' possessions too. So many leftovers. The place was a warehouse for the belongings of the dead.

In their awkward gratitude they could not begin by clearing out these photos, clothes, cushions, ornaments, pictures, place mats, all of which seemed to have more right to the house than they did. It felt hasty, greedy, ungenerous. But it meant there was nowhere to put anything. As so often happens, in a piecemeal way they settled in to what soon became normal. As there was room, they began by shifting things around, putting them out of sight, so that they did not have to decide whether to keep them. They fitted themselves in slowly, randomly, discovering a bit at a time the shape of their new lives.

They began by moving into the spare room. It was smaller than the main bedroom but had a beech tree outside a big window and was away from the leakage of the village green street light. And it felt less of a trespass. Eve fell onto the bed and slept for a couple of hours.

When she woke, Danny was out, driving back for the last load of their possessions. She went down to the kitchen, began emptying a box, adding their plates and mugs into cupboards already groaning with crockery. Sometime they would sort it out. They would have to. But not now. In the next cupboard along were the glasses, the familiar, heavy tumblers. She picked up two of them, put them on the table and poured a slug of whisky into each. She went to the living room, leafed through the recently played albums, still propped up on the hi-fi since Christopher had last played them. She selected a piece by Charles Ives. Christopher had loved it, had tried several times to convert her. She had got as far as appreciating his pleasure in the clarity and tension. She turned it up, went back to the kitchen and sat where she always sat, opposite Christopher's chair. She slowly drank one glass empty, then reached across the table for Christopher's glass and downed it. How was she ever going to deal with that empty chair? Taking the bottle and one glass, she went up to the studio, where she was at least used to being alone.

She approached the threshold with caution. The memories of her encounter with Demon had been scrubbed into a vague blur of general anxiety. She stopped in the doorway. The curtains were drawn, the room in half-light. The gloom and calm was welcoming. She sat down, remaining still for some time, the room settling around her. Eventually she picked up her acoustic guitar, always within reach of the chair. Once again, she sketched out the melody, as much of it as she could muster, as single notes. The notes made waves in air, she listened to the sounds, felt the resonance of the notes in her own body. Her gratitude and love for Christopher felt like weights at the base of her throat. She played the tune slowly, very slowly, holding her feelings of loss close, contained within the notes.

And all of it was slow and wordless.

And all of it was necessary.

That was as far as she got, just forming the notes, letting the tune exist in the medium of air, in the vibrations of her skin and bones. Anxious lest the moment be spoiled she stopped. It felt so little but enough to lift her up, reset her. She went down to the kitchen, put on Christopher's favourite Schoenberg concerto, sat at the table and poured another whisky.

I was glad that Demon was elsewhere, for it allowed her that little moment: respite and a precious reminder of who and what she was.

51

you
must at last
claim your waiting fate

It was summer, ordinary and fair. There was for a few glorious days a sense of letting go, a period of respite for all of us. Eve sat in the garden under the beech tree, I on the grass next to her. With Demon gone, I was almost back to my natural form.

Breeze swished the leaves, a patch of sunlight danced across her face. She slid down the old canvas deckchair into more reliable shade. She thought she should try and work. Maybe later. Beyond the first bits of tinkering, sketching out shapes of sound, she had yet to make a start on the score for the opera and none of her ideas were more than rudimentary. In composition there was always uncertainty and work, but now it felt so hard to come by, so unsupported by clarity and purpose.

The piece for Christopher, the requiem, was personal, and Christopher could not have known it would exist. It was safe to presume he had no expectations on that score. But he had loved the prospect of the opera, was so excited about it. This made it hard to ignore. If the requiem was a debt to herself, the opera was beginning to feel like a debt to Christopher.

Those debts must be paid, but not now.

For now, she was content to just sit. Or wander the house, or watch the television. It was as though disruption had settled to delicacy and she had entered a state of permanent convalescence. The languor of summer swaddled her, smoothed over the disjoint. Though unrepaired, she was calm and her headaches had settled.

With this return to stability, Danny felt able to pick up preparations for a long-planned tour with his band. He was spending a few days sweating in a stuffy rehearsal room, staying with the bass player. He could not let go of his worry and messaged her often. She looked forward to hearing from him and in this reflective time she noticed her dependence on him with both gratitude and anxiety.

She closed her eyes, felt the pull of blessings stretching along the drag of decline.

I should have known those precious, calm days of summer would not last. This gentle state, this recuperation, was due to the absence of Demon. He had been gone some days, off stirring his own weather.

52

**I
will
use force
where promise failed**

Demon came back towards evening. His dark glitter shone, all dullness banished. He glowered with jet intensity. The spells and sigils, the scars and markings shrank and multiplied, shimmering across his body. I was both relieved for him, and afraid.

All around him I felt an inclement cackle, the twisting of something other, a waiting cacophony. Wherever he was, the soft summer air began to strain with the holding of a storm. He was preparing for battle, stamping towards what could be no fair victory, so mismatched were the armouries.

As I grew once again with his return into my own majesty I was wary of what was to come, though I had longed for years for it to happen. Now, I feared the destruction of either Demon or Eve would be the price of the fight. Perhaps it was best for all if she just accepted what he brought to her, turn price into prize. One letter, so big a difference. Demon was here because she had called him. It was not his fault, nor was it hers, but there are battles, and sometimes we do not get to choose them. Sometimes all we can do is decide upon the mode of our participation. Sometimes walking calmly into defeat is, however regrettable, the only wise choice.

I could not so easily forgive the cost. This battle would destroy her life or take her soul. Both seemed too dreadful to contemplate.

But Demon was mine, I was his. I was bound by all that made me to hope he would win. Whatever destruction came as the price.

He picked me up, held me to his face. We stood for some time in stillness. His fingers clasped me tight, it hurt. I began to feel the intensity of his thoughts, the thrum of his ancient power. I felt within myself a strange new urgency, a will to fight. I felt for a moment the drooling, wrecking desire, to be fierce, a wolf. A wish to clamp jaws until death. A desire to vanquish. I was consumed by heat that was borrowed from Demon's burning core. He put me down and the feeling evaporated, and I was weak, shaky, almost ashamed.

I knew that the time had come; Eve must either succumb or destroy them both.

I shivered, for Eve and for Demon, but also for myself as I did not know what of that destruction might rip through me.

Demon took me under his arm and we went to the studio. Eve was there, as if by appointment. She was strumming some chords on her old acoustic guitar, to fill the time, to pass the day, to make a change from the beech tree or the television. Her wonderful interior world was gone. Her landscapes and crystalline planets, the arcing curves and gravitational slabs of sound awaiting her summoning had disappeared. She was without armour. She put down her guitar and sat in silence, waiting. She sat as though in acquiescence, as though acknowledging that her emptiness must one way or another be finally resolved.

There was a vast stretch of quiet, of nothing; a chill claimed the air, marking the seriousness of the negotiation that lay ahead. The atmosphere thickened with the cooling chill. It seemed from Eve's passive demeanour that the deal would at last be an easy one to make. But for a long time, nothing happened.

I started to hear fragments, a kind of conversing; the boom, as though at a great distance, of Demon, mumbled uncertainty in Eve's response. The air shimmered, turned harsh, liquid. I tried to listen, to hear more, tried to tune in as the intensity grew. The chill turned to heat. I felt breathless. Eve slid her hands to her head as a headache blurted its familiar pain across her skull. The room danced as though above hot desert tarmac. Everything swelled, shrank, pushed out, was punched in. The room seemed too much for the house, the world, this realm, to bear. Demon's voice surged. He got louder and louder, and I could no longer decipher all that he said. His voice boomed with the shiver of the room. Eve's words were incoherent, to me, but I could hear that she was pleading. She pressed her hands against her temples. She pressed against the pain, against the raging of her mind, the pulsating, unnatural exuberance of the air, the walls, the floor and ceiling. She shrank from it. She muttered. I did not know if Demon understood her but I could not. He grew, his voice began to shriek, his face contorted, pressed into hers, he grasped her.

She moaned, tried to pull back, then dropped forward as though into his arms. She scratched out screaming words, bleak sounds of desperation.

Demon roared.

Demon roared.

Demon roared.

Everything shook, to its smallest parts, the stitching loosened. I disintegrated. The light flickered and screamed itself into darkness.

53

you
thought a
demon gentle?

The noise must have stopped at some point, or the violent cacophony rendered me oblivious. Anyway I became insensible. I was held for an unknown span of hours in greyness, in nothing. Eventually, in turbid disarray, I began to come back into my existence. I had no clear idea of what had passed. Lingering giddiness quelled and slowly I felt myself to be driftingly present. The past night was a blur but consciousness returned bit by bit and I began to realign myself in the world. I was in the armchair in the studio. Night was gone, low morning sun came through the window. Was it the following morning or any number of mornings later? So overwhelming had been my malaise that I had no idea. I could not see Demon, but thankfully neither could I hear him. Though unsettled by his absence, I welcomed the quiet, for the recollection of his shrieking juddered a lively sickness through me.

As I became more aware of my surroundings I realised that I was not alone in the armchair, I was sitting in the lap of Eve. Her head was flung back, showing the pale and vulnerable stretch of her neck, the underside of her chin. I could not see her face. She was completely still. What had happened? Her hand was flung out over the chair arm, her palm facing upwards. I looked over her anxiously, noticing at last a pulse, the thread of a blue beat in the delicacy of her wrist. I did not know what to do – had Demon left me here for a purpose, so I could help in some way? I felt as unequal to the circumstances, as useless as I would have been had I remained a natural rabbit.

The sun moved, turning from us round the room. Demon did not appear, Eve did not wake. I sat, uncertain and timid, waiting for another to give me purpose. The sun moved. I waited.

I kept a close watch on Eve, nervously checking the pulse in her wrist, monitoring the shallow movement beneath me caused by her breaths. Sometimes I was alarmed to feel nothing – an absence followed by a gasp of inhalation, as her breathing tried to catch up.

I began to feel warm, too warm. First I thought the heat was from the sun growing into the day, but it did not come from the window, it came from the body of Eve. Her breathing became faster, shallower, more uncertain. I felt that something must be required of me. I stretched my front feet up onto her shoulder. The pallor of her face was interrupted by a scrape of red across each cheek. Her eyes fluttered and shallow breaths crept in and out through her nose and slightly open mouth. Sweat glistened at the edge of her scalp. I nudged my cheek along hers, wanting to bring her back into herself. She was too far gone. Where? A battlefield in another realm. The deepest secret core of herself. Demon's deep dark pocket. Was this the end?

I nuzzled her face again. I was alarmed, sad, and filled with terrible pity.

The sun moved. It was well into the day. I did not know what to expect but Eve's state worried me. She surely ought to be waking by now. But in her sleep, or whatever it was, she was barely present. And if rousing her were the better course, how was I to make it happen? I closed my eyes, trying to locate the point where, now and then, I had been able to hear the music of her thoughts. That elusive spot somewhere between us marked a connection; perhaps I could turn that connection to my own use, and make her hear me.

There was little enough to follow. There were many barriers. I eventually found a kind of darkness that I did not recognise as my own. *Eve. Eve*, I whispered, hopeful and afraid, into that void.

No words or thoughts came back to me. But then, a miracle. Perhaps only in the spasmodic actions of sleep, her arm swept back as though onto her lap, and I felt her hand as it came gently to rest on my back. It felt soothing, welcomely possessive, like Demon's hand in his settled moments, I treasured the gentle weight. It was delightful, disarming, strange, somewhere between deep pleasure and an unsettling intrusion. I had never felt the touch of a human before. Divinity separated Demon and I from mortals, we were forms that did not exist on the same plane. Perhaps she had been so wrung out by her encounter with the divine that she was still partially trapped in our realm. I felt dread for her, straddling the worlds in this way, and a kind of bumptious preening as though, in that rare connection, I had been chosen. And so I would have stayed, but as the day advanced, the heat of her seemed ready to burn us both up, taking in fire the scraps that Demon's fury had left behind. Her breathing quickened as though her life was further pared in the long tail of the night's travails. If we stayed here, still and silent as we were, I feared it would be unto death.

I sent my voice back, into the place where our darkness edged each into the other. I pleaded with her to wake. The effort rekindled my giddiness and I did not know if I was still in the room or somewhere else. But I kept on and perhaps she heard me at last, for I felt us both rise. I felt her carry me. I felt the echoes of my voice forming, as though a substance, around me. I felt her bearing us both through the house, and at last into her bed. The heavy curtain was still closed, day was shut out of the room. Eve put me down next to her on the rumpled sheet then curled up on her side. We both fell into deep sleep.

The dry heat of fever shrouded us. Along with his prize, Demon had taken his toll. Whether I was meant for the suffering or if so closely aligning myself to Eve had carelessly allowed contagion I did not know. I could barely rouse myself to check on her. So, for most of that day, we slept.

Later I began to wake. At first for seconds, before the heavy blurring of sleep obliterated consciousness again. Then for long enough to remember where we were and the cares of what had passed. Eve still had not moved; she curled around me like a sickle moon. As I felt my strength returning I did not dare leave, but tried to shine for her, to be her morning star. And still, the changeless hours wore on. Soon I was fully awake and able to give proper attention to my concerns for her. She was so pale, her breaths so slight and shaky. Silently I pleaded with Demon to return soon. I feared he had abandoned us both.

She could not have made such a poor deal that her end had come already. He could surely not be done with us just yet.

Night fell once again and the darkness was complete. I could just about make out the pallor of Eve's face, the faint gleam of stray moonlight on her shoulder. Her black hair anchored her in strands to the darkness and still she stayed under.

54

no
matter,
I gave you
what I truly am

The next time I woke, Eve's face was lit by the screen of her phone. She was reading messages from Danny that had arrived through the night, sending reassurances in her reply, telling him that she had been unwell but he should not worry. I was not myself certain of the truth of this.

She was perplexed by what had passed, putting it down to the terrible fever. Her confusion was soothed by presuming the cause an illness; her disquieting recollections, the sense she had that she had been away and was now returned could be made to fit the parameters of delirium cause by high fever and this afforded some peace of mind. I could feel immediately that the brief time, in that haven where we two were connected, had passed. I would not again feel her touch. I moved closer to her anyway, wanting instinctively to reassure, for I could feel her trying to quell her troubled mind. Such is the lot of a companion, and if Demon did not need my resources, meagre as they were, why should I not spend them elsewhere?

55

**We
both
may relish
the chance to rest**

The next few days passed in a dreary blur. Though we both were recovering I could no longer flatter myself that we were recovering together. That lovely moment, consumed by exhaustion, Eve resting her hand on my back and giving both of us comfort, did not leave me. In the midst of something terrible shone this jewel of deep joy. I was sad for the brevity of its light.

On the third day, Eve felt, at last, hungry, went down to the kitchen and made some toast. Danny was due back that afternoon. She was looking forward to seeing him. She was still weak; weaker I thought than Danny had known from their calls, for I could feel it in her core. It was as though the fever had been of her soul as much as her body. She was shaken, right through to the part of any being that should be touched by nothing. But Demon had loosened the locks and opened all the doors, Demon had holed the walls. Demon had rampaged, a fierce intrusion on her integrity. She was still baffled, her understanding of what had passed lost in vagueness. But she was getting better, perhaps happier for the slippery absence of true understanding. It may not have helped her to be too clear on what she had given up.

She ate the toast, she showered, she put on a clean t-shirt. She was looking forward to Danny's return. And she found no obstacle to that pleasure.

I was not satisfied, I wanted more than vague uncertainty, a loose recollection of torment in illness. I longed for understanding, both of what had passed and what was to come. I was curious about where and how her rewards would appear and thus to know for what, in the end, she had lost her soul. I had not expected the transition, the forging of the deal to be so perilous. Suddenly, realising how little I knew at all, I was frightened by Demon's absence. For a moment I was afraid he had lost, and was wandering a bleak hillside, clinging to the scratchy bark of a stunted mountain tree. But I had seen so much of his power, those few nights before, that I soon rejected this notion.

I tried to remember that I had a purpose; my true role, my allegiance was to Demon. Though since then, he has been a carefree creature and needed me less – he has taken more sport than comfort from our connection. And how irritating that sport became. Now, as we wait on the cliff for this final ending, he is almost languid.

These turns about the world, these collisions between human and divine, all seem so simple, so logical in the tales I spin for Demon. Thus and thus it happens, and lo, the divine being wins. But tales are always trimmed in the telling. Real life, even the reality that includes creatures from other realms, is slow, scrappy, saturated with an everyday messiness that must be wrung out to make a well-told tale. I could not expect it all to be laid out before me and had to trust that, over time, I would learn what happens to a woman who, however hard she at first fought, had willingly given up her soul.

Danny was due back in a few hours. Eve was longing to hear the sound of the door but she knew it would be a while until his return. She sat at the kitchen table, drinking water from one of the heavy tumblers. Her face was colourless, she had lost weight and looked sharply made. Her hair, still dyed bluish-black, curtained the pale planes of her face. She pushed a strand behind her ear, catching it on the silver hoops, the remnant of the days when her ears hung with dangly silver, crosses, charms. It reminded me of the first time we had met, that cold evening on the village green.

She put on one of her favourite of Christopher's records. For a while, time passed pleasantly. She was swaddled by sound. After a while she became distracted. I worried that she was falling into another headache, but then, I heard the melody, the haunting sound underneath the record, sneaking in at the side. It was the piece, still uncertain, unformed, that arrived to both soothe and torment her in the days following Christopher's death. The piece she knew she must someday complete for him.

When she was younger, before the distractions of recent times, whenever music asked for Eve's attention, she dropped everything, anything else she was doing, went to the studio and shut the door. In the middle of a conversation, barely affecting a polite termination, or halfway through any other chore, she would simply leave to find her guitar, or some other instrument. Whatever the glitch caused in the connections to those around her, she seamlessly entered a state that shut everything else out, kept her for hours. For these last months, it had led only to frustration. This time she went to the studio but did not stay, she brought her guitar down to the kitchen. She sat at the kitchen table, strummed and plucked the notes, skipping off on an elaboration then returning to the start, easing the melody into new shapes. She was becoming so absorbed, and I could feel her having to resist the temptation to go to the studio, shut out the world, record layers that she could play against and with.

Instead she waited for the sound of Danny's key in the door.

Though I was glad for the lift in her spirits, she was still frail and I felt the nag of worry for the arrival of a headache, that familiar, horrible pain that would assert its hold and interrupt the flow of her music. But it did not come. She played and, as the ideas began to form, she moved into them with caution, as though following a trickster sprite into an uncertain, magical land, wary of the wolf that might be hiding around the next corner. It was too easy. It was wonderfully easy. She slowed herself again, went back to the simple run of notes. What was she missing? Where was Demon?

She heard the sound of Danny returning, ran to the hall, and pulled him into a long embrace. She had been so wrung out the evening before that he was taken aback by her recovery, her smiling welcome.

Eve and Danny spent a happy few days, occupying the house as though on a holiday. They ate long breakfasts reading the paper, drank coffee under the beech tree while Danny told of the ups and downs of rehearsals. They had afternoon naps and long baths. Eve was as relaxed and happy as she had been for years. The weight of worry was lifted from Danny and he too was happier than his concerns for Eve had allowed for a long time.

This lovely intermission could not last longer than a few days because Danny was due to go on a tour of arts clubs and jazz festivals across Europe. He had half expected that he would need to pull out and dreaded the disruption and mayhem it would cause for his friends in the band. But Eve was so clearly better, not merely from the illness that had enveloped her over the last week but the malaise that had dragged her down for months; she was lighter and brighter, a burden had been lifted.

Did she truly not have the measure of that burden? Did she not know to what she had agreed? Or, was it simply that she now fully embraced it? I did not know then and I do not know now. Some of it became clearer, but not all of it and still I am waiting, hoping that these tormenting secrets will be opened to me at last.

To my knowledge, Demon was still absent. But I wondered if they talked together, out of my hearing. Perhaps now the privileged chamber of the soul had been ransacked, the key in Demon's hand, the conversations took place in a secrecy so deep that no one could overhear, let alone a lowly companion, a mere rabbit, cloaked in divinity's borrowed garb. I hope that my faithful service over these years will encourage Demon to gift me with answers, now our time is so nearly at an end.

Their conversations, if they still happened, must have become cordial for she was unburdened, as happy as I had ever seen her. And in the end, perhaps that was worth the price of her soul; if you give me your soul I will go away – I say it quietly but it does not seem a noble bargain.

Though I was relieved, eventually, to presume I need no longer fear drab eternity, I was sad to think of Eve finally succumbing to a deal.

A few days passed in this lovely, restful way, Danny and Eve spending time together, learning how to put down their cares. Then the time came for Danny to leave for the tour. He would be away for several weeks. He had asked her many times, if she was sure she would be ok while he was gone, and knew to trust her reassurance. Eve had at one time been dreading his departure, but now, though she would miss him, she was looking forward to being alone.

As soon as he was gone, the subtle thread of that mournful melody sprung demandingly before her. She had kissed Danny goodbye a final time and gone straight from the doorstep to the studio.

Eve worked on the requiem for hours each day. I pottered around her feet, unnoticed. I presumed that Demon was busy, laying paths, creating situations, constructing the framework of Eve's coming success. Whatever kept him busy he seemed not to need me.

But I was happy, sitting alongside Eve, listening to her work, listening to the twists and turns of invention; like water falling down a mountain stream, split here and there by rocks, rejoining, curving and falling, gathering for still moments in a pool.

It started with the sorrowful tune. It had caught her attention like a curtain seen in the side eye, blown gently by a breeze from an open window. A lifting, a wavering. But in itself it was too short, saying only 'I am sad.' And that was not enough. This music needed more.

She did want to honour, thank and mourn her friend.

That was the task.

To avoid sentimentality, to avoid obvious mournful triggers, doomy minor keys that painted 'sad' with a house brush.

Work and work.

She settled into herself, clothed in the gloom of her studio, in the emptiness of her dear friend's house.

56

**Not
true rest.
Not until I am
returned to my brethren**

Eve barely went out. When not in the studio she wandered the house, picking up and putting down, running her hand along the surfaces, a chair back, a bannister, the rounded edge of the kitchen table.

Cautiously she trespassed into drawers, cupboards they had not yet opened. Death had made each into a box of secrets; perfectly ordinary things, handkerchiefs, stationary, batteries, a calculator that did not work. All spaces behind cupboard doors, within furniture, were rendered as sites of intrusion, opening them a moment of almost blasphemous incursion into the intimacy of a passed life. She felt the burden of it.

She found a photograph of Christopher that was recent, looking like the man she knew, not a mysterious younger version. It had been taken by the look of it, perhaps by Jon on a holiday shortly before he died. Christopher was sitting in a cafe chair with a brightly sunny European city behind. Pale stone and pedestrian streets, passers by in sunglasses. She taped it to the wall of her studio.

All the time Danny was away Eve drifted, absorbed in and absorbed by the house, by her intentions for the piece. And this was work, and this was work.

She took to wearing the shirts and ties still hanging in the big wardrobe in the main bedroom. Jon's or Christophers, she did not know, but all crisply cotton, plain, too large for her. A range of colours she took pleasure in pairing. This blue with this dark red. This grey with this burnt orange. She tucked the shirts and the tie end into her usual battered jeans.

She had never paid much attention to Christopher's clothes. So much she did not know about him.

But that is always true. This much I know. The dead are instantly a mystery.

The stream of ideas tumbled, pooled, fell away, Eve found in the many possibilities a right way to shape the piece. It was, after all, a requiem, to honour and mourn the loss of a beloved friend.

The little scrap of melody had stretched and strengthened and grown, providing both structure and embellishment for the whole. There were nods to works she had discovered through the caring and passionate musical education she had received from him. The last part she worked on was a choral section, for which she needed many voices. A few would do for now, she could layer them so that they would, for working purposes, sound like a choir. She hoped that soon she would be able to perform the piece. When finally shared with others, it would be complete. For when is a work of art complete before it has crossed the distance between its maker and another? And I understand that. A story needs a listener, does it not, my dears? Otherwise it is just a collection of words.

It was a beautiful piece. Eve was working on a small refinement when two weeks later the taxi dropped Danny, his cello and backpack at the house. He came into the room, stopped for a moment to watch the back of her, headphones on, bent over the computer as she refined a section. He could hear a sigh and tut of annoyance, knew she was unaware of the sound she made because of the headphones. He walked over, touched her gently on the shoulder.

After they had embraced, he stepped back to look at her, taking in the shirt and tie.

'I like your look.' They smiled at each other, making an awkward way out of the door, arm in arm.

Later Eve played what she had so far over the speakers in the kitchen, anxious for Danny's response. He was overwhelmed, and she was glad. She believed it would be the most important piece she had written.

57

**So
many
threads of
chance or fate
knotted in my hands**

Demon came back eventually and I was very happy to see him. Perhaps had Eve once again known I was there, had I received some strokes, some encouraging words, it would have been enough. And perhaps it is silly, to feel left out by people who do not know you exist. All I know is I was glad to see Demon.

He carried me out to the model village where we sat upon the trimly mown grass of the roads, as a liquid gold sun set behind the trees.

'What have we, what have we, Rabbit? Tell me what you know?'

'It has been a quiet few weeks, lots of work. Is this the piece that will make her name?' Demon looked at me through narrow eyes, then his uncomfortable smile pulled across his face. He lifted that finger, wagged it at me.

'Ahhh, aha! We will see and we will see. Tell me how you think it, Rabbit? What could cunning old Demon have wrought?'

'I think that because she wrote a piece that was for Christopher, and because it is a piece that many find moves them, because you are allowing her to find it, you were able to show that her success would come from something that has ... value, she was finally able to embrace the temptations you created, and now you will fulfil your promise.' I looked up at him carefully. Even when invited I was wary of seeming presumptuous.

'Very clever, Rabbit, my hedgerow companion.' He turned over onto his back, eyes closed, hands behind his head. 'Yes, yes, who knows ay? Who knows, my divine little woodland friend?' He tipped up his head to observe and point at me.

His success had made him obnoxiously pleased with himself. Maddening thing.

After years with Demon as my only companion wishing for more playfulness, greater cheer, and now finding myself subject to his poorly wrought version of play, I remember the caution to be careful what you wish for; he was stubborn, repetitive and, though he knew it not, fallow and infuriating. And I sometimes feel moved to express, at least out of his hearing, that I have deserved more.

But soon I will know the ending – for all the players – for I already know well what will become of the two of us.

Luckily I have learned patience as much as I have learned storytelling, flattery, soft compliance, in my long apprenticeship as a divine companion. I suppose that he has done his best with the tools that he has. The recipe that made him, so long lost or hidden, was not a play at joyousness. But he has tried. Perhaps even tried on my account. And for all, divinity comes with a price.

Mine has been to pass my divine lifetime with one who finds little happiness, one who understands beauty and humour only clumsily.

I wonder where my predisposition, one could even say my talent, in so different a direction has come from? Perhaps like sturdy rootstock shaping a magnificently decorative tree, it is my rabbit ancestry not my divinity that has allowed me still to feel joy. Perhaps it is simply that joy cannot survive the harsh tests of eternity.

We rabbits are timid, fearful, because life is often perilous, but we are happy creatures. I did not in my hedgerow life know the wonder I now cherish, but perhaps wonder comes when a joyful mind is, over a finite period of time, allowed to expand in curiosity.

Wonder is the flickering of an uncanny, lovely light, filling the dark corners curiosity cannot yet illuminate with understanding.

It is no bad thing, wonder, no second rate superstition, best and soonest obliterated by the antiseptic swipe of science and fact. It is a blessing. This much I know.

What some have chosen to make with it, that may be quite a different matter.

58

I
pull
them in

Leon left it as long as he could, after Christopher's funeral, before he contacted Eve. But eventually impatience prompted him to act. He walked from the bungalow, through a maze of quiet roads until he reached what passed for a town centre, a few desultory businesses along a busy coastal road. A shop with a post office sold postcards with beach views, seagulls, the usual fare. He bought one, and a stamp, a biro. He leaned on the dome of the letter box, recalling the words he had settled on best to catch her. He wrote a short message. *So maybe we should get together in a while and talk properly about the opera? It would be a really brilliant tribute. What do you think? L.* The card slid into the post box, a flit of confident hope.

The idea of the opera had not gone away. It kept growing, until it was the only thing he cared about. He feared that Eve may no longer be interested, then hoped her love for Christopher might make her certain to complete it. Leon at last had a spark lit from the same fires that smouldered in Eve. Had Demon carried the ember? However it had begun, he burned for the opera, it consumed him, he was willing to do anything to make it happen.

Eve padded through the house in bare feet and put the kettle on for coffee; the usual way she began her day. Morning sun flared against a film of dust on the window. She blinked sleepily, tilting her face to meet the warmth. She pushed back shoulders tightened by days of bending over keyboards and mixers.

There were letters on the mat, the usual bills and statements, and the postcard from Leon. Sipping her coffee, she let her mind graze on the idea of the opera. There was so much there. It might even be fun. She called him that afternoon. They talked, finding the parameters, finding a loose form of agreement that would allow them to begin.

'I think it's important to make it about the reasons Jon built it as he did, the figures in the house,' Leon said.

'Yeah, of course,' Eve said. 'Do you know how to write a libretto? Because I haven't a clue.'

'No – but you did always say I could write decent lyrics,' said Leon. Eve nodded slowly.

'Hello?' said Leon.

'Sorry, yeah, was just thinking.'

'What? Do you think it could work?'

Demon was clutching the back of her chair, stretched as far as he could, if he breathed it would roar in her ears. But for once she showed no sign, took none of his tension into her body.

'Yeah,' she said slowly, 'yeah, it might be a really interesting thing to do. We should give it a go.'

'Amazing! I think so too. Look, why don't I put some ideas together, well, I have a few already actually and we'll talk more?'

'Yeah, good. But I need to take it slowly. It's – it's kind of all new, and I'd hate to do it badly.' Eve's confidence had been knocked by the failed pieces, all the works that never made it to completion; burnt and fallen moths, evidence of what now seemed her insurmountable limitations.

'You won't. You won't do it badly. But, I get it, no pressure, let's take it a step at a time.'

For Eve and for Leon it would shape and change their lives.

In those first weeks Leon was as happy as a perpetually hungry soul can be. He took to the writing with a new joy. Luckily, for he would not care to lay gratitude at Demon's feet, the pleasure at least in its fulfilment if not its genesis, was truly his own.

He knew he was writing as he never before had. He did not do happy things to celebrate. He did not smile, jump about, sing cheerful songs. But his hunger abated. Or, it shifted; he longed to taste only what he could himself provide.

It would be a depressing ratio for Leon, how much effort he had spent in achieving the admiration he so craved, set against the amount of time anyone even noticed he existed. For I have noticed that much of the time, humans do not think so much about each other, neither to elevate nor deflate.

Of course there are times, in most days, in most lives, when thoughts about another are an obsession. Or, if not the demanding insistence of obsession, a presence. Love is like that. Hate too. One focuses with intensity upon another. And the other may feel nothing of it. Unless the two are in lockstep, dancing love or hate, or both, together.

Most of human life passes much as it does for us rabbits. Days pass, filled by preoccupation with current needs, how they might be met. Of course, our rabbit days being simpler, may more easily unfold in a manner that can be counted a success.

So much of life, when reduced to the essentials, is set to this end: just to build a string of successful days. This much I know.

Even love, love that is supposed to give, to nurture, even love picks up the beloved and reforms them as a building block. A whole being repurposed, made a component in another's successful life.

Perhaps divinity is making me a cynic. For all could be rendered down to such basic material, and the magic of it would be lost in the bubble and the steam. Perhaps the magic of love is a remnant, a little gold leaf of divinity, stubbornly gilding in fragments the layers of earth-bound life.

'Demon?'
'Yes Rabbit?'
'What do you think about love?'
'It is a useful lever.'

'What do you think about music?'
'I don't think about music.'
'Not even when Eve was writing her best work?'
'Least of all then.'

Sometimes I wish Demon had picked up two rabbits, or another such as a mouse, or even, god forbid, a badger. At least I would have had someone to talk to about these things. Demon is as self-absorbed as any I have encountered.

59

A
twist
and turn,
a flick of fate

Leon's life was filled with useful coincidences; I presumed they came courtesy of Demon, though he never deigned to tell me what was going on. I have become good, I think, at reading between the events and between the overheard scraps that reach me from the minds of others. Chance encounters with old books, the spark of a memory playing out to the drift of a tune from a neighbour's window. Over weeks, prompts and gentle nudges guided him until he understood what was required.

It was absurd, daring, it would be completely unexpected. But Leon had, with or without Demon's prompting, conceived the idea of an opera written about Jon and his creation of the model village, and seemed to be making it happen. It felt certain, in that early flush of enthusiasm. It was to be a great work of art, and it would elevate both of them to new heights. And at last she would be grateful to him. A buried voice of tempered spite was revived in the heat – she would owe him.

There it was. Demon had plans for Eve's elevation – Leon, earning her gratification as his reward, was the hoist.

Leon looked up how to write a libretto.

He bought, even read, some books on opera and was heartened to discover the form was far more loose and comfortable with itself than he had at first assumed.

He wrote and then destroyed pages and pages of twee, tale-telling rhyme.

He went to productions when he could find them, listened to contemporary operas and came to love some of them.

He wrote a short story to act as a map.

He screwed it up and wrote another.

He resisted the urge to call Eve, to ask what she was thinking, to confess that he needed something from her, admiration, or gratitude.

He walked by the sea, listening for the loneliness of Jon, all those years before.

He felt at last something of Eve's attachment to the miniature village, just the fact of it, even without the secret that it held. He felt that he was on the verge of creating something that might define him. If only she would be there to make it happen.

The fragments were becoming skeins, starting to coalesce in loosely woven loveliness. It was time to create structure and narrative. Not the whole, for collaboration was required to make the whole. But he wanted enough to impress Eve, to show her how it could work, to tempt her, to pull her in. I do not know if he sensed the assistance of the divine in these endeavours, but Demon spent a lot of time with Leon.

He began with a song for Jon. He pictured him in a workshop, fitting pieces of board together, peering at a sketch in the light of a single cold bulb. Jon speaking absentmindedly to the friendly people he pictured living in the house he built.

He realised he was framing it to himself as an opera by writing 'Oh' too often, at the beginning of a verse. He crossed out eleven occurrences of 'Oh'. He lay down on the living room carpet, thought about what an opera was meant to be.

He veered at first into a murky and sordid tale, primed by his own reading. Night-time visits of forbidden lovers. A bit of rough underneath the fancy pretensions of an English village. Perhaps it was Demon who reminded him that Eve, with her love for Christopher, her gentle compassion for Jon, would not take to the tale told this way.

He sank with maudlin ease into picturing Jon as a reviled and lonely man. He imagined he knew how he felt. His better self clarified: there were greater tragedies than had been the brief experience of his own. But somewhere, in the core of his soul, he felt a pulse of it, buried deep.

Jon had made the model village at a time when love was not only absent but barred to him. Leon had been given love, uncomplicatedly, un-showily, and yet still not found himself to be worth loving. Are both not deserving of compassion? It has to be acknowledged though, that Jon was called by no one Jon the Prick.

I do not know why I keep finding room to pity Leon, but he was as stuck with his own nature as any. And shaped by it. He was a prick, for sure, but he was never quite told that he needed to learn not to be. Life gives some useful lessons and lets others slowly damn themselves.

As he worked out how Jon's story could be shaped for an opera, he developed a sense of obligation and care – he felt he should do right by this man, and furthermore knew he would not snare Eve if he failed to do so. But he did not want to create a biography. He chose a new name for the lonely model-builder, set a divergent path, a way for the story to take on its own life. Jon became Tom.

Leon set to inventing a path for Tom that justified the kind of finale demanded by an opera. Some grand ending to the tale. For though he was glad that there had been a loving and happy outcome in real life, he didn't feel that a fortuitous drift out of loneliness and into a lasting relationship would serve the tale as best it could.

He thought it might be necessary to make people cry.

60

each
finger
on a string

The collaboration between Eve and Leon began at last in earnest. Though Eve was intrigued and excited, she was also treading with care. Leon was intense, madly determined for the project's success. Both had reasons for caution but came to working together in a refreshing new way untainted by the past.

It was an unfamiliar form so the work had to be learned as well as made. Leon had written many lyrics and Eve had composed long pieces that in some manner proposed a story. But neither had written an opera. They presumed secrets of the form that were not there to uncover, then tripped over unanticipated obstacles just as they thought the path ahead was clear.

At the beginning, despite their reinvigorated enthusiasm, neither could predict whether or when it would be finished. They did not want to be bound by promises to others. Eve feared old habits resurfacing, taking the joy out of it, stifling the whole thing. Leon was wary of Eve taking flight, schooling himself to not apply pressure that might cause desertion. Faintly he even saw that it might be him, not the work, that caused such pressure; he took hold of his impulses as he never had before.

Both, in different ways, feared it might become another chance for Eve to destroy Leon's dreams.

The bounds of their shared endeavour were often stretched so thin it seemed shape and purpose would leach out and be lost. It was fidelity to the idea, become precious to both, that made them forgiving enough, tolerant enough, flexible enough to work together in closer step than they ever had.

As I wait for the end I am curious still, about how this arrangement was brought about. How Demon slotted Leon so tightly and so usefully into his plan. I have asked him, of course. Too many times, too curiously, too irritatingly, he would say. But for what seems a very long time now I have had to indulge Demon in his teasing, and that has been deeply irritating to me. So perhaps we are even.

I have to put up without knowing, and might never discover the answers, however much I burn for them. I have no choice. There is nowhere to seek answers that he will not himself provide, so secretive, so rare is his practice.

So much I have learned and all that is unknown still remains infinite. It has to be said that curiosity has been both an enlivening and burdensome part of my experience as the companion of a divine being. To while away the time, I turn to Demon.

'Demon, do you think it is good to be curious?'

'I have to be curious, Rabbit. It helps make the map of my cunning. Humans are curious because they can't help it.'

'What do you think makes it so?'

'Too much brain power, not enough sense.'

'Would they not believe, those curious people, that to be so makes a map of cunning for them too?'

'Yes, but so many make a map that is too big, too unruly. The fools do not know how to contain.'

'Perhaps it is your job to be part of the containment?'

'Perhaps. Perhaps had we been a never-sleeping army, we brothers, we should have fenced them in a little, made them more ruly. But what a cruelty that would be to us.'

'Well I can say, even without knowing how, you have been very clever to make it all work,' I tell him, hoping to cheer him again.

'I know,' he replies, lying back down on the grass. 'Cleverer than you know, Rabbit.' He gazes at the beckoning sky.

I cannot help it, despite Demon's warnings, my curiosity burns like an itch. There is so much still to know about these strange years, the tale I have seen unfold, the blessings I have been allowed and the peculiar burdens that have been my charge.

As so often I yearn for complete knowledge. I wish I could know it all. I long to be a curious fool, to make an unruly map as big as the cosmos.

I wish to know more about even the mysteries, so overlooked, of my life as a rabbit. Why had I been a rabbit? Why had all of us rabbits been so? To feed the foxes? To feel the sun upon our backs? I saw that we too would have needed stories, were our minds to fall more naturally to such thinking.

Magic, stories, music, they are also maps, also knowledge. This much I know.

What would be the harm in knowing everything? Perhaps for one such as I doomed to die before a new day begins, not much. I will not have the time to put the power of it to any ends.

To see the beginning, the dawn of the time of demons, the making of the spell that binds them. To see the seeding of it in the imitators, the weakling humans built so as to test, their very nature a test of all that has been created. Which human, which demon brother came together to first dance the deal? Which human soul ascended for the first time to that throne of realisation, the highest achievement of its own nature, then sank soulless into oblivion? For Demon does truly bestow a gift for what he takes in return.

To be as great as you could wish to be. To be mighty in the fulfilment of that wish. If you are built so, what is the crime in wanting to be magnificently so?

Do they pay with their souls as a warning of the dangers of such desire? Do they pay for wanting greatness without effort? What is so good about effort?

Are they allowed to reach greatness, such as is bestowed by the demon brothers, to inspire as well as caution? For I have seen more desire and longing, more wishes for elevation than I could believe possible. All those fervent prayers, invectives, silent dreams, grasping, scrabbling journeys, immaculate plans, all in pursuit of some form of greatness. It must be part of the design.

But do not recklessly wish for the divine, dear souls, for you will be emptied of meaning. You will become a husk. This much I know.

61

a
twitch
here and there

We sometimes took flight, when drifting with Eve and Leon into and out of their inventions became tedious. They were caught in the time of work; it can be both utterly boring and entirely thrilling. Swathes of time when thought pulls in, then out, then in. Never quite going anywhere, never quite managing to leave and go somewhere else. *What about this?* a mind will ask, again, not quite certain that this was not a question that had been posed and rejected many times. *What happens here?* a mind will ask, as it reaches the same blank wall it stared at an hour, a day, a week ago. A period of scratching around in tired old scraps, ended by forced play it is hoped will become invention. A period of tallying, combing, teasing the fragments in the hope of learning how they might knit together and be enhanced.

Sometimes it will happen that in and out, in and out, going nowhere changes in an instant, and there is a rip tide, a jet plane, a galloping horse and whole new vistas open up.

Like nature, parts grow, retreat, find their way in and around each other. And soon it is settled. Harmony, for now, is reached. A piece of music, and wilderness, will be steady, for a while, when the balance that holds all together is found. And slowly their work took balance.

They worked first on themes, outlines, the sense of the thing. Maybe we could, maybe he could, what if, why don't we. These questions and suggestions went back and forth.

For Eve the story was more about the model village, the strange fact of it, the vague reasoning behind creating a world in miniature rather than the story about why a particular model village was made by a particular man. She didn't relate so much to Tom, but to all the Toms, all the people terrorised by the heavy hand of 'normal'. All the people who in their exclusion might build their own smaller, kinder world. All those whose loneliness led them to make companions, hand carved make-believe friends. All the people, not so different to her, who found this small version of a big and complicated world strangely compelling, peculiarly logical, easier to navigate perhaps than the one scaled for them.

And let me be fair too, to Leon the Prick. He came to honour Tom's story in all its flat brutality. He came to respect the new discipline of writing in this pared-back way. None of his previous stock-cube sordidness, murky and dark, to flavour as though with depth, no laconic bombast to pique a taste of supposedly harsh and vivid truth. With such simple materials as words that do not clamour for their space, words set in a shape to be sung, a taut and elegant pattern must be designed. The beauty in his poetic shreds of writing, the words that floated free of him into midnight pages found a new form. And he began to do it well.

I was glad to find him come into this new, energised calm. He had purpose that extended at last beyond the dreary rating of his position in the eyes of others. And he had genuine confidence. It made him seem more like Eve. For all that she doubted her place in the world, her connection and worth to others, for all that these last years had knocked her off the path, leaving her distraught and disconnected from what she knew, she had never doubted the necessity of writing her music. She had never believed there was another who could do it, just this music, her music, better. It was not confidence born of assessing the terrain and deciding she could match it, of looking at the competition and thinking why not me? It was the return of her old confidence, based on certainty – she never had to ask the question. She did not have self belief, she did not need it; she had purpose.

Eve found new direction, a nuance of intention, in this work. She felt what she did was not only important for herself, but that it might be so for others. An act of sharing, recognising, honouring, a tale that must be told, alongside so many other tales, as many times as it was necessary to undo the tyranny of normal.

And here was Leon, basking almost, in similar clarity. Doubt, even so pushed out of sight, so hidden that he barely knew it was there, was truly gone.

He shut himself away in the bungalow to finish the libretto. Tom became so real it was as though Leon could see him. He wrote, discarded, read. He came back to long red wine drinking nights of scrawling in notebooks. Tom was there.

The two of them took a long walk into the countryside. Finding a pub, Leon bought himself a pint of lager, thinking about what Tom might usually drink. He stroked the smooth sides of his pint glass, cooled by the lager. He remembered the heavier-handled glasses with their beehive shape, the faceted surface. He stroked his fingers on smooth glass, through a thin spill of drink, imagined Tom's fingers, tougher, calloused from hours hand-working wood, whether the feel of the glass would be lost. Would pubs have served lager? Certainly not the one he drank, internationally branded and imported from some factory brewhouse.

He thought about a village pub, Tom's local, the local brew, the local people. He wondered whether it ever felt a place that Tom could easily go, once the idle speculation about him had become shaming fact. Every village, every town was home to men and women who had been forced into humiliating calculations about where and how they might belong, what risks and what rewards belonging would entail.

Leon watched the woman working behind the bar, attracted to her tight black t-shirt and her sternly bored demeanour. He thought about the curious attraction he had for some men, often there but never acted upon. He thought about Tom, how he would feel his desire for a stranger in a pub, a tea room, a train station, whether he would suppress it. Whether it would demand to be heard.

Leon ordered books, biographies and cultural studies; he devoured them. In these stories of courageous defiance and the twists of sad tales, he learned to admire. How resilient, how hard-worn must be the defiance of someone who knows that people hate and fear them. He felt the meagreness of his own rebellions, his easy option of standing out from the crowd. He learned admiration for the bravery of those who had not been given such a slack choice.

Tom's life took shape. He was, like Jon, the son of a prosperous staid man and a respectable staid woman living in one of the larger houses in a village. In that narrow community the father was admired. The family felt their worth and spent much effort in protecting and polishing their name. For a name is a magic spell and only has power if all choose to believe it. And with their careful attention to bearing, accent, clothing, manner, for a generation or so, many did choose to believe it.

The adherence to rules.

Ordinary people. A normal man and woman, married, careful, safe, obedient. Their cultivated name and their presumptuously tended status bestowing both privilege and protection.

From tyranny are such spells concocted.

Normal. If all that was most common was called usual then perhaps fewer would be excluded. Abnormal is so much more threatening than unusual. But then, it is the usage of a word over time that confers its meaning. Human mouths will soon enough flavour a word with distaste and scorn if it is distaste and scorn they require.

And so for Leon the story grew. It became something so much bigger than the thin ribbon of words he would be required to write for an opera. It was a sea from which Leon must reverse a slender stream. It became for him, even with this necessary reductive process, something like Eve's landscapes were to her.

He shut out his monitoring cares about Eve fully, for perhaps the first time. The voice, his own, that wheedled for her approval, the voice of hers that he invented, speaking of her contempt. Whether she would get what he was doing, whether she would approve – that was to come, and the prospect of it bothered him less that it ever had. He felt a certainty that brought him busy, restless peace.

Leon felt as though his days were spent in the company of Tom. He talked to him as he walked on the beach, as he wandered, strangely adrift in the neat flotilla of retirement bungalows. He wondered how Tom felt his loneliness, wondered vaguely at how he no longer felt his own. He was bound to Tom and together they dreamed a dishevelled dream. And at last Leon turned it into a story that could be told. A story that grew from Tom, not the people around him, nor the manner in which he was inexplicable to them.

62

a
pull
to tension
forms the game

Yes, Leon still longed to be admired, but nagging fear, so long his unrecognised companion, was gone. Where did it come from, this fear? Why be afraid of obscurity? I still cannot puzzle it out.

Perhaps I am the greatest rabbit who ever lived. But that I would long to be so is absurd. Perhaps I should enjoy this thought in the last few hours remaining to me. I am the greatest rabbit that ever did live on this earth. There may have been others by chance elevated in the companionship of a demon brother, equally I may be the only one. I am perhaps the only rabbit to ever be alive (if alive I am) under the sea, the only rabbit to dream my way through the cosmos, to befriend – yes, in this moment of deliberate pride, I will allow that, to befriend a divine being. I have soothed that divine being, diverted him, sometimes. I have done more than even Leon could dream, should he feed his dreams every day with the most preposterous of intentions. I allow a sense of my own greatness to puff up in my chest, to blunt my curiosity and awareness of what is around me, to raise my head, certainty setting my jaw at my own glory.

I suppose I can see how such a lure might tempt one to the hook.

But time is passing too quickly to wallow in this pompous state. Already I can see so much else is wiped from view when oneself fills the entire frame. Glorious me – perhaps there is a truth, and that truth is a small part of the wonder of it all. But it is not the interesting part. This much I know.

I have known Demon to raise himself thus when fully in the triumph of his cunning. Even that to me is strange. He is after all built to win the battles that are set him as his fate. He is well primed to outwit a mind often vulnerably in lockstep with his own. If he has to stretch himself a little for the win, is it so glorious? Should a horse feel the pride of victory in a running race with a donkey? For all that a decrepit horse may have once taken a beating at the hands of a particularly fine donkey, I think not. It is the order of things. And thus perhaps is an answer. It is the order of things for Demon to win as the powers of divinity have skewed the game in his favour.

He is sent to those who want him, plays them with an artful simulation of what they desire. There are more difficult battles. But then there are the marks such as Eve who make it hard.

And there is the grimacing wraith, clinging to the hawthorn, condemned to eternal nothing by a mark who would not deal. Good odds are not the same as certainties. Ask the decrepit horse that lost a race to the sprightly donkey. The odds of an easy win shift when the price for losing is so very high.

I kept asking Demon to tell me how he had worked this deal but he persisted, relentlessly, with his infuriating teasing. He was not very good at it but luckily I have learned to dissemble as I have learned to tell stories and I was able to make a convincing show of being delightedly frustrated by his poking.

'So, Rabbit, what do you think of it? What is to become of Eve?'

'Oh Demon, tell me, do!'

'Ah ha! No Rabbit, I will not!' he would invariably chuckle, a stiff series of chuck-chucks in the approximate shape of a laugh.

'I cannot bear it. You mean there is more to this tale and you will not tell me what?'

'No Rabbit, I will not!'

'How long must I wait? Oh please, dear Demon, tell me what your cunning has wrought!'

'Ahhhhhhh – you must wait, Rabbit. All of you must wait.'

'Oh dear oh dear, what will I do?' And so it went. By all that is sacred, he could keep the game going for hours. I noticed that I became more cartoon-like in my responses as boredom and laziness took hold, but if anything he seemed to like it more.

Demon stirs beside me on the grass now, he turns and gives me a look with a quick flash of suspicious malevolence; these recollections may be waking his interest, and so I will quiet them for I do not want him to feel he has been fooled.

63

**we
are
ready**

Eve was working on the requiem. A section in the middle needed more space, it needed to lose the thread and wander a little. She experimented with the ways that might happen, taking away and reforming. It was a puzzle but no longer a worry. She had been absorbed in the one section, the one fleeting idea of it many times, with only the pleasing burden of a problem to solve. It was coming together; the turmoil of the last months left her afraid of making false steps but really she felt herself restored.

She looked at the clock. Leon would be arriving soon.

Eve, Leon, and Danny sat at the kitchen table in high spirits. The libretto was complete. Danny leafed through, meditatively sipping his drink. Eve had read it earlier in the afternoon, alone in the studio. She could not wait to complete the music. Eve and Leon sat back in their chairs, toasting the opera, excited about what was to come.

It was thrilling for Eve imagining future casts, different directors taking her work into unexpected directions. She thought for the first time that in some ways, a work she had completed would in fact be forever nearing completion, subject to the reinvention of new singers, new players, new interpretations. An endless evolution.

Danny caught her smile and answered with his own, and a question.

'What, what's making you smile Eve?'

'Just thinking about the different groups who might perform this, what it might change. Maybe a school hall, or in some field. I dunno, it's just kind of exciting.'

'I'd love that. We could get a performance happening here in the village hall!' Leon grinned.

Some bright spark ideas I think must have come straight from Demon, judging from the way he reclined on the kitchen floor, his eyes shut, arms folded behind his head. He had barely leant over their shoulders for a laconic aside, let alone the usual hissy stream. Demon was perhaps the most content of all in the kitchen; everything was playing out as he intended.

Later, with Leon sleeping in the spare room, Danny already in bed, Eve slipped out to the bench. I followed, confident that now Demon was settled, relaxed even, the bond between us could be a little more elastic at my instigation as well as his. Eve let herself drift into old and new ideas for the opera score. I hopped up beside her onto the bench, leaned into her thigh, resting on the thick fold of her coat, and waited for her to take me on a ride.

She had returned to her habit of stretching her work into unusual shapes to test it, to come at it from a new angle. This time, she was imagining it small, first small enough to fit into the village hall. Seven instruments, three singers, and an audience of two dozen. She knew the sound of that village hall so well, but had not tested the acoustics with un-amplified sounds. She imagined the power of an opera singer's voice, blasting into the pre-war rafters, then muffled to a whisper. A woman of the village telling secrets about a man who lived in a house behind a rhododendron hedge.

She wondered what the voices of the model village would sound like – squeaky and tinny, or just quiet? Could tiny vocal chords and rib cage and diaphragm make a bass note? The makers and visitors would sound with the terrifying boom of the gods, filling the streets, squeezing through black-painted windows, echoing inside empty boxes where secret friendships flourished. She imagined herself shouting down to the rooftops, frightening the cowering little inhabitants. She wondered what the sound would mean to them.

Some kind of visitation.

Some kind of fearful demand.

Some kind of brush with the divine.

She began to hear a thin thread, from long ago, a clarinet, two clarinets, picking out a theme, a voice for the carved wooden figures. How would it sound, within the tiny box where the lovers hid in their bed. Two small voices telling big tales, two melodies weaving between the houses and over the rooftops.

Some of these swirling thoughts would coalesce, make it to the stave, some would be forgotten. Some would lurk, waiting for their chance to inform a future project, as though a fresh insight, however long they had been drifting in the storehouse of her mind.

It is the scale of this invention that makes humans so different to us rabbits. To other creatures too. I have seen crows and dogs invent games. Perhaps even in the play of little rabbits there is some invention for a game cannot exist without it. Older rabbits never instructed us when we were youngsters to chase and kick our legs and jump over each other but we did it anyway.

Perhaps it is all the result of a game, of curious exploration. From the smallest forms of life to the most complex. Trees, herbs, forests, creatures and their play, the habits and rituals of animal life. Demon and his sleeping brotherhood. A little stretch into the unknown here, an accidental discovery there, and slowly, something becomes. Time alone makes it feel immutable. For really, everything changes. This much I know.

Perhaps time knows when the demon brothers were given their role, or when they chose it. Perhaps they once knew all of it, their purpose, their charge, but sleep has made them forget. Perhaps Gravity remembers when she was first tasked with holding. Humans spin tales to hold memories, to tell general truths when facts are long gone or unreachable. Perhaps Sleep curses the brothers, filling all the time in which they might otherwise spin tales to bind the sense of their being. Perhaps because they have no time for tales, sleep is their only refuge against fear of the unknown.

I would love to talk to another about this but I will get nothing from Demon. And as the hours are passing, I must be content with my own speculations. After all, I can still thrill to the wonder of it all, for not knowing how something came to be does not infer its lack of magnificence.

We sat on the bench for some time, Eve and I. She thought about the fragments and the ideas, the loose scraps, the strange possibilities. Never one for a lengthy thesis, she thought about it in concepts, somewhere between words and pictures.

walls, boxes, restraint and protection
sounds echoing in chambers
sounds sliding through gaps
emptiness loneliness
the fullness of being loved
hope
making a body, carving a body, sacred objects
loving a statue – some myth, can't remember
a body in a box, but not a coffin
or, might as well be a coffin
getting out of the box and singing loudly
a duet

All of these loose and jumbled thoughts revolved, appeared again and again. Such lightweight, careless thoughts, and so very necessary. Like summoning a fog, a spell, a miasma in which to work.

64

to
meet
the end

Next day, Eve re-read the libretto, then set about translating it into a form that she could use as a guide in writing the music. On a roll of lining paper, she drew out a timeline in felt pen, so that she could measure it in a glance, a horizon line that would translate into music. Above the line she wrote in little snippets, codes for the ideas that were half formed; *rough, scratchy strings and backtrack. Wailing sad. Drift (Tom dreaming). Villagers hysterical bit.* Words were never her forte, but only she needed to know what they meant. Once it was laid out, she fell into studying, seeking patterns, so the blocks might heave and breathe, so the fissures and the folds would speak, so the spaces between had a chance to swell, narrow or split. Once more those glorious landscapes of sound came into being.

She ravelled and unravelled. Pulled back to the text in front of her before her imaginings took flight too far, too high, too free to be useful. She pushed and pulled between the possibilities of what it might become in the future and what she had before her now. There was much work to be done but her intention rang with a sweet clarity. It was the best place for Eve to find herself. At last, it seemed, Demon was rewarding her.

Days in the studio were long, time slipped unnoticed through hands, along strings, across keys and channels. She recorded digitally, each evening loading scraps and songs onto her phone to listen to fresh and first thing in the new light of dawn; though with such long days, little time accumulated to revive her ears.

Danny knew that Eve was entirely happy but still he persuaded her to step out into another version of the world, now and then, an afternoon, or just an hour with him in the garden, talking of other things.

Eve hit a stumbling block. She felt her response to one scene was flippant, cheery, shallow. Though Tom was imagining happiness, the circumstances were far from happy. She could not get the subtleties quite right. She called Leon, who invited her to visit, talk it over, see if a change of scene might help. The next afternoon she was there.

Leon was glad to see Eve. They were slowly learning a new appreciation of each other. They chatted for a little while, then went to walk on the beach. Low tide exposed bones of rock, seaweed smeared across it until the tide would return to set it wavering in the backwash.

Eve launched into the problem she was having, her inability to settle on the right tone for part of act two, an act that took place entirely in Tom's imagination. There were sections where he toyed with the idea of revenge, compromising his own character in the process. Perhaps it was better said that he was toyed with by the idea of revenge. Perhaps Tom had his own demon to work with. That latter section was working really well, but before it, in a passage where Tom pictured the happiness that he longed to embrace, the piece she had written had a sweetness or positivity that felt wrong. She could not make the section work.

'I just feel that what I'm doing is too coy. All kind of sweet, when really there's nothing sweet about someone having to imagine people liking them,' she told him. Leon nodded.

'When I was writing that, I imagined all the villagers dressed like clowns, you know, that kind of sinister misery masquerading as joyfulness.'

Eve stopped walking, shutting her eyes. 'That's really interesting. Yeah, I think that's really something like it.'

'I mean, you don't really need the full ya-ta diddle-diddle clown music – although ...'

They laughed.

'No, but something like it. A bit absurd, really, isn't it? It's that sad, absurd thing that's needed?' She looked to Leon for his answer. A little fist pump of triumph rose in him. It overlaid and obscured tiny champagne bubbles of gratitude.

'Yeah, exactly.'

'Yeah. Nice one. Thanks Leon, that's really helped.' Together they took another small step towards the realisation of the opera and, in her simple gratitude, Leon felt at last a little burst of triumph that he had so long coveted.

65

a
soul

The opera was at last complete. Clarity had come to Eve, the stretch of unknown between idea and execution had been filled with discovery, way signs and markers, and progress fell sweetly, a beautifully tiled path beneath her feet.

Leon and Eve stood side by side, as a full run through of The Model Village, an opera in Three Acts, unfolded onstage. Final adjustments were made, a stretch here, a lift there. Watching from the wings was so different to being on stage as a performer. It was a transition that Eve had already made, but it was new to Leon. On stage, they had shared collective energy that brought them closer than they were off it. Seeing others bring their work to life was a different thrill, but just as overwhelming. Leon paced, excitedly. Eve stood motionless, tension held in the curve of her fingers and held in her listening heart. Her head dipped a fraction, now and then, in anticipation of a swell, of a drop, of a moment of musical drama. And when it sounded as she hoped it would, she smiled. And then she listened again.

As the final notes died away, they looked at each other and grinned; it was perhaps the moment of purest connection they had ever had. Almost, a hug happened, as spontaneously Leon laid a hand on Eve's back, in honour of her work and his joy. Eve reciprocated awkwardly with her hand on his upper arm. They patted each other, feeling new, mirrored gratitude and warmth for this annoying person in their lives. Both knew they had created valuable work, only made possible because it was done together. Something about these two awkwardly shaped people really did fit well together, whether they liked it or not.

Demon, floating above the orchestra, took a bow.

66

to
take
me home

And then, the opera was out of their hands. Thanks to Demon, the timeline shrank in a series of fortuitous events, and the first performance was soon on posters and playbills.

The opening night took place at a prestigious music festival. The director had approached Leon, confessing that he was a long-term fan of Never. He had been utterly charmed by Leon and was thrilled to work with him. The German conductor, on board because of Eve's involvement, brought more excitement and attention.

Successes abounded. Of course much of this was thanks to the machinations of Demon, but surely (at least I hoped so) some could rightly be accorded to Eve on her own account. For she had received many accolades preceding her deal with a demon. Like a jealous parent I did not want another to take all her glory as his own.

They had made something strangely beautiful with this opera. It was clear to all who came to see it, that first night and all the nights after. The story explored the simple desire for one man not to be alone, and the complex, unkind emotions of a community that perceived this desire as a threat. The story, set in the specific, told something of the whole, and are they not the best kind of stories?

The music was wonderful, twining and splitting in subtle complexity. Threads tugged singly away and then knotted in ugly clumps, only to be teased apart again under the examination of different instruments, reforming in a new weave, a different pattern; melancholy and hope glimmered in a jacquard shimmer.

I do not know how, as a rabbit, I developed such a keen ear for music. I can say, as can all rabbits, I have spectacular ears if it is mere listening that is required. Maybe it was because I learned about music alongside a woman who thought almost exclusively in musical terms. Perhaps this girl, this woman had been my teacher as well as my study. I wished I could cross the barrier between us, and talk to her. But only Demon had that privilege and has no interest in what is not necessary to achieving his success.

Curiosity has been a gift, but it is also a curse, for it can never be sated. This much I know. I sit here now, in these last moments, still yearning to understand, still longing for answers. There are so many dark corners to illuminate. So many things I would ask of so many souls. Demon will only answer with irritation and so these last furls of longing, little hooks reaching for yet more knowledge, no matter how tempting to me, must be held in check to preserve our final hours.

But I risk another question.

'Demon, at the last moments, is there a connection between us – between you and the mark? Is there any talk? Do we say goodbye?'

'Sometimes.' It is all he says. He turns from me and closes his eyes.

Perhaps death is a cure for curiosity.

Now I am the petulant one.

I was so glad that we were there to see the opera. I discovered on that first night, the weight and feel of a new emotion. I was proud. I think that is the best way to describe it. Of course I had not directly influenced the creation of this marvellous piece of work. But I had helped Demon, guided him even, when he was lost, so perhaps I could allow myself a little claim on the fruits of a shared endeavour.

And pride has another form not related to the self. I saw two people in whom I had become deeply invested achieve something wonderful, something that made others take a deeper breath, feel the weight, the swing, the arc of life shifting through their bodies even as they sat in their seats, part of the audience. Eve and Leon had done so well and I was delighted for them, I was impressed by them.

I saw Eve after the show, deep in conversation with the conductor. Elaine stood awkwardly at her shoulder, smiling, uncertain and happy. She felt uncomfortably aware of the imposition of her need to congratulate her daughter more than she already had done. Just as she was about to wander away, mildly embarrassed by her inability to be part of the conversation, Eve turned, pulled Elaine in. She introduced her to the glamorous, dramatic conductor, and, miraculously, managed thereafter (for a short but gratifying while) to talk about the costumes, how people seemed to appreciate the show, what Munich, the conductor's hometown, was like at this time of year. I say she managed to talk of these things, but, in truth, it was more that she managed to listen and smile and interject appropriately, resisting the temptation to pull the conversation away and back to the music they had been speaking of. Though Eve did not know it, Elaine noticed and was touched.

Elaine (just as with Leon and his parents) has always understood Eve more than she has fully known. If she wished Eve to be a better communicator, a more careful and consistent pleaser of others, it was only in the hope that she would settle into the world in a way that would make the world kinder to her. It was the way Elaine had been raised. It is the way so many are. It is a useful strategy – to others perhaps more than themselves. Imagine how much would be released for the benefit of all, if the kindness of the world could be presumed?

I felt a sudden burst of great sadness thinking of how Elaine would feel to know in that moment of pride and happiness that her daughter hung by a demon thread. I pushed the thought aside, unwilling to sour my mood when the occasion was such a happy one.

The evening had been a great success and so much seemed to be dropping into place for Eve and Leon. To Leon's delight, a journalist, who had been a fan of Never and now worked as a columnist for a Sunday colour supplement, cornered him and asked if she could do a full profile. She even asked him about the book rumours – that old rejected novel, dusty and salty, now out of the drawer and in the hands of an enthusiastic agent, apparently. Leon was fit to bursting with the thrill of her knowing about it before it had even reached a publisher. Eve and Leon were in buoyant spirits as they said goodbye. Danny suggested they go for a celebratory meal but Eve was exhausted and Leon had to leave for a flight as soon as the performance was done.

Eve had been inspired by her work with the conductor and from it an idea for a musical exploration, a collaboration between them, was manifesting in a corner of her mind. Not yet a piece, or an intention, or a plan, but a place where she wished to make some musical play, to see if it might take shape.

In the taxi, she relayed the conversation with the conductor to Danny, what it had made her think, where she might try to take it. Danny smiled in the darkness, knowing that, her period of doubt now past, though she never stopped making music, and so in some ways was always working, she was rarely burdened by it. Even when she could not resolve something, she did not succumb to the anxiety or panic of a deadline, she simply sank further into the passage, the piece, the mood. Eve was, once again, fully, the music she wrote. He gratefully compared her now, returned to the woman he had first met, with the Eve who had struggled so long under the black moods he put down to grief and uncertainty.

In that sense, in a moment above all where she could expect to take a break from work it was not more work she was proposing. It was simply the continuation of her existence.

67

**but
first,
some time
for dreams –
I must make good
on my side of the deal**

Need I tell how well the opera was received? There is nothing like the helping hand of the divine to make the world take notice. Yes, everyone loved it, yes, it took the form to new audiences, yes, they clapped and cheered ecstatically. Eve's music reached the world. Demon had done his work well.

And yet, I know, I hope I know, that some of it would have happened without the guidance of a divine maestro. For it was a beautiful, strange, wonderful work. Perhaps there would not have been the unexpected surge of new young fans or the personal congratulations from presidents. Perhaps some of the more lavish offers for staging would not have been made.

But people would have cried, people would still cherish those hours in the dark. There still would be playbills tucked carefully into folders of keepsakes. There still would be some who wanted signed copies of the CDs.

The model village committee contacted Eve and Leon because they needed funds to repair some of the houses; a cannily opportunistic move that resulted in a well-supported amateur production of The Model Village, an Opera in Three Acts, to be performed in the village hall. It seemed absurdly possible that this was the grand finale to Eve's dream for she was so thrilled about it. Leon too. He even took time away from the excitement of his book and film deal to lend his fundraising cache and newly invigorated social media following to the efforts.

Eve wrote a new arrangement for the disparate array of instruments that were available. The singing ranged from appalling to surprisingly good. It was very moving, and a delightful mess thoroughly enjoyed by all. The money was enough to make all the necessary repairs and start work on a cafe gift shop, if a location could be agreed. Eve set up a generous fund from her income for ongoing and future necessities.

And Eve kept writing music. At last she completed the requiem.

Under the carapace of her shyness and in the slipstream of her invention, Eve softened, unfurled, learned the connections of music to the emotions of the listener. Finding it somewhere in herself she discovered the interplay of vulnerabilities and strengths, the quiet hope and tender sadness of people. Gem-like glints of an older woman's understanding began to seam through the geology of her invention. She never had been able to make small talk, to make a stranger feel comfortable, but she could now speak to them, and, more preciously, make them feel she heard.

Her music was not mawkish or sentimental. It remained beyond the taste of most. But for enough, it was beautiful, striking, ugly and compassionate. All the words that so inadequately describe what music does. She did not talk about it well, but her intensity was for some a kind of charm. Her hands would hang in the air, make gestures in a slow and rooted dance in an attempt to convey what she was trying to achieve. In the frustration of this process, she would look at people intently, willing them to understand. For Danny it had always caused a tender smile to hover that he well learnt to suppress so as not to annoy her further. Her endless focus, her frustration and the beauty of what resulted filled him with love.

68

**It
is time,
at last, to go**

The time came for Eve to share the piece she wrote for Christopher, in the first live performance, at the memorial event organised by Gordon.

She led the ensemble, and I saw in that hall a glimpse of Eve as she had imagined herself, years before. The Eve who formed in an idle moment of hope as she staved off the boredom of working in a little supermarket. Her hair was no longer shaved and messy but it was still dyed raven black. Her clothes were plain and sharp, she wore a black suit, just as she had imagined, over a mustard silk shirt and Christopher's burnt orange tie, as she had not imagined, in that younger age of banished colour. I smiled for her. She did not get it so wrong after all. Though her guitar did not lean against a chair, and the hall was less extraordinary, less heavenly high and confoundedly vaulted. It was built on a smaller scale. But still it had been designed in the service of the music that would be performed there.

She had been asked to speak to the audience, to talk about the piece, and the man it memorialised, but she would not. They all knew and loved him already. What was the use of added words? Eve did not want her audience to follow a precise arc, she wanted them to share a common experience, shaped in this case by grief and gratitude. And if not that, simply to allow a time for wonder. A time to feel human.

The piece began with a low hum, a deep note. After some seconds, the instruments joined in. It built up then split like water around rocks, into shreds of the sad melody that had begun the whole composition. As the piece developed, we could feel the pulse of the audience, the beats of their hearts answering each other and falling into one rhythm. We could feel the thickening in the throats – of those susceptible to the emotional triggers of music and those reminded of their own losses. We could feel the audience come into that beautiful state, of being many as one. We could feel it surge as it was echoed in the musicians, and in Eve. She did not allow her own emotion to take a part in this unfolding, but she had put every fleck, every slab, every wisp, in all the hours she had spent and the purpose she inhabited, into the expression of such emotion that others might share it.

There was silence before there was applause. There were tears and elation. Eve was strangely constrained, feeling spent and exposed. Unusually for her she cried later, from all that she had put into the work, and all that had come back to her from it. And for the sorrow of missing her dear friend.

It was welcomed then and became widely beloved.

And over the next few years, it escaped the confines of the self-selecting audience who already admired Eve's work. It became familiar to many. It became a song played at funerals, and even weddings. It became a piece turned to for solace, in a time of lonely need. It became folk music. It became shorthand for a common understanding of loss and suffering, and withall, hope. It reached nowhere near the heights of the most popular shared music, but for its kind, it was extraordinarily well known.

Eve found music in new and startling combinations. She wrote with a depth and breadth that was becoming more widely, deeply admired.

She had the luxury of time, spent in the ruckle, the waiting path between the moment an idea comes to mind and the time when a piece can be judged complete.

Though not as extravagant as some of Demon's stories, Eve had been rewarded. But whether there was more, or whatever else the reason, we were not yet ready for the finale. Demon was back and gone and here and there. Sometimes he took me with him. Sometimes he left, giving me a little smirk, a little finger wag, telling me I must be patient, things must be done and I would know all about it one day.

'One day when, Demon? How long must you wait?'

I meant how long must I wait.

Now, only moments or hours away, I am sanguine about the coming of death, but there were times, not knowing how long there was left, when it played on my mind. It made me anxious. But, not understanding my need I think, he would not tell me and my anxiety easily became irritation. I hid it, of course.

And then, of a sudden, Demon arrived. His face was blank. He blinked slowly.

'Rabbit, it's time to go.'

69

I
long
for sleep,
for blessed dark,
and hope they leave me be

That was yesterday, or today. Some hours ago. It has been hard to keep track.

We arrived at this unfamiliar place, settled on the grass and I understood that this is the last place I will be.

And now we are waiting. These last few hours seem to stretch and expand. I do not any longer know how long we have been here, how long it will be until the true end.

'Soon,' Demon almost croons. He is listening to my thoughts again.

And we wait, and time is passing.

And we wait and soon it will have passed.

What will it be like, the transition between living and not living? How does Demon journey home? Who will wake him next? I hope for his sake it will not happen for a long, long time.

'First sleep, long and lost sleep,' Demon mutters.

It is as though he is already gone and talks from that longed-for rest.

The sky is masked in cloud. Will I too pass beyond? I do not know what will become of my body. I do not truly know if I still have a body. Perhaps I will lie here in this spot returned to my old rabbit form. To be pecked by seagulls and worried by a stupid dog pulling on its lead until the owner notices with disgust what has caught its slobbering attention.

I choose to think I will become immaterial, passing through the thickness of the clouds, or into the dark mineral riches of the earth, still enough there to feel the passage, fading into the true nothing beyond. The memory of my old body, smaller, browner, may be tucked within the magnificent spell of being that carries me now, but how could it reappear? For I am not really a rabbit at all. I am an idea. Am I? I feel a little unmoored to suggest it but this talk of bodies brings me to such thoughts. And what would happen to the shimmer, the gleam and markings, the spellwork of that idea? Where would that go? Too much of a treasure and a giveaway, surely, as leavings for humans to find.

All that I do not know and never will.

70

I
have
loved you

Demon scrambles up to standing. He is poised, tense. I follow his gaze. An old man stares at the horizon while his dog sniffs and darts amongst the tall weeds. Some kids in school uniform shout more than they need, vape, push and joke at each other. A man in an overcoat walks the path. There is no one who looks like Eve. Perhaps Demon just knows she nears.

I realise that I do not even know if she will be physically here. I know nothing.

But Demon is waiting. And so, therefore, am I.

The kids pass us scattering insults and jokes to be blown inland by the wind. The older man stares at the sea, the dog wags its tail, obliviously, for no one shares its vacuous enthusiasm. The man in the overcoat walks along the path.

That man comes closer and I see it is Leon.

I am confused. Demon looks at me slyly, with the beginnings of a smile stretching across his face.

'I fooled you, Rabbit, oh I fooled you!' And though he suddenly seems mightily weary, pale, he is agitated with the pleasure of his triumph.

Leon seems to have no awareness of us. He sits on a bench by the path. Demon lowers himself to the grass as though his limbs ache.

I look from one to the other. Both are haggard, exhausted.

And I wait, and then no longer able to be patient, I prompt Demon, 'tell me, please tell me what happened?'

'That stupid girl would have damned me,' he says, looking at me from the corner of his eye.

I am elated. She rejected Demon's offers. She did not succumb. And then I am astonished, for Demon says to me 'you think I did not know that it is how you wanted it?' I am afraid that he is annoyed with me. But he looks at me with great tenderness. I feel for a fleeting second that there is after all a bond of love between us and I am overwhelmed.

'I never wished you to fail Demon,' I say, hoping that he understands that I too have cared for him.

'I know.'

When I am able to gather my thoughts I ask him again to tell me how it happened, the details, how he worked his plan. It is the first time for many years that my admiration is not a part put on for storytelling.

He looks so tired, his voice grates close to a whisper.

'Eve gave me Leon. Stupid woman, wanted me gone. I would have given up on her long before, for your peace of mind, Rabbit, and for mine, but until I am bade leave, I cannot. She dallied, shuffled around, oh, do I want this or that, or something pure, or precious or – well, it is of no account, for, once she knew she could release me from my bond by offering another, so she did and I was free. You remember that terrible day? Certainly you felt it though you could not know what passed. I nearly had her, nearly convinced her and still she said no. Then she ordered me to leave, offered another in her place. So simple, once you see that it is possible. Happily for me, she found her way to that point, then gave me Leon, and there he sits.'

We looked over at Leon, a man at rest on a clifftop bench by the sea. A man about to lose his soul.

Demon noticed a divine spark, yes, that is what he called it, in Leon when he began to write his scraps, his shattered moth wings, his poetic shreds. Despair swept away all Leon's dreary parameters, banished the overseers, the imaginary judges. For he was in turn a poor judge. What will people think is good, was his first and only thought. And he did not really know. And so it was no guidance.

Despair struck him open. Old habits, built by years of false reckoning, crumbled, leaving room for new discoveries, new ways. A little weather can revive, after all. And Leon, exposed, unhappy as he was, became a better man than he had been, swaddled in his old, careworn, yellowed shell.

He wrote words not meant to be seen. Not at least, ready to be seen. Not filtered through the eyes of those who would come to see. He wrote words, a few little scraps, for himself. And they rang with a frequency tuned to Demon's ear.

And Demon was close enough to hear the tiny mewling forms of those words.

And Demon, being adept in such matters could hear in those first soft mewls the beginning of what would become, in the right circumstance, a roar.

And Demon knew that he himself was the right circumstance.

And Demon knew a ripe mark when he saw one.

And Demon could see that Leon the Prick was as ready as any for a deal.

'In the end it was simple. An agent, a rights auction, dismayed publishers who'd missed out,' Demon says, 'and in the end, he got his parity with Eve.'

Leon looks over at us as though he too enjoys the tale, the story of his own glory, or his own folly. Perhaps he stares with vacant pleasure through us, to the distant clouds.

In his sapped state, I can see Demon is cherishing his chance to be the storyteller. And I cherish mine, as the rapt audience. I move closer, settle within the curve of his body.

'When the time was right, my study made, my offer honed, I went to him.'

'How did he receive you?'

'My offer fitted as though created in the chambers of his own heart. I knew him well enough by then. Literary prizes, someone and someone realising their huge mistake when they rejected his book, glory, movies, lovely excited people. Yes, all of that. He lived it well. And this one last garnish. He wanted parity with Eve, gratitude, even.' He turned to me, a true smile, just, hovering. 'I got him that, Rabbit, but you will know I sorely had to work for it. He barely knew it himself, but oh how hard he wanted parity with Eve. He wanted people to say of him as they said of her, yes, Leon is a real artist. He wanted her to be impressed by him.'

Demon had in the end used Eve as he had the stonemason. He did not require her soul. He needed her to compete the dreams of another. I looked up at him and wondered at this creature. So vast a presence, so powerful, and so beholden. Mighty, world-changer, servant. How I wish I had taken more care with all that I have known, how I wish I had noted everything. How I wish I could stay to tell the tale. But it is right that I go – to whom would I tell this story? Some old magical tavern rabbit, telling tales? I am Demon's comfort, nothing else.

Leon sits still on the bench; he is stolen over by vacancy, as though emptied already.

'Do you, have you his soul, Demon?'

'No. We must wait, just a little. It is not to be found like loose change in a pocket.'

Demon tells me that Leon wanted to shine above people, he wanted their desire so he could choose to reject it and their envy so he could choose to ignore it. He wanted most of all to be the best. To win the prize as the best. To be known as the best.

I thought back to what I had heard and ignored, Leon's visits to America, his sour old book resubmitted and finding favour. Never songs being used in adverts and film soundtracks. Enough, apparently, for Leon to make it to the sofas of early evening entertainment shows and the VIP lounges of cultural events.

'It is not my job to ask how long he wishes to be the best, to prompt him to keep me here, waffling through dreary years while he enjoys himself. So I made him the best. He won prizes. People were astounded. More importantly, they told him they were astounded. It was what he asked for.' He tails off, as though it is all in the end of no account.

We notice Leon, his thoughts once again waking. He rouses himself, pictures all that has gone before these last months and years. How bloody good it all felt.

And he smiles.

And Demon smiles, and we both know Leon has no regrets, he has no fear of the price. I am proud of him for that.

His soul comes to Demon.

It comes I know not how, but I know that it does.

Leon does not slump or stand or fall. His thoughts tumble and he empties. His body, still seated on the worn memorial bench, is emptied.

Demon is filling out. It is as though he is warming. He grows in light and warmth. He smiles. And at last it is a true smile. Beautiful. He is radiant.

He cups a hand around each side of my head, looks into my eyes as he never has done before. I am mesmerised. His voice is golden.

'Because you love and admire Eve, I am glad to tell you that she will live and die as all others. She will reach the blessing of death and a return to the thoughtless, wordless, unsplit stream of being. Before she dies, she will in her music capture the divine, but the divine will not capture her. She will not be world famous, as I could have made her, but she has her soul, and for some, her music will be miraculous.'

Demon grows more radiant yet. I stare into his beautiful eyes. He is magnificent. His body moves into the air, he keeps his hands cupped around my head, a last anchor. He drops a kiss on the top of my skull.

'Thank you, Rabbit, you have cared for me well and I have loved you.'

And he goes.

And he is gone.

I am, what am I?

Here, one time companion to a Demon. In wonder at what the claiming of a soul has wrought. Is that, after all, a reason why this game is played? Not for the human but for the divine?

All that I will never know.

And what am I?

Here, still, next to the absent Leon. I honour him for wanting to be everything that his nature made him. Is it dishonourable to want to be magnificent? If you are willing to pay? If it harms no one? It should not be. And is that not another good reason for the cranked reruns of this old story? Not to spite a soul for wishing it but to gift them with the wonder of fulfilment.

I slipped well enough into the might of divinity. Not all are suited to the meekness of rabbits.

And yet, as I fade, I long only to sink into the ground

I long for return, in the humble body of a dead creature

it is enough

I slide into the nothingness of death

once more I am of the earth

Acknowledgements

I would like to thank everyone at Bluemoose for their work on *Beast*. It is an honour to collaborate with people who have published so many wonderful books. Thank you.

Tom Sargeant who cast an eye over my portrayal of Jon's life – thank you for sharing your vast knowledge.

Thank you to early readers, Virginia, Sam, John, Pierre and Thea. It was precious to have your thoughts and your encouragement.

And Pierre, thank you for always rigorously reminding me of the path I wanted to take. Thank you for everything.

And Sam thank you my dear friend. You always help me do the thing – whatever the thing is.

Thank you to my family. Always.

Lils and Phoebs, I so love talking to you about what I am working on, or trying to do, or scrabbling at – you help me see the world in new and thrilling ways and it is a true blessing.

All my musician friends – I'm so glad you do what you do. None of you are Leon.